Dark Bloom

Molly Macabre

Edited by William J. Burkhardt and Anna Larsen Porter.

Book Cover by Hampton Lamoureux of TS95 Studios.

I dedicate this book to my mom: my biggest fan, most steadfast supporter, and harshest critic. Thank you for believing in me and always having your red pen ready. And for loving my apostrophes even when they don't belong. I l'ove y'ou s'o mu'ch!

Contents

1. Chapter 1 1
2. Chapter 2 4
3. Chapter 3 7
4. Chapter 4 14
5. Chapter 5 18
6. Chapter 6 21
7. Chapter 7 29
8. Chapter 8 31
9. Chapter 9 35
10. Chapter 10 37
11. Chapter 11 40
12. Chapter 12 44
13. Chapter 13 48
14. Chapter 14 50
15. Chapter 15 55
16. Chapter 16 57
17. Chapter 17 60
18. Chapter 18 62

19. Chapter 19 64
20. Chapter 20 68
21. Chapter 21 74
22. Chapter 22 76
23. Chapter 23 80
24. Chapter 24 85
25. Chapter 25 88
26. Chapter 26 92
27. Chapter 27 95
28. Chapter 28 103
29. Chapter 29 110
30. Chapter 30 115
31. Chapter 31 119
32. Chapter 32 122
33. Chapter 33 127
34. Chapter 34 131
35. Chapter 35 136
36. Chapter 36 138
37. Chapter 37 143
38. Chapter 38 148
39. Chapter 39 150
40. Chapter 40 155
41. Chapter 41 157
42. Chapter 42 160

43.	Chapter 43	165
44.	Chapter 44	168
45.	Chapter 45	171
46.	Chapter 46	174
47.	Chapter 47	176
48.	Chapter 48	180
49.	Chapter 49	183
50.	Chapter 50	187
51.	Chapter 51	191
52.	Chapter 52	195
53.	Chapter 53	197
54.	Chapter 54	200
55.	Chapter 55	205
56.	Chapter 56	208
57.	Chapter 57	211
58.	Chapter 58	216
59.	Chapter 59	220
60.	Chapter 60	227
61.	Chapter 61	231
62.	Chapter 62	233
63.	Chapter 63	236
64.	Chapter 64	240
65.	Chapter 65	243
66.	Chapter 66	246

67. Chapter 67 249

68. Chapter 68 252

69. Chapter 69 256

70. Chapter 70 259

71. Chapter 71 261

72. Chapter 72 264

73. Chapter 73 266

74. Chapter 74 269

75. Chapter 75 273

76. Chapter 76 276

Note From the Author 279

Dark Bloom Soundtrack 281

Acknowledgements 283

Chapter 1

The world outside was different than the cage Kate had grown accustomed to. The silence was predictable and punctuated. It did not seethe with dread or buzz with tension like the dingy basement that trapped her for so long.

Leaves crunched beneath her as she strode through the woods. Rocks and twigs poked her bare feet as she gently pressed each one onto the ground. After months of wandering through forests and trekking down gravel roads, the skin on her feet was hard and blistered, impervious to pain.

Wavy, black hair lay on the back of Kate's neck, creating a thin layer of sweat. The nights were starting to cool, while the days were still ignited with summer heat. Still, the warmth she felt was not overwhelming. Large oaks and pines shaded her, creating a cool atmosphere beneath their stately limbs.

Houses stood bare and streets were empty. Still, autumn relentlessly blanketed the silent planet. *Oh, to live with such confidence,* Kate thought. The seasons forced themselves upon the world, regardless of how big the audience. *Dance like nobody's watching*. And dance, they did.

Tiny feet scurried over the carcasses of dried, orange leaves, causing her head to jerk in that direction. A squirrel sat back on its haunches, gazing at her with wide, fearful eyes. Whiskers twitching in apprehension, the tiny creature looked just as surprised to see her.

Tension escaped Kate's lips in shaky breaths, and she crossed her arms around her middle, wrapping herself in a nervous hug. Rubbing her thumbs across her skin, her gaze fell on the track marks.

Couched carefully in the crease of her elbow, small red dots freckled the fragile skin. Though the bruising had subsided, and the punctures had closed, the emotional wounds were gaping.

Be careful what you wish for. It was the theme of countless tales. Kate had wished for freedom. Begged for it. Cried and pleaded and screamed for it. *Ask and you shall receive.*

And now Kate found herself wandering through a hushed forest, alone and barefoot with nothing to call her own but a small pack and the few supplies she snagged from that dreadful house months ago.

While aware that the state of the world was different, Kate had no idea what she would need before crossing the threshold and entering into the unknown. Gathering a steel water bottle, a few snacks, and a first aid kit she found beneath the sink, Kate set off out the door with nothing else except her memories, her trauma, and her track marks.

There were no bills to pay. No mindless job to attend daily. No house to clean or vehicle to upkeep. No toxic relationships. No relationships at all. Nothing but rural emptiness and the occasional smell of death. Freedom.

Creeping by several small houses Kate hoped were abandoned, one home in particular whisked away her train of thought. Mirages of the well-kept home played out before her: a husband working on an old car in the garage, a mother playing tag with her two children on the lawn.

The family's apparitions only evoked morose feelings, so Kate blinked them away, reducing them to the maggot-riddled corpses she assumed they were.

Still, Kate inched through the yard in cautious silence, in case the household was not decomposing, but watching her and waiting for the ideal moment to attack.

Arriving at the edge of the forest, Kate paused to take everything in and decide what her next moves would be.

A road once bustling with the strange mix of lake tourists and country folk was now deserted. A modest shopping center, out of place in the middle of nowhere, sprawled out before her in the space next to the road.

Having lived here all her life, it did not take long for Kate to inspect the businesses occupying the buildings. They were the same as they had always been: a cell phone store, a liquor store, a grocery store, a Chinese restaurant, and one of those pizza places that always had pies hot and ready to pick up.

Everything I need to survive all in one place, she laughed to herself.

Survive. It was only months ago that Kate wanted to die. The persistent yearning for the torment to end consumed each day. Just one strong blow would have taken her out, as weak as she was. One strong blow to break her free from the torment of the metal bars and basement walls into whatever afterlife would accept her broken soul.

Chapter 2

"How was your day at work?" he asked.

Despite being just a memory, his voice was as clear as if he had been standing in front of her. Sitting at a table in the back of the Chinese restaurant, Kate gazed out of the window which offered nothing more than an unsightly view of the parking lot.

"I asked you a question." His voice sliced into her reverie, and she focused her attention back to him. Narrowing his eyes, he watched Kate's features rearrange from an innocent, daydreaming girl to the dutiful, compliant woman she was supposed to be.

"It was fine," she replied, managing a disingenuous smile. Ice cubes tinkled against the drinking glass as she stirred her straw around in an absentminded manner, indulging a nervous tick.

"You left twenty minutes late." His low, harsh tones were even more frightening than if he had been screaming at her.

"The day was just so busy. I stayed to tie up a few loose ends. Phillip was going crazy between all the prescriptions and vaccines due," Kate explained, shifting in her seat.

Years before they had met, she started working at the pharmacy as a technician; something that did not require a degree or much training. The job often left Kate discouraged with long, unpredictable hours spent enduring patients' verbal abuse.

Once a month, at least, she made grandiose plans to get the hell out of that pharmacy, plotting a way to stay at home working from her computer or start her own business. Maybe she could write a best-seller and never have to work again.

It was all talk. Overwhelmed by her aching back and feet and consumed by exhaustion, the dreams faded. The time loop Kate was a victim of continued: waking up, going to work, coming home, cooking, cleaning, sleeping.

Eventually, she would concede to the idea that this was her life until she retired. A few weeks later, the fruitless daydreams of finding other methods to fund her life would begin again.

"Phillip." The name came out through clenched teeth. These days, every conversation with him felt more like an interrogation. Each time they spoke, his patience with her seemed to diminish a little more.

"Connor," Kate said. "He's the pharmacist I work for. I don't understand—"

"How long, Kate?" he growled. Her mouth hung open, grasping to comprehend the situation. "How long have you been fucking him?"

Snatching her wrist from across the table, Connor dug his thumb into the delicate veins of her forearm and peered into her eyes as if he might see the whole act in her irises. If he gazed long enough and with much concentration, he would see the two of them in the back of the pharmacy, their bodies bathed in the harsh light of a single fluorescent bulb, thrusting and heaving with passion. Kate closed her eyes and turned away from Connor—he would not find that there or anywhere.

"I'm not," she squeaked. Tears welled up behind her closed eyes. Repulsed, he tossed her wrist aside and sat back in his seat without saying a word. He did not need to.

When she finally dared to look again, his crossed arms and raging eyes gave away Connor's plans for her. Kate would need to prepare herself for pain.

Chapter 3

Kate shook the memories away. The ghosts of her past would have to find some other time to haunt her. Right now, she needed to focus.

Studying the buildings that made up the shopping center, Kate considered what she needed and where to find it. The two restaurants and the cell phone store were useless to her. The liquor store, well, that was tempting, but the grocery store was the source of her most dire supplies.

Taking a deep breath, she imagined the danger that lay within the walls. She had eaten her last bit of food the night before, and her canteen only held about a half cup of water. Taking the risk was imperative.

Kate broke into a hushed sprint until she was on the covered sidewalk of the shopping center. The windows of the cell phone store were intact and nothing inside seemed disturbed.

Next was the liquor store. It was no surprise that these windows were shattered and most of the shelves were empty. There was nothing more appropriate during the end of the world than the desire to drink away the pain of losing everything you knew and loved.

Kate stepped through the open window, careful to avoid the glass sprinkled on the floor like morbid confetti. She made her way to the tequila section, picked up a 25-ounce bottle of Casamigos Blanc, and secured it into her pack. She told herself it was for medical reasons. *You know, in case I need to sterilize a wound.* That was what she told herself, anyway.

Next, she came to the grocery store. The windows, smeared with the fingerprints of desperate souls demanding entrance, remained intact, though the metal was marred with gouges where they had been forced open. Turning sideways, Kate slipped through the gap and crept through the lobby past rows of carts that stood like metal skeletons—a reminder that her once-thriving world had been laid to rest.

The next set of automatic doors had also been forced open. Pausing in the doorway, she cast an anxious glance around the store for any signs of danger. The stillness and the quiet revealed nothing.

Putrid odors hit her like a brick to the face. Kate's stomach cartwheeled from the combination of sour meats and rotting vegetables. Taking a deep breath through her mouth instead of her nose, she demanded her senses to push through.

A portion of the stench was clear as she scanned the produce section and its moldy, wilting fruits. Rotten juices had trickled down the wooden bins, leaving dried, crusty puddles on the floor. *Nothing worth taking there.*

With soft footsteps, Kate moved between the first and second checkout lines, where she found the chips and soft drink aisle. Aside from a few cases of root beer and large bags of spicy chips, the shelves were empty. Spicy was not really her thing, but being picky was not a luxury Kate was afforded.

Rounding the corner, the next aisle contained snacks, crackers, and breakfast items. Kate tore open a box of trail mix in serving-size bags and dumped them into her pack along with some dark chocolate and almond granola bars.

Kate salivated at the thought of ripping open a foil package and sinking her teeth into a s'mores toaster pastry. The graham cracker crust and the marshmallow filling, she would kill for just a bite. *Ugh, dark chocolate and almond. Better than nothing, I guess.*

The next aisle had a lone case of bottled water that was unmolested. It was a 30 count of those cute, kid-sized bottles. Sitting on the floor, Kate emptied the little bottles into her canteen until it was full.

The silence she had grown comfortable in was broken by something being dragged across the floor from the next aisle over. A shuffling sound followed by a fleshy slap produced images of a gnarled foot sliding and smacking against linoleum.

Setting the empty plastic bottle on the ground, Kate twisted the top on her canteen and slipped it into her bag without a sound. Sliding the backpack over her shoulders would surely give away her position, so she picked it up by the handle.

The sound occurred closer, and this time, the skin squeaked as it grated against the ground. Low, choppy chuckles emanated from the aisle, like the excitement of a perverse child who had just found a house cat to torture.

Kate scaled the end cap and peered around the corner, only to confirm her suspicion that it was one of them—the Infected. One leg was bent forward, giving the impression the Infected was about to kneel, while the other leg was indented at the knee, forcing it to be unnaturally straight. Leaning hard to one side, its head almost rested on its shoulder. With convulsing fingers, the muscles in the creature's hand danced to a beat no one else could hear.

As she turned to duck back around the corner, it locked eyes with her. A high-pitched, shrieking laugh erupted from its lungs sending shivers through her.

Shit. Kate quelled the desperate urge to run. Where there was one plagued creature, more were sure to be nearby.

Skimming the signs that hung over each of the aisles, Kate found the one she was looking for: Cooking Utensils.

The Infected hobbled toward her, both crooked and straight legs somehow working together to close the distance between them. Shouldering her pack and speed-walking toward the aisle, the staggering feet of the Infected scuffed the ground as it followed.

Once in the aisle, she scanned the items with haste: aluminum pans, tongs, meat thermometers. The Infected rounded the corner to the aisle and a hungry hiss escaped what remained of its lips.

There! Kate almost screamed aloud as she grabbed the perfect cooking utensil that was destined to double as a killing apparatus. Holding the two-pronged meat fork as if she were about to throw a football, she squared her feet and prepared to fight.

The creature lunged toward her clumsily, and Kate thrust the fork into its left eye. Howling in pain, its searching arms drooped but continued their pursuit. *So much for a quiet attack.*

Grabbing another fork from the rack, she jammed the utensil into its head just above the ear. Blood gushed out around the metal prongs, but it was not enough.

With as much force as she could manage, she plunged another meat fork into the Infected's skull from the top of its head, straight into the brain. Anguished roars emerged from its throat as sheets of blood poured out over its brown teeth. The crooked legs trembled and the creature fell to its knees and then finally to the floor. Kate gaped at the monster sprawled out before her, forks sticking out of its head like a cheap imitation of Pinhead.

A feeling of triumph rose up through her belly and straight to her head. It was not the first Infected she had killed, but this death was certainly the most thrilling kill under her belt thus far.

Still stroking her ego, Kate plodded backward down the aisle but was stopped dead in her celebration by a sound from behind. Pivoting slowly, every muscle in her body tensed in dreadful awareness.

At the end of the aisle stood four Infected, all gazing at her with a desperate hunger. Two of them were laughing, the merriment and humor absent, jeering at her.

Kate took a deep breath and sprinted down the aisle in the opposite direction of certain death. Her feet hit the floor hard, bare skin thwacking against the linoleum. Pumping her arms forward and back, she propelled herself through the store. The Infected followed, and they were surprisingly spry despite their broken and twisted bodies.

Kate had planned on running out of the grocery store's dormant doors, through the parking lot, and back into the safety of the forest. But when she got there, two more Infected, attracted to the sounds of the struggle, stood in the doorway.

Keeping her pace, she broke right and sprinted down a hallway, passing bathrooms and the employees' break room. At the end of the hallway stood the door to an office. Twisting the knob, she fell into the room and scanned it for creatures.

When she found it empty, she closed and locked the door, resting her hands on her knees as she caught her breath. The Infected likely knew where she was, but being loud was as good as offering them her latitude and longitude.

Finally, her breathing had steadied, and she gazed around the room. Two heavy filing cabinets lined the wall next to a desk littered with papers. Centered in the desk's cutout, sat an office chair, a cardigan draped over the back. A window occupied the wall behind the desk, looking like the most picturesque route of escape Kate had ever seen.

The Infected heaved their lifeless bodies against the door. She wrapped her arms around the filing cabinet closest to the door and pulled as hard as she could, but it refused to budge. Positioning herself on the opposite side of the filing cabinet, she leaned her back against the cold metal and pushed against the floor with her feet. The cabinet began to slide.

Kate pushed harder, repositioning her feet when they started to get too far out. With one final thrust, the filing cabinet was in front of the door.

Ignoring the snarls and groans on the other side of the door, Kate rifled through the desk drawers for anything to aid her in escaping the room. Instead, she found useless things: pens, blank name tags, and a schedule book. Except in the bottom drawer, a box cutter looked up at her almost glowing like a video game quest item.

This will come in handy, she grinned victoriously.

Kate turned the catch on the window that kept it locked and the pane lifted. As she pushed the window open, the outside air enveloped her, smelling of falling leaves, crisp air, and escape. Willing her frantic fingers to cooperate, she used the box cutter to slice a hole into the screen big enough for her to slide out through.

The wooden door fractured into pieces and metal clunked to the floor as the first Infected burst into the office, knocking over the filing cabinet. Kate's feet hit the pavement outside, and she sprinted in the direction of the woods. Though her heart pounded and her feet ached, she kept running until she was sure the creatures were no longer behind her. Resting one hand against a tree, she doubled over, inhaling the sweet air of the protective forest.

After regaining some stamina, Kate briefly took in her surroundings, listening to the sounds of the woods.

Kate slid down against the tree, opened her backpack, and retrieved the bottle of Casamigos. Pressing the bottle to her lips, panting against the cool glass, she took a long swig. The liquid burned her nose and throat and swept her away into a memory that seemed older than it was.

Chapter 4

"Oh my God, this is my favorite song!" Rylee jumped up from the table and danced around the living room. Her arms swung wildly in the air while her hips shook from side to side with the rhythm. Like a horse's tail swatting flies, her long auburn hair whipped around her face.

"Every song is her 'favorite song'." Eden laughed, turning to Kate and rolling her eyes. Kate smiled and sipped her margarita. The ice chips were soothing against her swollen, bruised lip.

Eden gazed at Kate for several moments, deciding whether or not to bring up the obvious dilemma taking up space in the room. Kate despised the way she looked at her with those stormy eyes, her dark eyebrows furrowed in concern. Casting her attention to Rylee, Kate hoped Eden would follow her gaze. She even forced a giggle, but Eden would not budge.

"Kate," Eden said.

Here we go.

Kate was not even sure why she had come out tonight. Eden and Rylee had been her friends for as long as she could remember, but things had changed. Besides working a full-time job, Kate had been putting most of her time and energy into a new relationship.

Rylee had just finalized her divorce, and though she emitted party-girl vibes everywhere she went, those who knew Rylee best knew she was hurting, and it was all an act to protect her heart; it was a front.

Where Rylee was uninhibited and free, Eden was reserved and methodical. Months away from earning her doctorate, she allotted no time for dating or hobbies, considering them distractions from her goals.

Kate always wondered who Eden was trying to prove wrong, as she had spent most of her life in school, scooping up every credential she possibly could. By now, Kate had lost count of all of Eden's degrees and certifications.

These days, they found very little time for each other. Tonight, Rylee had called Eden asking to hang out. Except she had done so in Rylee style, making a joke about how 'hanging out with bitches even sadder than herself would be sure to boost her mood.'

Eden called Kate, explaining that Rylee's recent behavior warranted a girl's night. Heavy drinking and reckless nights with men had consumed Rylee's nights, leaving Eden disgusted and concerned.

Kate begrudgingly agreed to join them so long as they agreed not to go out, though she was sure it would not matter. Connor's accusations against her would be the same.

"What happened to your lip?" Eden asked, her voice firm but low enough that Rylee could not hear. Kate was not sure Rylee could hear anything over the sound of her self-proclaimed fabulousness.

Kate looked down at the table, her lips feeling like mush. Anything that spilled from them would surely sound like a lie, even if it were the truth.

"Nasty cold sore," she answered, impressed with how confident the words came out. Eden simply nodded, never looking away from her.

Kate's phone vibrated and she looked down to read a text message from Connor.

Hope you're having a great time. When will you be home?

Kate clicked the side button of her phone and put the screen to sleep. She returned her attention to Eden who was frowning at the phone.

The song ended and Rylee flung herself into the seat next to Eden. Panting, the sweat dripping from her forehead caused creamy beads of foundation to run down her temples. Eyeliner smeared in black clouds beneath her eyelids giving her the visage of someone who had not slept in a week. Rylee looked back and forth between the two women, trying to read the room.

"What did I miss?" she asked. Her eyes darted to the bottom of Kate's face. "What the fuck happened to your lip?"

Kate rolled her eyes. "It's nothing, okay?"

"I thought it was a cold sore," Eden said.

"That's the nastiest cold sore I've ever seen." Rylee drew back, disgusted.

"So, is it a cold sore? Or is it nothing?" Eden. Unrelenting Eden.

Kate's phone vibrated again, and she could not keep herself from glancing at it.

Kate?

She turned off the phone screen again.

"Did that motherfucker hit you?" Rylee asked, eyes wide.

"Kate, we're your friends. You can talk to us," Eden said calmly.

"No, I just—it's nothing, okay? It's really none of your business." Kate shut her eyes tightly, wishing it would all just go away. The interrogation. The texts.

Bzz, bzz. Her cell phone alerted again.

You better call me now bitch

"Look, I have to go. Thanks for the drinks." Kate stood up, pocketed her phone, and walked toward the door.

"Kate, please. We can help," Eden protested.

"I'll kill that asshole!" Rylee shouted, knocking over her mixed drink as she reached a clumsy hand in Kate's direction.

Without looking back, Kate left Eden's place, leaving the pleas of her friends trailing behind her. Although she did not know it, she felt it in her core; it was the last time Kate would see her friends.

Chapter 5

Kate opened her eyes to the earthy brown hues of the woods. Weariness weighed on her, and she might have drifted off to sleep if her memory had not left her feeling so loathsome.

She had been an idiot for not listening to her friends. Had she simply confessed to them the abuse she was enduring, she could have saved herself a lot of pain and maintained her dignity. The funny thing was, she would probably still end up the same way, sitting under a tree drinking tequila following a battle with the undead.

Kate thought about who she was before meeting Connor. Surviving a childhood torn apart by divorce, she was forced to grow up quickly, managing her parents' matters long before she was old enough to understand them.

The time she spent with her mother was filled with routine: schoolwork, sports, and after-school activities. It was wholesome. Normal.

At her father's, Kate indulged in drinking, smoking cigarettes, and spending time with boys a few years older than herself. The yin and yang left her feeling empty and ashamed.

Kate developed a deep depression that she would hold hands with for the rest of her life. Many nights were spent lying on her bedroom floor weeping as she lost herself in rock music. Crying out to Underoath and Taking Back Sunday, scribbling the raw, heart-wrenching lyrics over everything she owned, those songs were the only thing that saved her.

Most of Kate's friends were listening to pop music and the upbeat energy only frustrated her, making her wonder why she was denied the joy expressed in the songs.

Others were listening to country music which was either upbeat or expressed a sadness that could be pinpointed. He was sad because his wife left him. Or she was sad because her babies were growing up and life was moving too fast.

But rock, more specifically metal, that she could relate to. Vocalists cried out in voices trembling with agony, singing intense lyrics that did not feel obligated to parade around false hopes or unreachable joy. Hopeless screams mimicked the dismal, confusing feelings that left her a crinkled pile of tears on the ground. The growls and gutturals left her light-headed with a power drawn from pain rather than contentment.

When Kate blasted the music into her ears, it did not make her feel better. But to know she was not the only one who had ever felt so downcast was indispensable. When Kate listened, she was not alone. In fact, she found somewhere she belonged.

Fitting in at school proved to be difficult. Passing through many phases, Kate never knew who she was or who she wanted to be. She hung out with the kids who drank and skipped school and she dated boys who confessed their love for her but ended up sleeping with her friend or leaving her entirely.

Kate did a stint in college, pursuing a psychology degree, but made the mistake of revisiting an old flame who had often accused her of being unfaithful while she was away. She dropped out, moved back home, and moved in with him, but the accusations never ended.

Working entry-level jobs, she exhausted herself to pay the bills while he sat around smoking weed with their roommates who never cleaned up after themselves.

Their arguments escalated daily. Each time she tried to leave, he would threaten to kill himself. Without a proper outlet for her frustration, Kate would punch the walls and destroy their room. Once, she even threw their TV to the ground in a fit of rage.

Kate confronted him when he started seeing another woman. Twisting everything around, he had convinced her that she was to blame so she learned to keep quiet, accepting that he was a cheater and she was trapped. Fighting with him achieved nothing and she was left with only a pillow to catch her tears.

Eventually, he overdosed on hard drugs that Kate was not even aware he was using. Then again, she was not privy to most of his extracurriculars.

After his death, Kate had only a small window of freedom before she met Connor. If the saying is true, that women marry their fathers, then falling for Connor made sense. He was a combination of every horrible man she had ever dated with an additional serving of degeneracy. Of course, he had not revealed his true self to her until it was far too late.

Sitting beneath the trees in the tranquil forest, Kate decided this new life was not bad at all. The trees guarded her like silent, steadfast protectors. She was a nobody. No one knew her name. No one was looking for her. No one cared where she was. She was only responsible for herself.

Kate had spent her whole life taking directions from others, and most of them did not have her best interests in mind. Now, she had to find her own direction and learn how to survive alone. The hardest part was learning to love the only person she was left with. Herself.

Chapter 6

Asphalt heated the soles of her feet with evening warmth. The tequila and bleak memories had her trudging lazily down a back-country road. Passing modest houses and run-down barns, she began walking parallel to a fence surrounding a farmer's field.

Cow carcasses littered the field and the smell of decay assaulted Kate's nose. Left to fend for themselves, animals starved, died of thirst, or succumbed to disease.

Commotion from a bush against the fence startled Kate and she stopped dead in her tracks. Listening, she groped for the box cutter in her pocket and clicked the blade out to its full extension.

The branches continued to sway and the leaves rustled, amplifying the reverberations of her heart. Inching toward the bush, Kate held the box cutter out and at the ready, disguising her fear with false bravado. She peered around the bush, careful to keep her distance.

A small furry body erupted from the bush, took off across the road, and dashed into the foliage on the other side. She sighed, closing her eyes and steadying her breath.

Just a raccoon, stupid girl.

That was when Kate heard it. A voice up ahead. Her eyes shot open, and she ducked into the bushes that had concealed the raccoon so well.

"You don't have to hide from me, sweetheart," a deep voice called after her. Frightened and angry, Kate had told herself never to walk the roads. It was too dangerous. Avoid the roads and this was why.

His boots crunched on loose asphalt as he started toward her. She parted ways with the concealment of the bush and sprinted down the road. The intervals between footsteps shortened, the soles of his shoes thumping hard against the pavement. He was picking up speed. He was coming after her.

Something sharp, a twig or a rock, pierced the sole of her foot. She lost her footing and the box cutter hit the pavement, shattering the plastic case that held the razor blade. She gave it a wistful glance but compelled her legs to keep moving.

Kate reached an old farmhouse, the one that belonged to the field of bovine remains, and ducked inside, hoping to find somewhere to hide.

Hoping to throw the man off her trail, she slammed the door to the first room she passed but kept moving. If he started his search there, she would have more time to figure a way out of this predicament.

Pressing on down the main hallway, she threw herself into the last bedroom on the right and closed the door. A skeleton key jutted from a metal plate just below the doorknob. She gripped the key just as his boots jarred the metal strip of the front door jamb. The skeleton key colliding with the lock engagement would offer up her location. She could not risk it, so she let go.

Kate pushed her pack under the bed and slid her body in next to it, laying face up and stiff as a board. Eyes wide as the mouth of a grave, she focused on slowing her breathing. If Kate made a sound, she would be dead.

The man's footsteps grew closer, thudding like an ominous heartbeat. They stopped right outside the room, and she let out a small gasp.

The doorknob turned slowly, and the door creaked open. Thundering into the room, the man entered and closed the door behind him.

Kate's attempt at misdirection was a failure. He knew she was here. Tremors racked her body. Terror gripped her, and she willed him away with everything she had.

"I just wanna talk. I'm not gonna hurt you," the man said, his voice unnaturally high-pitched, trying to achieve a false sense of security. It only frightened her more.

He knew she was in this room, but not sure where. Perhaps he would glance around and then give up; move on.

Careful, Kate. She scolded herself. *That sounds a bit like hope. Hope only disappoints.*

Investigating the room, he peered into corners, behind the desk, and even in the closet. Then, the toes of his shoes were inches away from her face.

Dizziness washed over her, and she realized she had been holding her breath. Because her life depended on it, she let out the air as slowly as possible and then drew in quietly.

The man's breathing was labored and heavy with adrenaline. He was so close that she could smell him: a mixture of body odor and motor oil. A bead of sweat dropped from his forehead onto the floor next to her arm.

The room fell eerily silent. She thought maybe he was about to relent. Maybe he was about to turn away and leave. Dropping to his knees, his face filled the gap between the bed and the floor, meeting her wide eyes.

Kate thrust a clenched fist at his face, but he dodged it with ease. He lunged for her head, catching a handful of hair, and pulled until only her bottom half was still under the bed. She grabbed at his fingers and tried to pry them away from her but each time she pulled one finger away another took its place. Wriggling violently, she hoped to break his grasp, but her efforts were in vain.

The man hauled her to her feet and slammed her down on the bed, pressing his left elbow on her throat until her trachea burned. Kate gasped for air and clawed at his arm. Surprisingly, he let go.

Repositioning his arms, he held her shoulders down, his knee digging into her hip to keep control of her lower half. Then, he smiled at her. Not a kind smile, but a smile that gave away his perverse intentions.

"Don't fight it, baby. We're just gonna have some fun," the man rasped in her ear; his facial hair tickled Kate's cheek.

Tears began to fall as years of suffering smacked her in the face. As if she were not just stuck in this one moment of anguish, but in every agonizing horror she had ever been subject to. His hands slid recklessly underneath her shirt and across her breasts. He pressed his groin against hers and she could feel how disgustingly erect he was.

In a moment of renewed strength, she ripped one arm free of his grasp and clipped him in the nose with an elbow. He recoiled from the blow, but it did nothing but rouse a burning anger. Closing his eyes, he blew out a long breath full of rage.

The man regained his grip on her arm and slowly turned his face toward her. The sickening desire in his eyes went up in flames, replaced by a fury she had seen many times before but from a different set of eyes.

"Bitch." He gritted his teeth and drew his fist back. The punch landed solid and heavy, connecting with the bottom half of one eye and the side of her nose. Blood streamed down her cheek, dripping on her neck and into her hair.

The collar of her shirt in his fist, the man pulled until the fabric ripped apart, leaving her top half exposed. He loosened the button of her jeans and pulled the zipper down violently.

In a few swift jerks, her pants were down to the middle of her buttocks. Any strength she had left drained from her muscles as she struggled under his weight. He fumbled with the belt around his waist and her body collapsed.

It was over. This was happening. She squeezed her eyes shut tight and tried to conjure up an escape in her mind—something to distract herself from the depraved act her body was about to endure.

Then, his head arched upwards, unnaturally, as if he were trying to look at her and the ceiling at the same time. A large hunting knife emerged from behind him. The sharp end took its place against his throat and cut, from right to left; a macabre violin bow playing one deadly chord to end a horrendous symphony.

Thick, red blood fell like a curtain from the opening in his neck. It was his turn to be wide-eyed with terror. His mouth hung open and dark, viscous blood gushed from his lips. Gurgling sounds bubbled over his tongue, and he coughed, painting her face in flecks of crimson.

Kate kept still, hardly comprehending what she was seeing. The drumbeats of her panicked heart refused to slow to a steadier cadence. She demanded composure from her limbs and lungs. *Get a hold of yourself.*

Finally, her vision cleared. A hand held her attacker by the hair as he bled out. Using its grip on the hair, the hand pulled the man off of her and threw the body to the ground. It landed with a sickening but satisfying thud; the sound of nothing more than a meaningless object colliding with a wooden floor.

Without moving, Kate looked up to see another man standing over her, still holding the large hunting knife dripping with the blood of her assailer. His long-sleeved shirt was stained with the crimson lifeforce along with dirt and sweat. There were several small tears in the fabric, and his dusty blue jeans mirrored the same wear and tear—the latest fashion: survival apparel.

Though a five o'clock shadow darkened his chin, his face was otherwise clean-shaven and set with high cheekbones. His light blue eyes were deep set, but Kate could find no anger in them, giving him a stoic appearance. Long on top with shaved sides, his brown hair was disheveled, sprouting and curling upwards in defiance.

Give or take a few years, Kate supposed he was around her age. She was always terrible at determining people's ages, especially in near-death situations.

Arms relaxed, his stance was non-threatening, and his eyes were calm, maybe even concerned. She opened her mouth to speak but the fire from her aggressor's assault on her throat returned.

"Are you okay?" his voice cut the silence, stern but warm. Kate nodded.

Realizing she was almost naked, Kate moved her arms across her body, trying to provide herself with a bit of modesty. Racked with fear, she trembled from head to toe. His eyes fell on her shaking hands and it made her feel weak.

The man promptly turned away from Kate in her state of undress. He knelt to the man he had turned into a corpse and wiped the blood of the hunting knife on his shirt. Standing, he put the knife away and started to lift his long-sleeved shirt over his head.

Terror swept through Kate once again. This man had only rescued her so that he could have her for himself. Did she think he was some knight in shining armor? *Stupid girl.*

But Kate had no fight left in her. With muscles aching for rest and a mind desperate for sleep, she would just have to let it happen. She had only one request. "Please, please, be gentle."

The man pulled his arms and head out of the long sleeve, revealing an undershirt that clung tightly to his torso. Without looking up at her, he stopped as he stumbled over her words. Perplexion became understanding, and his cheeks flushed with shame. He tossed the shirt to the end of the bed.

"It's for you to cover up with," he said meekly and turned around to give her privacy.

Kate reached for the shirt warily, like an abused animal deciding if it could trust the extended hand of an unfamiliar human. The ripped-up T-shirt that once covered her body lay shredded on the floor. She pulled the long sleeve over her head and repositioned her jeans where they belonged, snug around her waist.

Far from being able to celebrate, Kate allowed herself a subtle triumph as she eyed the body on the floor; the repugnant piece of shit had almost defiled her. Almost.

A sound sliced through her thoughts as quickly as her would-be rapist had been. Just above the antique skeleton key, the doorknob rolled slowly to one side, then the other. Their heads pivoted towards the sound as the knob turned again, and when it did not open, Kate realized when the man snuck in, he must have locked it. Kate was impressed by the forethought.

The man in the room with her, the one who still maintained a pulse, quietly opened the only window, while Kate retrieved her pack from under the bed.

The attempts on the door grew more aggressive, more urgent, and the creature begged for entry with deep bellows. Its laughter echoed off the wooden door, distorting the sound so that it seemed louder, closer than it was.

Extending his hand to her, the man lowered her out of the window and onto the grass below. The turning of the doorknob stopped and whatever was on the other side, surely one of the Infected had resorted to throwing itself against the door. The wood splintered as the outdated lock gave way.

As the man's feet hit the ground, the Infected crashed against the door a final time, sending metal and wood fragments across the floor. After pulling the windowpane down to meet the sill, he started toward the woods with Kate following close behind.

Twigs and rocks pierced her feet, but she had to ignore it. She had to keep running. The man was faster than her, always a few feet ahead, but he looked back every few seconds to ensure she was keeping up.

The dark of night was blinding. The moon was barely a sliver in the sky and its light was meager at best. The man would only see trees when they were but a foot in front of him. When he swerved to one side or the other, she followed, trusting.

Trusting. What the hell was she thinking?

Chapter 7

Kate and the man crashed through the trees into a clearing. The trees had disappeared, replaced by empty night air. Reality crept over Kate and she froze in place. What was she doing, following this man? Where were they going? He could not be trusted.

"We should keep going." The man turned to Kate, gesturing forward, but she remained still. Her thoughts were racing and her stomach was caving in from anxiety.

"I can't." Her voice was small and quivered when she spoke. Perplexed, and slightly irritated, he took a deep breath, inhaling patience, exhaling frustration.

The man found her actions to be inconceivable. Was the Infected still rushing towards them? Was this entire clearing blanketed by undead creatures lying in wait? He regarded the woman, what she had just been through, and whatever else had occurred in her life to make a death by Infected more appealing than trusting him.

"Listen," he said, but his voice was deafening. Surely, it could be heard for miles. He stepped towards her until he was only a few inches away. Standing almost a foot over her, his stance provoked her to shrink even further within herself. With trembling hands, she dared not look him in the eyes.

"Hey." His tone was gentle and hushed. "I am not going to hurt you. You can do what you want but it is not safe for you out here alone.

If you don't trust me, fine, don't trust me but taking what doesn't belong to me? That's not my thing."

Kate assessed his words. He was right. She could take her chances on her own again. But how long until she fell into a horde of Infected that she could not fight off? How long until she ran into another sadistic rapist?

Kate answered him with nothing but a reluctant nod, and they continued on.

Chapter 8

"My name's Nick, by the way," the man said in a hushed tone. Though Kate could not see his face in the dark, she knew his eyes were on her, waiting for her half of the introduction.

"I'm Kate," she offered with a sore, crackled voice.

"I'd say it's nice to meet you, but the circumstances weren't exactly pleasant." Nick's voice trailed off as his words stumbled out, awkward and shaky.

"Clearly," Kate replied, cutting the conversation short.

Nick and Kate walked another half mile until it was evident that they were not trekking through a clearing but a residential plot. Bathed in what little light the moon had to offer, a house stood encompassed by shrubs. As they drew nearer, the features of the home gradually revealed themselves. The vinyl siding, yellow or white, the dark shutters only for looks, and the red door.

Creeping up the steps of the two-story home, Nick paused and withdrew the hunting knife from the back of his jeans. With a firm grip on the blade, he opened the door slowly and willed his eyes to adjust to the darkness within. An Infected could be standing in front of him, and he would be blind to it.

Tiptoeing across the hardwood floor, his boots hardly made a sound. Kate's bare feet were just as silent as she stayed in step behind him. As his pupils enlarged, he finally made out his surroundings.

Faced with a hallway and the stairs leading up to the second level, he proceeded down the hall.

Entering the living room, a dusty blue couch faced an entertainment center that housed a TV he imagined had not played a show in almost a year. Family photos hung on the wall in a diamond shape above the couch.

Next was a dining area with a small, round wooden table. Four chairs were pushed in around it and two children's plates remained on the table; a last meal sat frozen in time.

The counters in the kitchen were littered with dirty dishes, food wrappers, a fruit bowl, and a daily planner scribbled with appointments, sports events, and teacher conferences only to be thrust into a world where time lay crumbled and meaningless.

Focused on making sure the domicile was safe, Nick had not looked back at Kate. Somehow, he could sense her close behind him though she remained silent. After making it full circle through the main floor, they determined it was free of Infected and moved on to the rest of the home.

They crept up the stairs and together, cleared the three bedrooms. They found nothing but beds that a family once slept in and toys that little girls no longer played with.

One part of the home remained unsearched. Heading back downstairs, Nick and Kate investigated the garage. Tools lay strewn on a workbench, storage boxes collected dust in a corner—no monsters.

Some of their anxieties subsided, a silent announcement of the home's safety. Kate hurried back to the front door, which had been left ajar as an easy route of escape if needed. Closing it tightly, she locked both the doorknob and the deadbolt.

Drawers opened and contents were sifted through, drawing Kate into the kitchen. Curious but suspicious, Kate watched as Nick rummaged through the room's inventory. He found a first aid kit beneath the sink, opened it, and produced a few of its supplies.

"Can I take care of that eye?" he asked, holding up the first aid kit. Kate nodded and sat down.

Pulling a chair in front of hers, Nick sat and took her chin in his hand. He cleaned away the blood from her face and disinfected the cut beneath her swollen, throbbing eye.

Their proximity was uncomfortable as he applied antibiotic ointment to her skin. The pair found themselves periodically sneaking glances at each other and pondering their newfound acquaintance.

Struggling to overcome his distrust, Kate was making certain she held onto hers. She had found no good ever came from trusting a man.

"We should get some sleep. I'd prefer we slept in the same room in case anything happens. It would be safer. But if you're uncomfortable with that, I can sleep somewhere else."

Kate only shrugged, wariness prickled her skin, but fatigue tugged at her eyelids.

Nick led them upstairs to the master bedroom and gestured towards the bed. Even in the dark, he could see that her eyelids sagged and her tired body only carried her around out of necessity.

Waiting for his eyes to reveal dark motives or ill intentions, she gazed at him but only found exhaustion. Besides, she was too depleted to give in to her anxieties. If he were going to hurt her, he would manage it one way or the other.

After setting her pack beside the bed, Kate crawled onto the cool mattress. A feeling she had not contended with in a long time stirred within her though she could not quite put her finger on the word for it. Though Kate was in a strange house with an unfamiliar man, she felt almost safe somehow. Wrapping herself in the comforter, she was whisked away into a deep sleep.

Nick watched over Kate for a moment as her eyes closed and her entire body fell into a much-needed rest. Taking a few blankets and pillows from the hall closet, he laid them out on the floor next to the king-size bed.

Nick closed and locked the bedroom door, set his backpack next to hers, and lowered his body onto his makeshift cot. Setting the gun beside his pillow, his eyelids grew heavier than they had ever felt in his life. Sleep came in an instant.

Chapter 9

Kate's eyes fluttered open and the real world seeped in. Sweating and frightened, she sprang up, wildly taking in her surroundings: the black and white comforter, black bedroom walls, brown oak dressers, and the man sleeping on the floor. Unsure of the time, sunlight invaded the corners of the blackout curtains on either side of the room.

Kate's panicked breaths stirred Nick and he jumped out of his sleep. Undergoing the same process she had, he gathered his thoughts and quieted his nerves.

"How's your eye?" Nick croaked, his voice adjusting to the new day.

A million questions dashed through his mind. He wanted to know everything—where she was going and where she had come from—but he thought that might overwhelm her. This was a start.

Touching the place beneath her eye, she pushed in on the warm, swollen pouch of skin, and pain shot through her face.

"It's okay." Her voice came out hoarse and her trachea ached.

The man's long-sleeved shirt caught her eye. It was about two sizes too big for her, and the sight of it revived the terrifying events of her close call the day before. "Thank you for..." She trailed off, not wanting to put what had happened into words.

A nod of his head assured her it need not be repeated. Nick's face grew solemn as he recalled the attack.

Killing the Infected had always been easy for him. Finding new ways to do it became a sort of morbid game. Nick had stabbed them, slit their throats, and lit them on fire. He had even beheaded one with hedge shears.

Since the world came crashing to a halt, Nick had not killed anyone except the Infected. He had not come across many others, and those he did find, he hid from or ran.

The end of the world had a funny way of changing people. Law-abiding citizens confined to the prisons of work and home life now became dangerous survivalists doing anything they could to get ahead. No one could be trusted, and it was best to stay out of their way.

Nick decided the man he killed *was* afflicted by a disease, just not the kind most were suffering from. This man was worse than those killing and stealing to survive. He was willing to do so for his own pleasures, and the world was better off without him.

The result of his death transformed Nick from a lone survivor, hiding and looting his way through the world's devastation, to a hero. And more than that, he was no longer alone.

Chapter 10

Downstairs, Nick regarded the layout of the kitchen as he threw away trash and old food, put dishes in the sink, and rummaged through cupboards.

Opening the pantry, filled with snacks months past their expiration, Nick took inventory of the food inside. The roof of the pantry sloped downward, making room for the stairs that led to the second floor. The house's water heater sat at the back and a small space opened up behind it.

Stepping carefully between a roll of paper towels and a box of ramen noodles, and balancing on his front leg, he peered behind the water heater. *Fuck yes,* he thought to himself as he discovered a stack of canned goods. Sweet corn, green beans, whole potatoes, and that was just what he could see from his awkward pose.

The cans squirreled away behind the water heater seemed like an emergency supply. Nick regarded the home's previous occupants. Had they been stockpiling in the event of society's deterioration? If they had the insight to prepare for something like this, where were they now?

Choosing a can of baked beans, he took a pot down from the rack over the kitchen island and faced the stove. The stove ran on gas and he sighed in relief as the front right burner ignited upon the first try. He poured the beans into the pot and heated them on the stove.

Upstairs, Kate opened the door to the master bathroom and took in its full array of soaps, shampoos, lotions, perfumes, and hair styling tools. Twisting the knob on the sink, she frowned in disappointment when no water came from the spigot.

Kate rifled through the contents in the cabinets beneath the sink, finding a pack of wet wipes. Removing her clothes, Kate wiped away dirt and oils that had built up throughout her travels in the wilderness.

A clanking sound cut through her repose and tore her from her thoughts. Panicked, she locked eyes on the bathroom's doorknob. She had checked this lock three times before getting undressed.

The lock remained intact. The clamor resounded and she realized the noise was downstairs—a utensil hitting ceramic.

Nick's kitchen soundtrack was calming. The mundane sounds had not been a part of her daily routine for a long time. They lulled her back to her place of comfort and rumination as she coated herself in a lavender-scented lotion.

Kate thought about Nick, her accidental hero, and wondered what he gained by saving her life, or at least her dignity. Furthermore, why let her tag along with him now? What did he want? There were few things more frightening in the world than the unknown intentions of a man.

Kate wrapped herself in a towel and stood before the large double vanity. Over each sink were oval mirrors that had been painted black. In between the mirrors hung a wreath made from twigs and adorned with faux black and white roses.

The wife's side of the counter must have been the left side as it was topped with a small make-up mirror, a hair straightener, and hair spray. Affixed to the wall was a black coffin-shaped shelf full of makeup.

I like this woman's style, Kate thought to herself and grinned.

Gazing at her face in the mirror, Kate hardly recognized the woman staring back at her. The swollen skin beneath one eye was an abstract painting, shades of eggplant and maroon. Deep creases in her forehead and sunken cheekbones made her appear older than she was. Choosing a few items from the coffin shelf, she got to work.

Moments later, Kate stared into the mirror and was pleased with the face that returned her gaze. Concealer had smoothed out her uneven tone and hidden most of the blemishes. Eyeliner had given her eyes some depth and mascara had elongated her lashes, creating a more feminine appearance.

Kate smiled. The beauty she felt was a stranger to her, trying to pluck out all the demeaning words that had been worked into her skin all her life. If only the degradation had not been rooted so deep.

CHAPTER 11

Just as Nick placed two bowls of hot beans on the table, Kate walked into the dining room and sat down. She wore blue jeans and a black t-shirt borrowed from the master closet. The closet offered more flattering, lavish options, but the state of things demanded more practical attire.

Though she was bathed and wearing clean clothes, she opted to don the long-sleeved shirt Nick had given her. For some reason, it was like armor to her, providing a sense of safety.

Nick glanced up at her, then looked down at his bowl, but his eyes found their way to her again. The bruising under her eye was barely visible. Glowing, her eyes were vibrant and defined. Feeling the heat of a blush, he sat down at the table and focused on his meal.

"Morning," Nick said in a colorless tone, without looking up.

"Good morning," Kate responded, looking straight at him. He seemed to be avoiding her gaze and she scrambled to reason why, but her confidence conquered. With fresh clothes, clean skin, and a face full of makeup, she felt rejuvenated. A chance to clean up and have a warm meal on the same day? It did not get better than that.

Kate finished her meal, dropped her spoon into the bowl, and let out a satiated sigh. "Thank you," she said. "That was delicious."

Opening his mouth to tell her she was most welcome, he chuckled instead. She looked up at him, surprised.

"You ought to be grateful," he scolded lightheartedly. "It took me hours to pick those beans and even longer to get the flavor just right. I'm surprised I managed to sleep at all as long as I've been slaving over the stove."

Though the joke was weak, they laughed, those deep bellows that came straight from the stomach. The laughter was rare and medicinal. Kate thought her belly would burst open between the meal and how hard she was giggling.

"Ah, yes. Cooking beans, the pinnacle of culinary achievement."

"Dangerous, too. There was an incident... with the can opener. Almost lost a finger." Nick looked down at one hand, shaking his head as though recalling a terrible memory. Unable to keep a straight face, his lips curled into a smirk and the two laughed even harder,

Looking past Nick, Kate eyed the empty can of beans on the counter. When she saw that the can had a pull tab, she shot him a playful, questioning look. The laughter died down, and they sat in silence once again.

As Nick gazed at her from across the table, restrained humor lingered on Kate's face in a thoughtful smile. Black hair fell onto her shoulders, wavy with ends that looked soft enough to touch. Her shoulders were slim but carried a certain undefinable strength in them. That same strength could be seen in her bluish-gray eyes, but there was something he could not quite detect.

At first glance, Kate's eyes revealed a normalcy, maybe even a shallow regard, but Nick suspected it was a ruse. After staring a bit longer, he could see a heavy pain within those pupils. The gray hues washed away the blue ones and shaped into storm clouds. He was uncertain what tempestuous thing was tormenting Kate, but whatever it was, she had been using it to survive. It had been her fuel.

Once again, he felt inquisitive but reminded himself that her past life was none of his business. Only the present mattered.

"So, where are you headed?" Nick asked.

The million-dollar question, she thought. Looking at him with guarded eyes, she simply shrugged.

"You... don't know?" he asked.

"I've just been trying to survive, I guess," she answered him, at the same time explaining to herself what she had been doing all these months. The truth was, she never had a particular destination in mind. *Don't die.* That had been her mantra. "You?"

"There's a Marine Corps base about 40 miles north of here. I was stationed there years ago. Before everything got bad, I had heard about people taking refuge there. I figured it might be worth a shot," Nick replied. Trying to sound hopeful, doubt crept through his voice the way the smell of shit always finds its way to your nostrils, no matter how many candles you burn or how much air freshener you spray.

"Sounds promising." Kate tried to sound genuine, but the inflection of her tone betrayed her obvious disinterest. It was nice of her to at least humor the idea because he knew it sounded too good to be true.

The naive part of him truly believed there might be a safe place somewhere. A place where people were living, thriving, and helping each other. Even after all the death he had seen, he still held on to such an ignorant, childish ambition.

"You could come with me," Nick offered, his voice sounding sunnier than before. "We could travel together. You know, strength in numbers, or some shit." Feeling his cheeks redden, he was embarrassed by the desperation that snuck out between his words. He had meant for it to sound like he would be doing Kate a favor. Instead, it seemed as if he were begging her.

Kate paused for a long time, carefully considering the options and weighing out the pros and cons. After a while, the only response she offered was another shrug.

Chapter 12

After their breakfast, Nick and Kate collected supplies from around the house: batteries, rope, medical supplies, non-perishable foods that would not weigh down their packs too much, and whatever else they thought might be useful.

Sitting at the dining room table, Nick rifled through his pack for a handgun that he kept for the most dire situations. He set it on the table, along with a magazine loaded with bullets and a box of ammo. Nick sighed, unsettled at the amount of firepower he had remaining.

"How much ammo do you think you'll need?" Kate asked.

"Not sure," he answered. "But however much I need, I want to have more than that."

"The closet!" Kate's eyes lit up. "Come on." She ushered Nick upstairs and into the closet of the master bedroom. In the back, half hidden by suit jackets and hoodies, stood a gun safe. "Think there's any ammo in there?"

"God, I hope so," Nick replied as he cased the safe, noting the type of door and the thickness of the metal. Retreating down the stairs and into the kitchen, he opened every drawer until he found the one he was looking for, the one he was sure would be there: the infamous junk drawer.

Sifting through the random items, a Phillip's head screwdriver, three nails, a few rubber bands, pencils, scissors, and utility tape, he found it. A paper clip.

Nick rushed back upstairs while straightening the paper clip and jammed it into the gun safe lock. He twisted it around for several minutes with no luck.

"Fuck," he muttered and threw the paper clip to the ground. Glancing around, he noticed Kate was no longer in the closet, or the master bedroom. In fact, she did not seem to be upstairs at all. "Kate?" No response.

Nick walked down the stairs until he was about halfway down, he heard a door open and close; one that sounded heavier than a regular bedroom or bathroom door.

Drawing his pistol from the back of his jeans, he side-stepped down the stairs, keeping the weapon close and ready. His left hand cupped the grip of the pistol while his right index finger hovered just above the trigger.

"Kate?" he called again, quiet and commanding. The only response was a frightening stillness that Nick was now acutely aware of as the silence pulsed in his ears. A procession of what-ifs marched through his mind.

Had one of the Infected gotten in and was tearing her to pieces somewhere? Did Kate decide he could not be trusted and flee the home?

Just as Nick reached the last stair, Kate appeared at the end of the hallway with a booklet in her hand.

"Were you calling me?" she asked but he was unable to respond as he stood bent over, the fear escaping him in exhales of relief.

"Shit!" Nick finally exclaimed. "Where did you go? Why didn't you answer me?" His heart thrummed with unspent adrenaline as he rehomed the handgun into the small of his back. Like a child being reprimanded, Kate looked down at her feet.

"I—I didn't hear you. I'm sorry." Her fragile voice stumbled over each word. Nick's irritation dropped into the pit of his stomach where an empathetic guilt was born.

Piece of shit, Nick scolded himself.

Kate's hands started to tremble the way they did when Nick first met her. Just a few sentences and his inability to contain his temper had shattered Kate all over again. That was not what Nick wanted. Releasing the tension in his shoulders, he dropped his domineering pose and prepared to soften his voice.

"No, it's okay. I just didn't know where you were. I thought—" Nick stopped himself before he projected a needlessly concocted scenario onto Kate. "I just didn't know where you went."

Kate waited a moment to discern if he was done speaking or if there would be more. Finally, she held up the booklet. "When we searched the garage last night, I saw a filing cabinet. I used to keep one in my bedroom and I'd put all my important papers in it. One thing I was sure to keep was warranties and instruction booklets. So, I went through the papers in their filing cabinet, found the gun safe booklet, and the code was written in the back."

Disbelief overtook Nick's expression for a moment before amusement took its place.

"Shit, you're amazing. I was about to look for a circular saw. It would've been loud, taken a while, and might not have even gotten through. It's a sturdy safe. You just saved us a ton of time and effort," Nick said.

A shy smile played on Kate's lips as she handed him the booklet and they ascended the stairs to the closet once more.

Nick twisted the dial on the safe to the appropriate numbers, laughing in triumph when it opened. He moved documents aside, pieces of paper that were important in a world that no longer existed. Four boxes of .45 caliber hollow points emerged in his hands. If the power behind the projectile was not enough stopping force, the hollow point expanding and ripping through an enemy should do the trick.

"The Lord's caliber" Nick laughed and stacked the boxes in his arms to carry them downstairs. Kate had no idea what that meant, but enjoyed the excitement on his face. She smiled, but it faded as she considered the purpose of the ammo. Killing. Fighting. *Don't die.*

"It's just a safety net," Nick reassured. Kate's eyes revealed her sinister apprehensions. She nodded but his reassurances did little to calm her fears. "Also, we should talk about that."

Nick pointed down to Kate's bare feet. Puzzled, she followed his gaze. "I know why you don't wear shoes. It makes for quiet travel. But you don't have to be so quiet anymore. This journey will have all kinds of terrain. And I need you to be fast, not quiet. You need proper footwear."

Kate agreed and perused the shoes on a shelf above the coat hangers. Passing over the high heels, motorcycle boots, and flip-flops, she grabbed a pair of black sneakers and checked the tongue for the label. Size 7. Slightly too big for her small feet but they would work. Taking a pair of socks from the wife's dresser, she clad her feet in the borrowed footwear. Nick nodded, and they descended the stairs.

Taking one last look around the house, Nick and Kate bid it farewell.

Chapter 13

"Millions have now been affected by this disease... doctors are saying it is some sort of mutation of the Kuru disease... contaminated brain particles... hundreds of thousands dead... close up your open wounds, people!"

Kate strained to hear the upstairs television as the news reporter spouted off about some deadly pandemic. The voices were lower now. The bastard must have turned the volume down.

What the hell is going on? Whatever was unfolding, strange disappointment befell her when she guessed the impact of it would miss her. The world she was confined to was much smaller than most.

Kate practiced her daily routine of testing the ties around her wrists, the ones that held her firmly to the bedposts in a macabre bedroom crucifixion. It came as no surprise when the bindings showed no sign of relenting.

Connor strode down the stairs holding a syringe, and just as Kate readied for protest, he stumbled. His right leg gave out from under him. Squinting her eyes, she studied him curiously. Placing a hand at the foot of the bed for support, he steadied himself.

The evil in his eyes was familiar. But there was something else. Anxiety. Terror, maybe.

Connor shook his head and continued toward the bed. Grabbing her wrist, he steadied the syringe at the crease in her elbow.

"Connor! No, please!" she pleaded as he plunged the drug deep into her veins. As her consciousness faded, Connor fixed his glassy eyes on her, struggling to focus. Looking like a broken doll, his head tilted to one side and his arms hung loosely from his body.

As she fought the urge to sleep, an unfamiliar sound broke through her delirium. Maybe she imagined it, but she swore she heard him laughing.

Chapter 14

Kate lifted her head from against the tree and forced the memories back into the disturbing box she tried to keep sealed up tight. The thought of her past made her stomach churn, and Kate could not afford to focus on anything but the present.

After a few hours of walking, she and Nick had taken a break. They sat side by side against trees, resting their bodies and minds. Leaning his head back against the wood, his eyes closed, she wondered if he had also been recalling some grotesque memory.

"How long do you think it will take to get there?" Kate asked. Nick's eyes fluttered behind his eyelids as her voice disrupted his thoughts.

"About two days. That's with stopping to rest, sleeping at night, and eating," he replied, opening his eyes and scanning the forest. A mutual silence had hung between them for most of their trek. Making any sound was dangerous. But here, Nick and Kate were close enough to carry on a quiet conversation.

Kate took a granola bar from her pack, took a bite, then offered it to Nick. After eating a small piece, he handed the rest back to her. They sat silently for some time until Kate jumped up without warning.

"Did you hear that?" she whispered, twisting her head around frantically. After listening for a moment, he shook his head. All Nick could hear was the wind lapping at the leaves in gentle waves.

Kate pulled her pack around her shoulders and walked with purpose in a northeast direction. Nick followed, staying on her heels.

Then, he heard it. A soft whimper—barely even a sound. Looking for confirmation, Kate turned to him, and this time, he nodded.

The sound grew louder until it became a soft, crying. Pushing past a thick veil of Virginia creeper, they eyed a small, broken-down structure. A low sobbing emanated from the long-abandoned wooden building. Perhaps a house at one time, there was a gaping hole on its east side where time and the environment had taken it away, board by board.

The weeping carried on as Kate tiptoed toward the opening in the house. Nick touched her elbow, and she whirled around to meet his uncertain gaze.

"There's someone in there," she whispered sternly and continued. Rounding the edge of the rotten wall, the inside of the structure opened up before them.

Against the farthest wall, a small form sat atop the withered floorboards—a little girl. Frail hands covered her eyes as she cried into them. A curtain of brown curls fell over her hands and the sides of her knees. A dress that had once been brilliantly white was now a tattered heap around her, dyed with soil and age and wet with tears. Beneath the hem of the dress, dirt-smeared toes peeked out, mottled with angry, red sores.

Kate approached the child on crouched knees, shrinking herself to be smaller and less threatening.

"Sweetheart," Kate called, trying to sound reassuring but the word drifted out on a wave of uncertainty. The child went on crying as if she had not heard her.

Everything in Nick's body tensed up as if bracing for a terrible impact. Unfastening the machete hanging from the right side of his backpack, he inched it out of its sheath. With the blade ready, he stayed in arm's reach behind Kate.

"Hey, it's okay." Kate tried again.

The child did not move but the sounds of her sobs changed. What started as steady, quiet weeping sped up and the child's pitch increased. Breathy and inconsistent, the cries grew louder as they echoed into her shaking hands. The child was shrieking now, except she was no longer crying. As the haunting tones rang out, they morphed into a disjointed cadence of unhinged cackling.

The little girl pushed herself to her feet and stared at the duo. Chocolate whisps of hair hung in front of her face but behind the strands... Kate gasped. The child had no eyes.

Kate stared a moment longer at the girl's face, whose lips curled up into a sinister grin. Kate realized she did have eyes, but they were black. Not just the pupils or the irises but the entirety of what filled the child's eye sockets was devoid of color.

It reminded Kate of the doctor's offices her mother had taken her to growing up. They would spend what felt like hours in the waiting room and Kate would flip through the magazines strewn about on cheap coffee tables. The words in them never mattered much to her—articles about the trendiest kitchens or whose bed a celebrity was spending their time in—but the images always caught her eye. It never failed that in at least half of the magazines, some bored patient with a pen had colored in the eyes and teeth of a model, an actress, or a musician. Sometimes, they had even added devil horns to their otherwise perfect heads.

In those waiting rooms, Kate had found it deviously funny. Now, staring at the little girl's eyes, she could find no humor in what she saw. There was no life, no soul left in them, and they were set intently on Kate.

Kate's hands shook and her feet were fastened to the floor. The little girl lunged at her with crooked, groping fingers. A guttural noise escaped the girl's lips, but the sound was not hers alone. Underneath was a deep bellow as if a grown man screamed simultaneously from the same throat.

Nick pushed Kate out of the way, and she stumbled to the floor. Just between the stomach and rib cage, he sunk the machete deep into the child's chest. A howl of pain filled the room, and this time, the sounds were only that of a small child.

Nick kicked the girl's body backward and pulled the blade out of her torso. Wrapping both hands around the butt of the machete, he plunged it into the child's head, through her left ear and temple. The sickening separation of tissue echoed around the decrepit building and out into the woods.

Blood dripped from the edge of the machete and pooled around Kate's feet. The girl's face hung lifeless from the blade, her mouth hanging open in a death tableau. The black, soulless eyes were no longer fixed on them.

Nick grabbed the top of the girl's head and pulled his machete out of her. He pushed the girl backward, and her body thumped to the ground, unmoving. After sheathing the machete, he worked to stabilize his hammering heart.

Finally, Nick recomposed himself.

Kate fell to the ground, curled into the fetal position, and began to sob. Nick dropped to his knees, cupped his arm under her head, and pulled her to his chest. She quaked as she wept, wetting his shirt with tears.

The sudden, encompassing sorrow was lost on Kate. Hoping to help the little girl, she knew how it felt to be so small and lost in a large, vicious world and be in dire need of rescue.

Nick almost whispered to her that he was sorry, except that would have been a lie. He was not sorry about killing the girl, and he was angry that Kate had fallen for such a deception. The Infected were no longer human. They no longer thought like rational beings, yet they still had a cunning about them. Preying on people's weaknesses, they knew how to use them to their advantage. The children especially knew how to be tricky.

But there was no point in being angry. It served no purpose to either of them. And while he could not fathom it for himself, Kate must have thought she could save this girl. Perhaps she reminded Kate of herself as a child. Or perhaps the girl had reminded Kate of a daughter she had lost. Either way, Kate would have been praying every minute of every day that someone would find her, save her, protect her. And Kate had wanted to fulfill that promise herself.

Nick held her until her chest, heaving with sobs, dissipated into gentle mourning. And though it was not time, and she was not ready, Nick whispered to her that it was time to go.

Chapter 15

Marching through overgrown fields and abandoned farmland, Nick and Kate passed by the remnants of a former life, remaining quiet and thoughtful.

The day was hotter than usual. Sweat poured down their faces leaving their shirts damp. They trekked through an especially thick portion of woods, profuse with evergreens and vines clinging to every branch. Navigating through it took time and Kate confessed, only to herself, that she was grateful to be wearing shoes. The sharp bristles surely would have torn her feet to shreds.

The dense vegetation provided a coolness that both were grateful for. At times, Kate even felt a chill as her sweat-soaked clothes clung wet and cool against her skin.

Kate spotted a small clearing up ahead with a large rock bathed in sunlight. Nick, a few feet behind her, kept his head on a swivel, constantly surveying their surroundings.

As her foot connected with the rock, a surge of pain shot through her leg. Crying out, she yanked her leg away and Nick rushed to her side. Inspecting the rock, they spotted it at the same time. She had stepped on a snake, and it responded with a bite to her ankle.

The snake was tan with dark brown bands that striped its body from head to tail. Nick feared it was an Eastern Copperhead, a venomous snake that heavily populated the East Coast. The serpent sat coiled up with its head erect, prepared to strike again.

Nick retrieved his pocket knife, pressed the toe of his boot to the snake's head, and severed it from the body. Picking up the detached head, he observed its features. The head was round and eased into the rest of its body without indentation. There were no venom sacs, typically portrayed by a triangular-shaped head.

"Not venomous," Nick reassured. Dropping the head to the ground, he sat on the rock next to Kate as she whimpered in pain, teeth clenched to avoid making too much noise.

Nick retrieved the first aid kit from his backpack and picked up Kate's leg, resting it across his knees. He checked the wound to ensure the snake's fangs were not lodged inside, then sifted through the medical supplies looking for disinfectant. Preferring something more potent, he set down a triple antibiotic ointment on the rock beside him but continued searching.

Kate opened her pack and pulled out the bottle of Casamigos Blanc, offering it to him with a shrug. He nodded and took the bottle. The tequila would cleanse the wound perfectly.

Making a gap between his legs for the liquid to fall through, he twisted the top from the bottle and looked at her uneasily. This was going to burn, his face implied. Kate nodded and squeezed her eyes shut.

The wound was set ablaze as he doused it with the alcohol. It dripped off her ankle, a diluted orange as the blood and alcohol mixed together.

Nick recapped the bottle, and Kate let out a deep breath as the pain began subsiding to a dull ache. He wrapped the snakebite in gauze and found his mind drifting to a place he had nearly forgotten for some time.

Chapter 16

The heat intensified and Nick's skin crawled with sweat beneath his desert camouflage. The sounds of bullets raining down on the area pierced his ears. The rifle was heavy in his hands but the weight of it produced a sense of safety in his mind. Nick clutched it tighter against his chest as his breath heaved with heat and tension. Rubble from fallen buildings lay all around, and the landscape's dust engulfed the town in a thick cloud.

"Help!" a voice yelled from behind him. Darting between cars and debris, he peeked around the corner, rifle ready, and observed the street. The gunshots grew louder and more sporadic.

A man lay in the street, a pool of blood staining a uniform the same color as Nick's. Two Marines kneeled beside him, attempting life-saving efforts and speaking in frenzied voices.

Movement in a three-story building to Nick's right caught his eye. The muzzle of a rifle emerged from a window and was aimed at his allies. Nick brought the scope of the gun to his eye, put the enemy in the sights, and squeezed the trigger. With a newfound hole in his head, the enemy fell backward, disappearing into the darkness of the building. The rifle dropped with a clunking sound out of the window. Nick scanned the area for more hostiles. When there were none to be seen, he dashed towards the Marines.

Upon reaching them, he recognized that the two men on their knees beside the wounded were from his unit: a sergeant and lance corporal.

Through the blood and dirt that covered the man's face, Nick realized with horror that the bloody man on the ground was Ryan Adler, his best friend. Panic swelled within him but he quieted it as best he could. He did not have time for panic.

Together, the Marines picked Adler up as carefully as they could and dragged him into the house closest to them. The face of the building was nearly destroyed, so they took him in a bit farther, concealing him behind the walls that still stood.

Nick tore off his tactical bag, fingers ripping through the supplies inside until he found the first aid kit. Tugging the Velcro apart on Adler's Kevlar vest, he rested the front plate above his head and tore his shirt open.

Adler's sternum had been shredded by shrapnel and he had an injury the size of a baseball, descending deep into the caverns of his chest. The middle of the wound produced a thick viscous spew of blood that seemed never-ending while the edges were burnt by hot metal.

Nick fumbled with a tourniquet, tossed aside disinfectant, and stared blankly at a pack of gauze. None of these items were going to save Adler. Nick knew that but he had to do something. Adler's fingers reached up to Nick's elbow, putting resistance against Nick's efforts, but he pulled his elbow away and cut him a vexed look.

"Stop," Adler gurgled, his throat coated in blood.

The other Marines kneeled beside Nick and Adler, exchanging worried looks as the sound of enemy fire grew closer.

"No." Nick dismissed him, and his movements became frenzied. The blood oozed out around his fingers making Adler's military uniform hardly discernible. Adler's eyes started to roll back into his head. The strength in his body waning, he could hardly maintain consciousness.

"Hey!" Nick's voice cracked. "Stay with me, brother. Please!"

Tears filled Nick's eyes and he swiped them away with the back of his sleeve.

An explosion just outside jolted the other two Marines to their feet.

"Gunny, we gotta go!" the lance corporal said, his voice thick with dread.

"No! I can do this!" Nick's hands quaked, and his head was swimming, overwhelmed with his task and the sounds of impending war.

"They're closing in on us!" the sergeant urged.

"I'm not fucking leaving him here!" Nick screamed and tears cascaded down his cheeks leaving trails of clear skin through dirt and soot. "Adler, stay with me!"

Nick shook his best friend gently. Adler's eyelids were fluttering as he struggled to focus on Nick's face. Taking Adler's chin in his hands, Nick's tears fell onto Adler's neck. His friend's lips struggled to move, and Nick lowered his head so he could hear what he was trying to say.

"Go," Adler whispered to him. Just as another explosion broke down the wall, Nick felt hands pull him up and further into the building.

Reluctantly, Nick pushed on with his brothers, away from the war conditions they were outnumbered in and away from the body of his best friend, leaving him to die alone on the floor.

Chapter 17

As Nick finished wrapping Kate's ankle, she looked to him gratefully, offering a soft smile that vanished when he appeared to be deep in thought. Eyes glassy as if on the brink of tears, his gaze was lost out into the woods. His hands rested idly on either side of the snake bite, no longer performing any actions.

Kate stole the opportunity to study him. Bright and stormy, his light blue eyes resembled the sky itself. The crop of hair on top of his head was tidy except for one lock that swept across his forehead. She wondered how Nick kept his face and the sides of his hair so clean-cut, then deduced that it was not entirely unheard of to use a razor blade during the apocalypse.

Jaw tense and teeth clenched, Nick's mouth was set in a tight line. The storm in his mind rained down a barrage of intense thoughts as he picked at the hem of his black tactical pants. A navy blue henley covered his torso, the top button undone, revealing the black lines of a tattoo hidden on his chest beneath.

Curiosity about the tattoo opened the floodgates to more questions Kate wanted to ask. What was his past like? How had he managed to avoid the disease, and why he was so hellbent on keeping her safe?

"Are you okay?" Kate asked, placing a hesitant hand on Nick's forearm. Blinking away his memories, he turned and gave her a melancholy smile.

"I'm okay," Nick replied, lowering her ankle to the ground.

After putting away the medical supplies, they closed up their packs and shouldered them. Taking both her hands, he helped her up and they walked a few feet together to test her ability to carry on. Her pace was slow as her ankle swelled and burned with pain at every step, making her walk with a wobbling limp.

Though they had not gone far, she grew frustrated and stopped, her injured foot hovering inches above the ground. Cupping her elbow in support, he observed her grave expression as she searched for the right words.

"I'll slow you down," Kate said. "It'll take us another day to get there or more. You should just...go"

This hit Nick like a ton of bricks. An ache consumed his heart as he stared at Kate; the images of Adler resurfaced in his mind. *How could she even suggest this?*

"No," he answered sternly. At first, Kate feared he was angry with her, but his mind was somewhere else entirely.

Chapter 18

The short distance Nick and Kate had achieved took them into late evening. Kate's ankle throbbed with pain and her breathing was ragged as walking grew more arduous. Nick knew she would have to rest soon.

Nick lowered Kate to the base of a tree where she sat with her legs straight out, leaning her head against the cool bark. Closing her eyes, she sighed as the pain in her leg eased up. Nick sat against a tree adjacent to hers, his muscles and feet equally thankful to find repose after the day's walk. He had hoped to find a house, like before, but this would have to do for now.

As he gazed out among the trees and into the field beyond them, Nick thought about the soldiers who traversed this land nearly one hundred and sixty years ago. Men clad in blue and gray uniforms trudging towards each other through these exact woods. Visions materialized of smoking cannons, marching drummers performing spirited cadences, and flag bearers proudly carrying themselves toward their demise.

War had been different then. Men had honor, and carried a moral compass with them. Nick had read stories about battles that ensued during the day, and at night the opposing soldiers would gather by the river, trading items and playing cards.

Obeying the rules of war, they had fought to accomplish a goal rather than to massacre an entire group of people. Soldiers of that time did not shoot men while they slept or strap bombs on their own children in some religious act of justice. They did not arm women and send them out into enemy territory to bait bullets. No, they fought like men, and they died as heroes.

Nick was not much of a believer in the paranormal, but he wondered if any of their souls still inhabited the land. Perhaps not so much as literal ghosts. He doubted one could sit here in the still of the night and see a transparent Confederate soldier traipsing through the woods, searching for his dead comrades. Perhaps they occupied this land in more subtle ways. The blood shed from battle mixed in with soil where a tree now stood tall. Maybe when the wind blew just right, one could discern the faintest smell of cannon smoke.

The land here was rich with a history that Nick had been fascinated with ever since he was a boy and now, a new history was being written. If the world recovered from this, children a hundred years from now might sit in this very forest and contemplate the past. While playing hide and seek or hunting deer with their fathers, they might think about the people who used these woods as passage to escape the horrors of the undead.

Chapter 19

A twig snapped in the distance and Nick sat upright, tense and watchful. Rising to his feet, he helped Kate to hers. Groaning under the weight, her leg ached with pressure, but she said nothing.

Nick drew up the pistol in his hand and they stood in silence, their eyes wide as their pupils adjusted to the darkness enveloping them.

Another twig snapped, closer this time, and Kate was sure she heard soft whispering.

Can the Infected whisper?

Nick clicked on the flashlight attached to the bottom of his handgun and set the woods around them aglow.

Unsheathing Nick's machete from his pack, Kate held it in one hand, her other arm wrapped around Nick's so she could balance on one leg. Nick felt her grip tighten as the whispering grew louder and seemed to surround them. Their approaching company was not the undead.

The panic Nick felt multiplied until he was nearly choking on it. Shining the flashlight in each direction, he searched every inch of woods the light would reach but he saw nothing.

Seven figures, four men and three women emerged from the woods in a circle and surrounded them in one swift movement. Kate raised the machete and Nick took turns aiming the gun at each of them.

Nick swung the gun barrel toward one of the men as he stepped toward the frightened pair. When the light hit the man's eyes, he squinted and looked away, annoyed.

Whether a blade, a blunt object, or a gun, each person held a weapon though they did not have them pointed at him or Kate.

"Gonna shoot all of us, friend?" the man irritated by Nick's flashlight asked. Arms folded across his chest, his face displayed amusement rather than alarm.

"What do you want?" Nick asked, adrenaline and fear dripping from his voice.

"Seems we could ask y'all the same thing. See, we live here. These woods are ours. We heard y'all trekking through and came to protect what's ours," the man answered.

He approached with measured steps, and Nick kept the gun trained to the man's head as he circled them, scrutinizing them. He lifted an eyebrow at Nick's pistol aimed at him, glanced at their packs, and then fixated on Kate's ankle wrapped in gauze. "What happened there?"

"Snakebite," Nick answered. "Non-venomous but hurts like hell. Look, we're not going to cause you any trouble. If you could just let us keep moving, she really needs to rest."

"If y'all need a place to enjoy a hot meal and sleep the night off, you're welcome to join us. Otherwise, so long as you're just passing through, we'll leave you be. You'll have to pardon our eerie introduction, but you can't be too careful, nowadays."

Hard pass, Nick thought, but he started to imagine what their night would look like. Kate might make it far enough to find an abandoned house they could call home for the night. With only his flashlight, they would have to secure it in the dark. They had accomplished that before, but how long would it be before they found the next building?

This crew held most of the area so they would have to travel beyond however far their property reached.

Sleeping beneath a tree was an option, but exposure to the cold, the animals, and the undead roaming the area in the night posed too many dangers. With only a small amount of food in their packs, they had nothing that constituted a meal, much less a warm one. Sleeping in a group was safer. If attacked, there would be more of them to fight, or more of them to distract an attacker while Nick got them both the hell out of there.

The fact there were women in the group put Nick at ease. Though he was unable to presume the group's relations, having females implied that the men were not starved for intimacy.

Nick looked to Kate for help in making the right decision. As he weighed their options, she could see the gears in his head turning, but the pain in her leg was blocking any clear thoughts. She shrugged at him. *Up to you.*

Finally, Nick nodded to the man, lowered his pistol, and clicked off the flashlight.

"That snake bite," the man said. "We're gonna need to see it before y'all come back with us. Sorry, but I gotta keep my people safe."

It was a reasonable request. Nick bent down, set the pistol on the ground beside Kate's foot, and began unwrapping the gauze from her wound. She placed a hand on his shoulder to keep from falling over.

The man pulled something from his belt. A clicking sound caused Nick to drop the piece of gauze in his hand and grab for his gun. When the item turned out to be a flashlight in the man's hand, Nick sighed and set the pistol down again.

The light illuminated Kate's ankle and the two perfect puncture wounds left there by small fangs. Smeared blood decorated two dark purple holes. The skin surrounding was an angry pink and had started to swell.

Satisfied that an Infected creature was not involved, the man turned off the light and returned it to his belt. Nick rewrapped the pierced skin, collected his pistol, and stood to face the man and his group.

The men of the group looked somewhat wary but mostly unconcerned. Incredibly, the women looked as if they had better things to do than bother with strange people found in the woods. Nick wondered if this was the confidence that came with living in a group. Coming upon two strangers was hardly a threat when that threat was greatly outnumbered.

Kate shivered in pain as she struggled to keep herself upright so Nick took the machete from her hands, sheathing the blade and stowing the pistol in his waistline. As he turned to see why her hold on his arm grew heavier, the torment of her injury swallowed her consciousness. Her body went limp, her knees buckled and Nick caught her before she hit the ground.

With Kate slack in his arms, Nick stayed in step behind the group of seven as they led the way through the unfamiliar woods blanketed in deep, obscure darkness.

Chapter 20

The walk through the woods was only about a quarter of a mile, but by the time they reached their destination, Nick's back ached. Kate seemed to grow heavier in his arms with every step. Sweat had formed at the creases of his elbows where he supported the back of her neck and the crook of her knees. As he walked, he tried to make sure Kate's legs did not swing out, imagining the pain that would ignite in her ankle.

Walking comfortably through the darkness, it was evident that the group was familiar with the woods here as if they had occupied it long before society's downfall.

Nick had heard of such places where cults lived deep in the woods, people surviving on only what the land provided. Without being subject to societal norms, they often enjoyed practices outside of what was legal. The stories he heard were almost always synonymous with bizarre rituals or heinous sexual offenses. Looking down at Kate, Nick hoped he was not walking them into a nightmare.

As they broke through the woods, large metal walls loomed before them. The leader of the group unlocked two huge double gates, and the other members helped push them open. Nick stepped inside to see that the place was a scrap yard.

Rusted metal panels enclosed an area the size of a football field. The dilapidated bodies of vehicles occupied most of the space, stacked like metal pancakes. Jagged metal and specks of glass littered the dusty, barren ground. Various piles of discarded car parts were strewn about.

In one corner, tires lay atop each other, the black rubber cracked and dried out from years in the sun. In another corner, a pile of car doors with busted windows sat, trim peeling off and slithering out in every direction.

Nick was impressed. He never would have thought a junkyard to be an apt venue for safety during the downfall of the world, but the metal walls provided fortification while the layout was messy and confusing to anyone unfamiliar with it.

"The RV is where Layla and I stay, but there's some extra tents. You're welcome to sleep there. It ain't the Holiday Inn, but it's a place to rest your head." The group's leader gestured to a rundown RV parked in the middle of a clearing. Surely, it was inoperable, but provided some semblance of a real home.

One of the men was already getting to work at starting a fire. He stacked logs against each other, ripped up newspaper, and stuffed wads of it beneath the logs. Retrieving a lighter from his pocket, he flicked the spark wheel until it generated a small flame which he held to the newspaper until it shriveled with heat and caught fire.

One of the women gestured for Nick to follow her to the grouping of tents just beyond the campfire.

"These tents on the right are taken. Those blue and yellow ones at the end are up for grabs. One for each of you," the woman explained.

"Thanks, we just need one," Nick replied, heading toward the yellow tent at the end of the row. Crouching through the open flap, he dropped to his knees and laid Kate down on the canvas floor. Pausing, he watched her a moment until he was sure the movement had not roused her.

Removing the pack from around his shoulders, Nick sifted through it until he found a sweatshirt to drape over Kate's torso. It was not much, but he hoped it would help against the cool night air.

Nick touched the small of his back and felt the reassuring outline of his pistol. Exiting the tent, he zipped it closed and sat on a tree stump around the campfire. One of the women brought out a pot of sausages slathered in tomato sauce and rested them atop a grate over the fire to heat them up. The logs were engulfed in flames now, orange and yellow heat dancing up toward the sky.

The man in charge sat beside Nick and produced a cigar from his shirt pocket. He held a lighter to it for some time until the end of the cigar was red with hot embers. Smoke wafted from the lit tobacco, a stormy gray vapor against the white smoke of the campfire.

The man took a puff, then held the cigar out to Nick, who politely declined. Most of the men Nick served with overseas enjoyed smoking. Over a game of cards one night with some of his Marines, Nick accepted a cigarette offered to him. The day had reached a miserable temperature, and coupled with an intense battle in a nearby town, Nick figured he would give it a try. After one inhale of the tobacco, he started coughing and the taste made him sick to his stomach.

"Name's Jeff by the way," the man offered, taking a long drag on his cigar. He blew the smoke out in a ring above his head and it lingered for a moment before dissipating into the night air.

"Nick," he replied.

Though Nick had expected to feel relieved to sit down and rest his muscles, he was tense, and nervous to be around so many people he did not trust, especially with Kate being incapacitated. If something were to happen, he was completely at the will of this group.

Somehow the thought brought him a bit of comfort. They could decide to do anything and there was very little Nick could do that would promise survival. It was a coward's sense of relief, giving in to inevitable powerlessness and he hated himself for it.

"And her?" Jeff gestured toward the yellow tent.

"Kate." Nick narrowed his eyes, reluctant to offer her name.

"She gonna be okay?" Jeff puffed on his cigar again, staring into the bonfire. The flames licked at the logs smoldering with embers. The smoke was mesmerizing, white and gray dancing together until the colors reached the height of the trees, disappearing forever.

"She'll be fine," Nick said. Jeff's eyes sparkled as he grinned knowingly at him.

The women prepared bowls of food and handed them out. For several minutes, the only sounds were the clanking of metal utensils as everyone ate with haste.

One of the men brought out a bottle of bourbon and the group members took nips off of it as they passed it around. When it reached Jeff, he downed several large gulps of the liquor, and then held it out to Nick who shook his head. He would not compromise his mental state, no matter how tempting a taste of the smoky spirit was.

"You ain't gotta be so overprotective, boy." Jeff lowered his voice, but his tone was friendly, maybe even more so than before. "Yeah, I see it in your eyes. I know that look too well. I get the same way about my Layla." Jeff chuckled as he looked over at the slim, blonde woman collecting dishes. "How long you and your lady been together?"

Nick paused for a moment, deciding how to answer.

"A long time," he lied.

Telling him the truth would undermine his and Kate's bond, therefore making them more vulnerable to the group. If this bunch had any ill intentions, he wanted them to think that he and Kate would do anything to protect each other because that made them more dangerous.

Jeff chuckled some more. "You better get that shit straight in your head. She find out you don't know your anniversary, she'll have you by the balls."

Nick faked a laugh and shrugged. "What good is it to know an anniversary? I don't even know what damn day it is."

"Shit, ain't that the truth."

In between puffs of his cigar, Jeff pointed to each of the group members and gave Nick their names. Layla had moved across the campfire to sit next to a blonde woman named Emily, the two deep in conversation. Phoenix, hardly twenty years old, sat on the ground propped against a log, feet crossed and reading a magazine years out of date.

A dark-haired man, David, leaned back in a patio chair near the RV, pushing against the ground so that only two of the chair's legs were on the ground. Whittling the end of a stick with a utility knife, he hummed a low tune Nick did not recognize.

One of the men, Sam, had already gone to sleep and the brunette woman, Julia, sat on the other side of Jeff, staring into the fire and sipping from the bourbon bottle.

"Welp, Layla and I are gonna hit the hay. Been a long day. I suggest you do the same." Jeff crushed his cigar out against the log, careful to save what was left for another night.

Nick nodded and bid the pair goodnight.

Hoping there were leftovers, Nick asked Julia for a bowl of food for Kate. When she awoke, she would likely be damn near starving. The woman rolled her eyes as she handed him a bowl of the slimy, warm sausages along with a spoon. Nick thanked her and retreated to his tent.

The inside of the yellow tent was anything but spacious. Nick found there was only enough room for two people, and their packs took up the space of one person.

Positioning their packs in between him and Kate, Nick placed the bowl of food in the back corner, hoping he would not knock it over in his sleep. He took a rag from his backpack and draped it over the bowl to keep bugs out. Laying down on his back with his hands behind his head, Nick's eyes grew heavy, and drifted off to sleep.

Chapter 21

"You ready to have some fun tonight, dollface?" Connor asked, descending the stairs to the basement and entering the room where Kate lay groggy from the night before. God, she must have slept all day. Her empty stomach growled, and her eyes were puffy from crying. Taking a key from his pocket, he unlocked the black chest against the wall.

"Please, Connor. I can't take another night of this," Kate pleaded. Purple and red bruises marked her broken body. The sheets beneath her were stained with dried blood, sweat, and semen.

Connor pulled several sex toys and torture implements from the chest and displayed them on the nightstand beside her. Revulsions and dread darkened her face as she imagined the damage each tool would do to her.

"Don't worry, babe. It's not gonna be like last night. Tonight, we have some company. I know how much you love to be the center of attention," Connor said, making an attempt at reassurance but his words only terrified her further.

Moments later, two men she had never seen before slunk down the stairs toward her. The first wore a malevolent smile, licking his lips with a revolting thirst. An eerie seriousness held tight on the face of the second man as if the ordeal was a business transaction.

Kate thrashed at the binds that secured her wrists, silently praying to whoever might be listening to spare her.

Please, don't fucking let them do this.

Just as she felt hands sliding up her legs, Connor stuck a needle into her arm, depressed the plunger and her world went dark.

Chapter 22

The memory forced Kate to wake with a jolt, sweating and terrified. Groping around in the darkness of the tent, her fingers landed on fabric she identified as the canvas and mesh of her backpack. Reaching further, she took a handful of Nick's shirt in the middle of his chest.

Alarmed, Nick's eyes shot open. He sat straight up and grabbed her hand in a defensive motion. In his half-conscious state, he aimed to rip the hand away, but her dainty fingers, her frightened grip, and her panicked breaths brought him to realization.

"It's okay! Hey, it's me! It's Nick," he reassured, keeping quiet so as not to wake the others. "You're okay." □

The sound of his voice abated most of the memory's anguish and Kate let go of his shirt; he released his grip on her hand. Grasping to rein in what emotions remained, she pulled her knees to her chest.

"We followed that group back to their camp and we're staying in one of their tents. You passed out along the way, and you've been resting since we got here," Nick explained, assuming her discomfort was due to disorientation.

"I passed out?" Kate asked.

"Yeah, I think the pain was too much. How does your leg feel now?"

"You just followed them back? No questions asked? We don't even know them. What if they hurt us?" Kate asked aloud all the questions Nick had on repeat in his own mind.

"I know. Trust me, I tried to come up with a better option but there just wasn't one. There was no way you could continue traveling on that leg."

"How did I even get here?"

"I—I carried you," Nick stuttered. There was a long pause and Nick longed to see her in the dark, to read her eyes so he had a shot at guessing what was going on in her mind.

"I need to pee," Kate said finally.

"Yeah, me too." Nick picked up the pistol from beside him and clicked on the flashlight. Unzipping the tent, he stepped out of the tent opening and scanned the area with the light. All seemed quiet. Nothing out of place. He helped Kate out of the tent and led her to a back corner of the junkyard, navigating around the twisted metal and shards of glass.

Pistol in hand, he kept watch as she relieved herself. When she finished, he handed her the gun. Kate stood there, the pistol heavy in her hand, and the light pointed at the ground. Her soundtrack of the night was a symphony of crickets and Nick's steady stream.

Had their situation been different, she would have thought these precautions were ridiculous. Extreme, even. But, given their circumstances, the safety measures they had implemented seemed to fall short of what was necessary.

Making their way back to the tent, Nick took the flashlight from the end of his handgun and positioned it upwards so that the light hit the ceiling and bounced off, creating a soft glow around them.

"Let me see your leg," Nick said, pulling supplies from his first aid kit. He handed her the bowl of food, which still held a slight warmth, and she ate while he worked diligently.

Blood had soaked through the gauze and stuck to her skin as he pulled it away. The punctures sat amid flesh puffy with inflammation. Dried blood flaked off her ankle like tiny burnt pieces of paper drifting from a house fire. Coating the wound in antibiotic ointment, he placed a bandage over the snakebite and wrapped it in clean gauze.

"Why are you doing this?" Kate asked. Confusion spread across Nick's face, and he looked between her and her bandaged leg.

"Um, well, we have to keep the wound clean. If not, you'll get an infection and—"

"No, not that." Kate shook her head. After devouring the beans, she sat the bowl down at the front of the tent. Pulling her leg back to her body, she looked down at her hands, trying to find the right words.

"I mean, all of this. When I was being...attacked, you could've ignored it. You could've kept moving. We would've never known of each other's existence. Or after, we could've gone our separate ways in the woods. Or this morning, after we rested and ate, we could've parted. After the snake bit me, I told you to go."

Nick looked down and ran his fingers through his hair, searching for a way to respond. He knew the answer, or at least the way the answer felt. But what words was the answer made of?

"I... I don't know. From the start, it just felt right. Once we jumped out of that window, splitting up just never seemed like an option. I felt like we could trust each other. Like we could help each other survive."

Still looking down, Kate nodded, unable to meet his eyes. If she were to look at him, things would become too real. He might have seen her for who she really was, might have caught a glimpse of the darkness.

"Thank you," Kate whispered.

A twinge of pain in Kate's ankle made her wince, and she decided to lie down. Nick followed suit on the other side of the backpack barrier. Turning off the flashlight, he laid his head back on interlaced fingers and stared up at the shapes that played in the blackness of the tent.

Thoughts and questions teased at the fringes of his mind until he was wholly overwhelmed. Squeezing his eyes shut he willed his brain to be silent until finally sleep found him.

Chapter 23

"Three of a kind, bitch." Adler laid down his three jacks on the table, smirking. Sitting on his cot, Nick tossed his pile of cards down, defeated.

"What the fuck," Nick mumbled. Adler picked up the cards, shuffled them, and dealt them out.

On a tour of duty in Afghanistan, they sat playing poker under a large modular tent that housed ten Marines. Their cots were lined up against the wall of the tent using clothing and blankets as makeshift dividers.

"Sucks to suck, bro." Adler laughed, eyeing the cards in his hand closely as three Marines burst in.

"Guess what, boys, we got ourselves a prisoner of war," one of them stated, lips twisted in a vile sneer. Nick's jovial mood dropped, and he set down his hand of cards.

"Prisoner?" Nick asked, conjuring images of a Taliban member chained up and being tortured.

"Yeah, Gunny. Come check it out, bro," another Marine said, urging Nick to follow him. Exchanging uneasy looks, Nick and Adler stood up and followed the men.

Along with their fellow Marines, Nick and Adler walked down a dirt path toward an old, concrete building at the back of the base. The metal groaned as the heavy door opened, revealing a room barely lit with dim fluorescent lights. The men stepped in and closed the door behind them.

A metal chair sat at the center of the room with a figure tied to the arms and legs. Nick walked around it, and his face fell when he surveyed the prisoner.

"That's a civilian," Nick said, confused. He looked at Adler, who shared his perplexity. "A woman."

A dark-haired Middle Eastern woman sat in the chair, paracord wrapped tightly around her wrists and legs. Her head hung low, facing the ground and Nick was not sure she was even conscious.

A long, green robe flowed from her torso down to her ankles. Her black hijab had been ripped off of her and thrown to the ground. Nick's eyes traveled from one Marine to the next until he determined who the highest ranking was and settled his gaze on him.

"Sergeant Morris, what the fuck is this about?" Nick asked, his teeth clenched in anger and horrified at what his comrades had in mind. Adler crossed his arms and looked at each man expectantly.

The sound of the men's voices stirred the captive woman, who tugged at her restraints, uttering words they could not understand. It did not take a fluent speaker of the language to recognize when someone was pleading for their life.

"We found her traveling the barrier near the base. They know better than to come that close. She was practically begging to be caught," Morris snickered and the two men with him nodded in agreement.

Morris, the apparent ringleader of this misguided capture, rested his hands on the woman's shoulders and shushed her in a way that was anything but comforting. Her foreign pleas grew louder the more frantic she became and her voice quavered with fear. Nick placed a stern hand on Morris's chest and pushed him away from her.

“Let her go, Morris,” Nick commanded. The smirks and chuckles among the men stopped, and they all turned to stare at him. Two of the Marines unknowingly stood at attention as they watched Nick for further direction while Morris raised a defiant eyebrow at Nick. An unhinged smile framed his teeth, bared like an alpha wolf ready to pounce.

“Look, Gunny, you don’t have to be involved but this bitch isn’t going anywhere,” Morris said. The woman continued to beg for her freedom in her own language and Morris sighed, disgusted. His fist came down hard on her face and the force caused a whimper to escape her lips along with a spurt of blood.

“Hey!” Nick shouted. Taking his attention away from the woman, Morris squared up to Nick, challenging him.

Adler yelled at the other Marines to go back to their tents, and they scampered away. To ensure they reached their proper destination without any detours, Adler followed closely.

“Go back to your tent, Gunny. This doesn’t concern you. This is a matter only the most.... patriotic can handle.” Morris gripped the woman’s chin tightly and spat into her face. Nick released the service pistol from its holster and aimed it at Morris's head.

“Get. The fuck. Away from her,” Nick barked through gritted teeth. Morris’s eyes widened as he stared down the barrel of Nick’s gun, raising his hands in surrender.

The concrete door swung open, and Adler stepped in, returning to make certain the situation was under Nick’s control. Morris’s head swiveled toward him, but Nick’s gaze never left the ringleader’s face, his expression squinted into anger and disgust.

Adler moved to stand beside Nick, and the two of them watched Morris warily, prepared for any move he might make.

Looking between Nick, Adler, and the Middle Eastern woman, Morris weighed his options, deciding what his next move would be. Finally, he threw his hands up in defeat.

"Fuck you guys," he said and walked out of the building. Nick lowered his pistol and holstered it.□Adler approached the female prisoner, wiped the blood and spit from her face, and then untied her. After helping her to her feet, he retrieved her hijab which she quickly wrapped around her head while Nick and Adler respectfully looked away. Adler led her gently by the arm out of the building as Nick held the door. They headed toward the barricade surrounding the base.

Moving past the barricade, they walked down the road to the edge of the village the woman came from. Knowing this was further than the Marines could safely go, they stopped to regard each other.

Bringing a hand to her chest, the woman placed it over her heart and smiled at the men. Nick and Adler repeated the gesture, and Nick's eyes watered as tears threatened to fall. After giving Nick a thoughtful glance, she waved goodbye to them and they watched her walk into the town until she was out of view.

Nick and Adler walked back to base, trying to wrap their heads around the events that had taken place. Though the measures he took to ensure an innocent person's safety were drastic, Nick knew he had made the right decision.

When they entered the tent, they were met with intense stares from every Marine within. The atmosphere sizzled with masculine tension. Morris sat on his cot, glaring at Nick. Unsure what he told the rest of the unit, Nick needed to address the men.

"Let's get something straight. We are here to do a job and fight against those threatening this country and their freedoms. We are here to *protect* citizens. We don't fuck with civilians unless they pose a threat. We don't snatch up innocent people and treat them like shit because we hate members of their country. We don't go off on our own fucking program without consulting a superior. If anyone has an issue with that, come see me," Nick said, sternly looking at each Marine as he spoke.

Some looked at him, confused and unaware of the situation. Unwilling to meet his eyes, the ones involved stared at the floor.

With his speech over, Nick took his place back at the card table and Adler followed. They continued their poker game, but Nick was distracted, staring off into space, and Adler had to keep getting his attention when it was his turn.

Nick felt betrayed by the men around him, the men he shared a housing unit with, the men he trusted with his life. But mostly, he was haunted by the thought that someone could contain so much hate that they could torment an innocent woman. If there was one man in his group of ten, there were millions in the world with the same mindset.

Nick would fight alongside these men. He would protect them and even give his life for them. But he would not trust them.

Chapter 24

Kate stirred from her sleep to find Nick lying awake, arms behind his head and staring at the peak of the tent. Throwing one arm across her backpack, she laid her head on it and looked at him.

"Good morning," she whispered. Nick glanced over, shot her a shy smile, and looked back at the ceiling. "What are you doing?"

Nick pointed to his ear and then towards the group, speaking in low whispers outside the tent. He was listening, eavesdropping. "Anything good?"

Nick shook his head. Much of the group's conversations were too quiet and he only caught simple morning chatter: what meals would be cooked for the day, how much of a certain supply they had left, where they would loot next.

"Oh, I should mention," Nick said. "Jeff, he seems to be the leader of this group. He, um, sort of presumed we were a couple, and I... Well, I didn't correct him. I thought it would make us seem vulnerable if he knew we had just met." Nick braced himself, expecting her to be angry or uncomfortable but she thought it over and nodded.

"That's smart," she agreed.

Nick and Kate emerged from the tent and Nick helped Kate to a spot around the bonfire. The pain was rampant in her lower half and her leg was more swollen now than it had been the day before, though she tried to ignore it.

“Well, look who’s up and at ‘em,” Jeff boomed, bringing each of them a bowl of warm potatoes. “I was startin’ to think y’all died in there.” □

Layla and the others joined Nick and Kate around the bonfire. They seemed to have already eaten as most of them stared curiously at the duo as they chowed down on their meals. Jeff sat down next to Layla and threw a lazy arm around her shoulders.

“Yeah, this snake bite has really taken a lot out of me,” Kate explained, looking down at her bandaged leg.

“I can’t imagine,” Layla said with genuine pity. “It must have been terrifying.”

“Must’ve hurt like hell,” Sam said.

Nick noticed the man had not taken his eyes off Kate since she sat down. The group members continued to speak with Kate, but Nick drowned them out, narrowing his eyes at this man. Watching him watch Kate. Who was he? What role did he have in this group? Why could he not pry his fucking eyes away from her?

“Right, Nick?” Kate asked. Nick turned to her, dumbfounded. Focusing only on the man across the campfire and succumbing to his intrusive thoughts, he had tuned out the entire conversation. Everyone awaited his answer as he blinked dumbly, trying to recall anything about the discussion.

“Uh, yeah. Right,” Nick replied and Kate laughed.

“I was telling them we were headed northwest. We’d heard of a sanctuary that had formed near the caverns there and we were going to check it out. See if we might find a safe place to call home for a while.” Kate wrapped her warm fingers around Nick’s hand.

Nick stared down at it, realizing she had lied to the group. Their destination was actually northeast. When they left here, heading north, it would seem believable but they could cut towards the right after a while, and if the group tried to follow them, they would be heading in the wrong direction. *Damn, smart move,* Nick thought.

Kate squeezed Nick's hand subtly, bringing him back to the present. Fearing his actions had conjured suspicions among the group members, he plastered on a fake smile. Lifting his thumb to meet Kate's hand, he caressed it softly back and forth.

"It's worth a try," Nick agreed.

"We'll, for y'all's sake, I hope you find what you're lookin' for. I guess not everyone can have their own little slice of heaven like we got here." Jeff chuckled, looking around at the scrapyard and its constituents. "Julia, would you collect the dishes, please."

A slender brunette, the woman who showed Nick the available tents, moved from person to person, stacking bowls and utensils in her arms. When she got to Nick, she lingered, examining him with a coy smile. He looked up at her, forced a smile, and nodded, intending to send a "move along" message. After standing over him a bit longer, she pivoted towards the next person with an exaggerated twist of her waist, making her curves appear more prominent.

Embarrassed, Nick glanced at Kate who raised an eyebrow. Rolling his eyes, he looked away but could not help but smile—a real one this time.

Chapter 25

"Alright, here's the plan for the day. There's a quaint little country store about two miles from here. We've done some scoutin' and it looks like it ain't been hit yet. Nick, I was hopin' you'd come along and help out. You know, as a thank you for us letting y'all crash here." Jeff grinned at Nick, his teeth yellow with tobacco stains and years of dental neglect.

"Everyone's going?" Nick asked, considering Kate's injury.

"I figured all us men could go. Let the ladies have some time to clean up, prepare the rest of the meals for the day, maybe even bond a bit. We'll leave David here to protect the ladies." Jeff took a step closer to Nick and lowered his voice. "Besides, he can be a clumsy son of a bitch."

The color drained out of Nick's face. David. He was the man who had been eyeing Kate incessantly. Clenching his fists, he rapidly mapped out this dilemma and all possible avenues.

"Sure," was all Nick could come up with. "I'll need some time to grab supplies and check on Kate's leg."

"We'll meet at the gates in about ten minutes." Jeff nodded and the men parted ways.

Nick unzipped the tent opening and slid inside. Kate was rummaging through her pack, taking an inventory of what supplies they had left. Zipping the tent closed, Nick listened and when he was sure none of the group members were nearby, he sat across from Kate.

"Fuck," he growled through gritted teeth.

"What's wrong?" Kate looked up at him, eyes wide with alarm.

"I knew this was going to fucking happen. They're trying to separate us," Nick said aloud but Kate was unsure if he was talking to her or himself.

"What are you talking about?" she asked and finally, he looked at her.

"Jeff wants me to go on a supply run with them. He said as a thank you for letting us stay but I saw it in his eyes. He meant as a thank you for not shooting us dead. It's only two miles but you'd never make it. And if I say no..." Nick ran his fingers over his head and squeezed his eyes shut. "And that fucking creep is staying behind. To protect the women, Jeff claimed. Bullshit."

"What creep?" Kate thought about the group members and was uncertain whom he was referring to.

"His name's David. He's got short brown hair, about our age, and has this twisted look in his eyes. He's always staring at you. Drives me fucking crazy," Nick described.

Kate knew who he was talking about but had not noticed him watching her. Eye contact made her uncomfortable so she had a tendency not to look at people.

Nick's distress stirred up panic within her, yet something else simmered beneath it. Something so naive that it made her sick. Surely, someone who had been through the things she had was not allowed to feel this way about a man. Nick's covetous demeanor sparked a shameful thrill that left her dizzy and disgusted. Discarding the emotions, she returned her attention to his dilemma.

"Here." Nick took the gun from behind his back and handed it to her. "Take this."

"No, I can't. You'll need it," Kate protested, but he shook his head.

"I won't." He patted the machete hanging from his pack. "I'll be fine."

"Where do I even keep it?" Kate asked.

Propping himself up on his knees, Nick pulled the waist of his jeans out with his thumb and slid the gun barrel in, facing down. He released his jeans and the gun hung there, the grip partially emerging from his waistline. "Like that."

Kate nodded and Nick removed the gun, holding it out to her.

"Listen, this is a Glock, so there's no safety to worry about. There's a bullet in the chamber. It is ready to roll. It's got about a six pound trigger weight which doesn't sound like a lot, but it can be if you've never shot before. If things go south, you aim and squeeze the shit out of it." Kate nodded, absorbing his instructions.

"You've got fourteen rounds. If you use all of them," Nick stopped to pull out another magazine from his pocket. "And you'll know because this slide will come back and stop there. You hit this button, drop the magazine, and I mean fucking drop it. Don't worry about grabbing it, putting it in your pocket, keeping it. It no longer exists. You drop it, slam this mag in, and pull the slide back. It'll chamber another bullet and you've got another thirteen rounds."

"And what happens when I use all of those?" Kate smirked, working against Nick's steely expression.

"This is a 45-caliber gun. Whatever, whoever you shoot, it'll turn them into Swiss cheese," and with that, he handed her the gun, sighing.

Kate positioned the gun into the front of her waistband, moving it around until it felt comfortable there, then pulled at the hem of her shirt to cover it up.

"Don't take any naps. I know your injury takes a lot out of you but please do not sleep until I get back. Do not eat any food they offer. Eat what we have here. Just... be careful, please," Nick said, taking the food from his pack and piling it into hers.

"I will," Kate promised. They looked at each other in silence for a long moment. "Nick, please come back."

The precariousness that had dominated Nick's features for most of their conversation faded and a fearless confidence replaced it. His lips pulled up into a half-smile. "There's not a fucking thing that could stop me from coming back."

Nick slung his backpack around his shoulders and braced Kate as she limped beside him toward the front gate. Jeff and the other group members were already assembled there, chatting as they waited.

Nick watched from the corner of his eye as Jeff pulled Layla in for a hug and kissed her goodbye. Turning to Kate, Nick placed his arms on either side of her shoulders and kissed her forehead.

"See you soon," he grinned. She returned a smile, laced with worry as she watched the gates open and the group disappear.

Kate lingered there a few moments, considering the kiss. It was meant to be a performance. Hiding behind the rouse of a relationship, they were actors playing any part they needed to survive. Yet the way his lips met her skin with fervor, the yearning behind his touch...

Chapter 26

While the three women of the group were engaged in various activities to pass the time, Kate sat in front of the unlit bonfire. Julia lay half out of her tent, basking in the sun and reading a book. Layla hummed a soft tune while she knit blue fabric together, and the third woman drank from a water bottle on a log across from Kate.

Shaving off strips of wood with a knife, David sat in a chair against Jeff's RV whittling a stick into a spear. Clad in thick leather boots, his feet were propped up on an old tire. His eyes, hollow and dark, made Kate shudder every time his gaze landed in her direction. She was careful not to make eye contact.

"You've got such pretty hair," the woman with the water bottle said. Streaked with natural low lights, her blonde hair framed her face and ended just below her chin. She had a slightly plump figure, but given the loose skin that hung from her underarms, Kate imagined she must have been heavier before the world's food sources deteriorated.

"Thank you," Kate smiled.

"I'm Emily," the woman said. "Can I braid your hair?"

Kate drew in a breath, her mouth poised to answer. Only a hesitant exhale came out. Flooded with embarrassment, Emily looked down, picking at a hangnail.

"I know how to French braid!" Emily added with a renewed giddiness.

Kate thought about Nick's vigilant warnings. Having this woman sit at her back for a long time seemed a good way to put herself in a bad position.

"Um—"

"No, it's okay. I shouldn't have asked. It was a weird thing to ask someone you just met. I'm just so bored," Emily explained, drumming restless fingers on the side of the log.

Kate examined her, the skintight yellow shirt that clung above her waist, exposing her pudgy stomach, and the lowrider shorts that squeezed the skin around her hips. Kate saw no bulges from her pockets and no imprints of guns or weapons.

If something happened while Emily sat behind her, she would have easy access to the gun in her waistline and should be able to manage the situation. Besides, who could pass up a French braid?

"I'd like that, actually," Kate said and Emily's eyes lit up.

"Oh, thank God. I thought I was gonna have to resort to counting grass blades."

The two laughed and Emily went to her tent to retrieve a comb and several hair ties. Taking the opportunity to steal a glance at Julia, Kate expected her to be engulfed in reading as she was before. Their eyes met, Julia glaring at her, and Kate jerked her gaze away just as Emily returned.

"Moving around too much really kills my leg. Do you mind if we set up here?" Kate asked, wanting to keep the other junkyard occupants in her line of vision.

"Of course!" Emily agreed.

Kate scooted off the log and onto the ground, relying on the strength of her arms so as not to put too much pressure on her leg. Emily started brushing through her hair on the log behind her.

"So, how long have you all been set up here?" Kate asked.

"Oh," Emily laughed. "We've been living the apocalypse life since before it was cool. We've always been out here, just enjoying the freedom and living off the land. But this whole thing did disrupt us a little. We had a large area next to the river, big plots of land where we grew all kinds of food and lived in actual houses. We had these cute little cabins. There were more of us, too, but it wasn't secure. We got attacked within the first few days and had to take off."

"I'm sorry," Kate said, picturing the event in her mind.

"No worries," Emily said. "We're doing all right here. Nothing to do now but to keep going."

Emily's fingers pulled Kate's hair tightly to her scalp as she moved her fingers over each other, intertwining the hair into neat plaits. Closing her eyes, Kate listened to the sounds of a decayed world—Emily's rhythmic breathing, David's knife scraping against wood, the occasional sound of Julia turning pages in her book, Layla's knitting needles clinking together.

Rather than enjoying the sweet cacophony of mundane sounds, Kate thought about Nick. He had no right to promise her that he would return. Knots formed in her stomach as she pictured all the sick, horrific ways he could break his vow. Would one of the Infected rip his flesh apart? Would the men Nick was forced to put his trust in shoot him in the back of the head and leave his corpse to rot in the woods?

Chapter 27

The afternoon sun blazed through the treetops, blanketing the men in a sticky humidity as they walked. Autumn leaves and broken twigs crunched beneath their feet. Occasionally, they could hear an animal off in the distance—a squirrel scurrying through the brush or a startled deer sprinting through the woods.

Nick's stomach ached with anxiety, imagining every terrible scenario that could occur back at the camp. Forcing himself to listen to the steady reverberations of their footsteps and the sounds of the forest, he narrowed his focus on the present, the only thing he could control. While Nick did not trust any of the men he was with, he had to admit that traveling in a group made him feel safer.

"Where's your gun?" Jeff wondered, his own gripped in his palm.

"I prefer to fight with a blade. Quieter," Nick answered, the question steering his mind back to Kate with the handgun tucked in her waistline.

"Y'all come across any others in the area?" Jeff asked.

"Two days ago, about 20 miles south of here, a man attacked Kate. I slit his throat. Pretty certain he was by himself." Nick used the opportunity as a power play; someone had threatened them and now they ceased to exist.

"Hell yeah," Jeff nodded and raised his eyebrows in astonishment. "Gotta protect your lady. You got a pretty one there, boy."

"Sure do." Nick preferred to fight a horde of Infected with a toothpick than discuss Kate with this man.

After walking for some time, they reached a clearing where a mock log cabin stood. The sign out front read 'Miller's Country Store'. Instead of the convenience store Nick was expecting, he found a purveyor of all sorts of goods: food, medicine, cooking supplies, souvenirs, hunting, fishing, and camping gear. The sign even boasted a small supply of arms. Nick wondered what that entailed. Guns? Ammo? Bows? Regardless, he could see why this group was eager to loot here. It seemed to have everything a survivalist could need.

Nick unsheathed his machete as they approached the front door. As far as they could tell, the place was untouched. No broken windows, and no doors ajar. They tried the main entrance, but the door was locked—a good sign.

Finding the rest of the doors locked, they gathered around a window, weapons ready.

"Brace yourselves," Sam advised in a daunting manner, picking up a large rock and slamming it into the glass. Cracks spiderwebbed across the pane but it did not give way. Backing up to provide more momentum, Sam heaved the rock into the glass once more, and the cracks burst open, fragments spraying into the store like rainfall.

As the store's dank air wafted from the window, they listened for any Infected disturbed by the clamor. The atmosphere was quiet and still.

"Go on in, tough guy." With his gun righted in his hand, Jeff motioned with it for Nick to go in first.

Testing the mettle of the new guy, Nick thought. *Fuck it, let's go.*

Nick stepped through the window frame, boots crunching on broken glass, until fully inside. The remaining men poured in, sorting through the items on shelves and stuffing them into their bags.

In a glass display at the back of the store, Nick found a .38 revolver and three boxes of ammo, a small silver pocket knife, a compact set of binoculars, and a can of pepper spray. The lock on the display was not engaged so he slid the glass door open and dumped the items into his backpack.

Before he could secure the pepper spray, a clatter from behind startled him. An Infected burst through an office door and hobbled toward him, its jawbone detached from its face and swinging as if on hinges. With light brown hair matted with blood and stuck to the middle of its face, Nick wondered how it could see.

Nick shot the Infected in the eyes with the pepper spray. The creature covered its face with gray, shredded hands and wailed as the liquid burned its black eyes. Shoving the can of spray into his pocket, Nick swung the machete into the Infected's veiny neck. Still holding its eyes, the creature staggered backward and shrieked louder. The machete had sliced halfway through, flaying the throat into a mangled mess, but the creature stood firm.

Nick raised the machete again and swung, even harder, into the opposite side of its neck, and this time, it cut all the way through, severing muscles and glands, and slammed with force into the wall beside them. The head thudded onto the ground, the monster's black eyes peering up at him.

Nick turned, panting, as Sam and Phoenix gaped at him with wide eyes. Jeff smiled, nodding in approval.

Thanks for the help, guys, Nick thought. Then again, it was better this way. He did not want to feel as if he owed them more than he already did.

"That was fucking awesome," Sam said.

"Bro, that was brutal!" Phoenix added.

Nick could not help but smile as he stood there with his chest puffed out like a badass. It was one thing to talk about it, but he had gotten a chance to show them how deadly he could be.

All compliments were stopped short when they heard a light thumping against the bathroom door followed by muffled, sinister laughter. Turning their heads toward the sound, smiles faded and eyes filled with alarm. Nick approached the door with careful steps, and the men followed cautiously behind him.

The bathroom door, thick and wooden with no knob, had a large metal plate engraved with the word "push". The Infected must have been trying to push from the other side but after hearing the men's voices, their attempts turned frantic and ravenous. The wood cracked and splintered as the pressure of their weight against the door increased.

Looking back at the men, Nick counted on his fingers. *One. Two. Three.* On three, he kicked open the door and plagued creatures spilled out of it. Nick sank his machete into the first one and it dropped to the floor.

The second fumbled over the first and lurched toward the other men. A third Infected tripped over the first and hit the floor hard. Nick swung the machete down into the gray, wrinkled skin of its face, severing an ear and grazing the tip of its nose. Another swing into the base of its neck made sure the creature did not get back up.

In his periphery, Nick noticed more Infected lunging at the men. A struggle ensued between them and before he could assist, two more creatures emerged from the bathroom toward him. Grabbing the can of pepper spray from his pocket, he shot a stream into both of their eyes and they stumbled backward, screaming in pain.

One of the creatures had flanked around to his backside, unnoticed until its claws gripped at Nick's shirt. Spinning to face it, Nick kicked it in the chest to provide space between them, chopping the machete through the air but missing as the Infected stumbled out of reach.

Gnarled fingers clutched at Nick's shoulders as the other Infected accosted him from the side. With a forceful push, the creature sent Nick sprawling into a glass display. The machete slid across the floor and hit the wall with a foreboding clatter. The glass and wood caved in, and Nick fell to the floor, shards piercing his back, his underarms, and his neck.

Without any attempt to brace its fall, the Infected fell straight on Nick's chest, knocking the wind out of him as it landed. Nick's lungs seized inside of him, desperately grappling for air. The creature spewed hot breath on his face as its mouth opened and prepared to feed.

Nick held resistance against the monster's head with one forearm and groped around on the floor until he felt a good-sized shard of glass. It broke the skin of his palm as he clutched the shard and shoved the sharp edge into the Infected's neck. The creature howled as Nick dug the makeshift weapon through each layer of skin until the glass was buried.

Nick pierced the Infected a second time, plunging the glass into its eye. Blood cascaded over his hand as the viscous orb split open, leaving the Infected screaming and writhing wildly.

Abandoning the small fragment of glass, Nick felt around on the floor again. He needed something bigger. Anything. Switching up hands, he searched the other side of the ground, and almost instantly, his fingers brushed against a long metal pole that had made up the frame of the glass display.

Nick clutched the pole, ignoring the stinging pain in his palm. Blood from his injured hand coated the metal, creating a slippery surface, so he gripped it tighter and drove the pole into the side of the Infected's face.

Driving the coarse metal into the creature's flesh, Nick pushed the pole through the soft flesh of its temple. The Infected thrashed against Nick until the makeshift weapon was deep enough to pierce its brain, stopping all motor functions. Staining his shirt maroon, the Infected's life force gushed out of the wound's entrance, slathering his face and neck. Pushing the creature off of him, it landed heavily to one side as he stood up, careful not to puncture himself further in the bed of glass.

Glass tinkled to the floor as Nick shook out his clothes. Swiping blood off his face, a piece of glass embedded in his knuckle cut a small gash under his eye. He picked the glass out, threw it to the ground, and used the bottom of his shirt to soak up the blood dripping from his cheek. The other men finished off the last of the undead, allowing Nick a moment to steady his breath.

"Everyone okay?" Nick called out as he collected his machete.

"Holy shit!" Phoenix exclaimed. "That was fucking insane!"

The men talked excitedly amongst themselves, exchanging their experiences, and reenacting their kills. Nick had no interest in measuring dicks with Jeff's goons; he headed to the bathroom, machete in his bloodied hand. He pushed open the door and peeked around the corner slowly, finding the small hallway inside clear. Proceeding with silent steps, he pivoted the final corner and stood in front of three bathroom stalls.

Each of the stall doors were propped open. Bodies lay in two out of the three stalls, two females with fatal wounds. A dried halo of brown, crusted blood encircled each body and met in the middle where the metal walls separated the stalls.

The first woman was older; Nick could still recognize some gray in the bloodied hair. The second woman was younger, and Nick could not discern any features that gave away much about her.

Both bodies had been partially devoured, the second woman's face almost completely eaten away. Thoughts of Kate surfaced, and Nick had to pull himself away from gawking at the corpses.

After determining the bathroom was safe, Nick closed the door and moved on. The men had finally resumed their search for useful items. Jeff approached Nick and patted him on the shoulder.

"You good?" Jeff asked.

"I'm good," Nick nodded, glancing around at the other men. "Any scratches or bites?"

"If they was bein' honest, none. But I'm gonna keep a close eye," Jeff answered reassuringly. "Now go get you some good shit." Jeff clapped him a final time on the shoulder, unknowingly smashing a sliver of glass further into Nick's skin, causing him to wince in pain.

Browsing the store, Nick gathered canned food, batteries, bandages, and isopropyl alcohol. A small autumn display full of knick-knacks and pumpkin-shaped things caught his eye. A fluffy stuffed bat with tiny fangs protruding from its grin gawked at him with wide, silly eyes. After a moment of debating with himself, Nick slipped it into his backpack.

Wandering into the back office where the first Infected escaped from, Nick found a purse hanging from an office chair and poured the contents onto the desk. Typical things women kept in purses spilled out: a mirror, a wallet, lipstick, five lip balms, and tampons.

An orange bottle rolled out from the purse and across the table and Nick snatched it before it could fall off the edge. The label read 'Oxycodone' and instructions indicated that they were pain pills. Kate might benefit from some pain relief, he thought, and then added them to his pack.

Nick collected the tampons as well. Maybe Kate could make use of them. If nothing else, he would put them in his first aid kit.

Nick thought about opening the wallet, curious about the name on the ID he was likely to find inside. Surely belonging to one of the corpses in the bathroom, he held the leather trifold with hesitation.

Would the photo on the card inside resemble the dead body at all? Imagining pictures of family members within, their smiling faces peered at him in his mind. He could hear their accusatory voices in his head. *Why are you taking my mother's things? They don't belong to you! Please, let her rest in peace!*

Sweeping the wallet onto the floor, he assured himself that he was gathering supplies to survive, and not stealing little pieces of people long gone to carry them out into a twisted, fucked up world.

Nick exited the office to regroup with his companions gathered around the window through which they had entered.

"Y'all set?" Jeff asked. Nick nodded. Now that the convenience store was declared properly looted, the men climbed through the window and set off toward the junkyard.

Chapter 28

Kate reclined on her back inside the tent, feet propped up on her pack, eating a granola bar. The other women had gone off to attend to tasks Kate could not help with because of her injury. David still sat beside the RV, whittling and watching.

Footsteps approaching the camp made Kate's heart skip a beat. Scrambling out of the tent as fast as possible without aggravating her leg, she limped toward the gate just as it began to open.

As two of the men pushed the large metal doors open, Jeff and Nick entered side by side. Layla rushed past Kate and threw her arms around Jeff. Though she wanted to run to Nick, Kate knew her injury would not permit such movement.

Nick's anxiety released its grip on his insides as his eyes found Kate and he started toward her intently.

As her eyes took Nick in, the gash on his cheek, his blood-soaked shirt, and the crimson trails that had trickled down his arms and dried, Kate's face went pale with worry.

Nick clutched her in a tight hug, one arm around the small of her back, the other around her shoulder blades. Kate returned the hug with force, making almost every cut on his back sing with pain, but he did not mind. When they released, Kate seized his shoulders and looked Nick over.

"What happened? Are you okay?" Kate asked. Nick laced his fingers with hers on his shoulders, offering a reassuring smile.

"I'm fine," he answered, nodding his head toward the tent.

Nick helped her hobble toward the tent, unzipped the opening, and led her inside. Kate sat behind him, examining his wounds as he ran bloodied fingers through his hair and sighed.

"The building was full of Infected, but we got what we needed," Nick described, remembering how close his face had been to one of the creatures, its rancid breath still present in his olfactory memories. His mind recreated the shape of every tooth that sought to sink into his skin.

"Are these from..." Kate ran gentle fingers over the tiny slices in Nick's shirt, each tear bordered with gore.

"Glass," Nick answered.

"Okay, you need to take this off," Kate ordered, pulled his shirt up by the hem, and then stopped, nervous about irritating his injuries. Crossing his arms, he grabbed the bottom of his shirt with each hand and pulled the shirt over his head.

Kate stared at his smooth, muscular back covered in tiny gashes, and speckled with blood. Mountainous biceps transitioned into sculpted shoulders. These were not muscles earned at the gym by lifting weights, but muscles developed out of necessity and forged by survival.

The intricate tattoo sprawling the entire surface of Nick's back made Kate pause as she studied it. A zombie wearing a tattered military uniform and glowing eyes extended curled fingers toward her. In an eagerness to feed, decaying teeth jutted out from a face that sagged with rotting skin. Dog tags swung from its neck with the name "Adler" written across the sleek metal.

Clouds of explosions and pillars of flames stood as the landscape behind the zombie, resembling a war-torn city. Amid the remains of buildings, broken and rusted automatic weapons lay partially buried beneath the rubble.

The line work was amazing, the scene so immersive Kate forgot what she was doing.

"Everything okay?" Nick asked.

Wanting to ask who Adler was, Kate did not answer right away. The scene on his back spoke for itself and Kate decided he had been through enough today.

"Yeah." Kate pulled the first aid kit from her pack and retrieved a pair of tweezers. Opening the empty granola bar wrapper, she set it beside her, picked out pieces of glass, and placed them in the plastic.

While Kate worked, he used a few medical supplies to sterilize and wrap the deep slash on his palm. Pain rushed him from all angles yet he caught himself smiling. The throbs and aches were drowned out by the knowledge that he was back at the camp without incident.

"Things went okay here?" Nick asked as Kate went on picking out the glass.

"Actually, yeah. I'd say boredom was the scariest part of my day. David spent the whole day being creepy, but he didn't do anything concerning." Kate answered, still applying the tweezers to Nick's punctures.

"Good. I like your hair," Nick remarked, and Kate laughed.

"Thanks. Emily braided it for me. She's sweet. Layla spent most of the day knitting. Who knew that would become such a useful skill? Julia just read and looked angry all day." Kate picked the last piece of glass from his back, instructed Nick to lie on his stomach, and began picking shrapnel from his calves.

Ink covered the skin on his legs, as well. Nothing quite as detailed as the one on his back, Kate noted the designs seemed to be a mash-up of random items: an eagle in flight, a wooden shield etched with symbols along the outer edge, and an electric guitar, to name some.

Seemingly random to Kate, each one was a puzzle piece that would reveal her companion as a whole. If only she knew how to fit them together.

"I don't know what Julia's problem is," Nick said through gritted teeth as Kate pulled out a large piece of glass near his Achilles heel. Blood trickled from the incision and Kate blotted it with gauze.

"I know what her problem is. She's in loooove," Kate sang playfully and giggled.

"I mean, who can resist a guy covered in blood with shards of glass sticking out of him?"

"About that, I love that you're finding new hobbies, but starting a glass collection really doesn't work for me." Kate jested, pinching another fragment between the tweezers and dropping it into the wrapper.

"But you're so good at picking out the pieces." Nick turned his head so he could see her, his lips curled in a wry smile.

"What a skill. I'll add it to my resume."

"Don't forget 'snake wrangler'," Nick added.

Kate poked him in the arm with the tweezers and he yelped, chuckling.

"Asshole." Kate poked him again, both of them laughing until they were out of breath.

When the last of the shards were removed, she bundled up the granola bar wrapper and set it on the ground near the front of the tent, out of the way.

Nick pulled his pack to him and rifled through the items inside, while Kate surveyed the tent floor for any rogue slivers of glass. As Nick's eyes fell upon the stuffed bat, embarrassment heated up his face. When he had seen it at the store, he thought Kate would find it adorable, and appreciate him for bringing it back to her. Now, he feared it was juvenile and a strange gesture.

"This will help with the next step," Nick said, closing the pack and handing her a bottle of isopropyl alcohol.

Kate dampened a handful of gauze with the sterilizing liquid, and began dabbing at each cut on Nick's back, sanitizing and wiping away blood. Moving on, Kate applied the same process to the cuts on his legs and bandaged the gashes deep enough to require it.

"Thank you." Nick sat up to face her and she grimaced at the gash on his cheek. "Hold on, before you clean that one, I got something for you." Nick threw out his insecurities and took a chance on making her smile.

Pulling the fluffy stuffed bat from his bag, he handed it to her and watched her eyes light up and her lips part into a wide grin. Tilting her head to the side, she looked quizzically at the bat and then back to Nick again.

"So, let me get this straight. In between traveling with a bunch of guys you don't trust, fighting your way through a horde of Infected, and looting for life-saving supplies, you found this adorable little bat, and thought 'Kate would love this'?" she asked, looking at him incredulously, the smile never leaving her face.

"It went *exactly* like that," Nick replied and smiled back.

"Thank you. I love him." Kate squeezed the bat in a hug, and Nick laughed, relieved she enjoyed the gift and proud of himself for changing his mind.

Kate picked up a clean square of gauze, dripped alcohol onto it, and lightly touched it to Nick's face as she cleaned the open gash beneath his eye.

While Kate focused on not causing him too much pain, Nick studied her. The wide smile he caused faded somewhat, but not completely. Her eyes sparkled in a way he suspected they had not for a long time. With the braids pulling the hair away from her face, her soft facial features were more readily apparent.

Beautiful...

Having been so focused on survival and moving forward to the next safe place he had not taken time to truly notice her.

Hell, even some of the female Infected had decent faces or a body that made him take a second glance. At the end of the day, he was only a man. Something dark and unforgiving in Kate's eyes told Nick not to look too closely, and so he looked away.

"Your turn," Nick said, pointing to her leg. With her ankle resting on his knee, he pulled away the old wrappings. Purple bruising swallowed up the bite marks and the flesh surrounding them. Nick smeared antibiotic ointment on the wounds and wrapped them in clean gauze.

"I guess this is life now. Finding someone who will patch up your wounds," Kate surmised.

"Speaking of, I got you something else. Not nearly as cute but certainly more useful." Nick's hand disappeared in his pack and resurfaced holding the pain pills. "After we eat, you can take one and lie down. It'll help take the edge off. Should help you sleep, too."

Kate stared at the orange vial, remembering all the times she had been incapacitated because of heavy drugs.

Nick watched the color drain from her face, and he shoved the tablets back into his backpack. "You don't have to take any. But we have them in case the pain gets too bad."

The tampons sat in Nick's pack, gazing up at him, nagging. "Uh, I grabbed these, too." Nick held up the tampons, his voice low and sheepish. "I'm not sure if they're... something you need. But they're here. I'll keep them in the first aid kit."

Kate glared at the sanitary products as Nick put them away in his medical kit. Her nostrils flared, her breathing became shaky, and she bit her lower lip to stop tears from falling. It was a kind gesture, so she tried to force that thought to the forefront as grief and anger prepared to wage war in her mind.

The damage Connor had done to her body had left her barren, unable to conceive life within. A few months after the captivity began, her body had stopped operating the way it was supposed to. Kate concluded it was because of the stress, and told herself that if she was ever allowed to participate in a normal life again, her body would correct itself.

After escaping from confinement, the months came and went. Kate was lost somewhere between hoping to find blood between her legs and being thankful she did not have to add that to the list of things to worry about during the uncertainty of the dangerous world she was learning to survive in. It had been some time since she had thought about her feminine uselessness, but Nick's act of kindness had unintentionally rekindled the feelings of loss.

Nick opened his mouth to speak, observing the unsettling hurt in her eyes, but a voice from outside cut him off.

"Dinner's ready!" Layla shouted.

Nick was prepared to ignore the dinner call and address the anguish written all over Kate's face, but she plastered on a fake smile and unzipped the tent.

Nick helped her out, and they took their places around the bonfire. Emily passed out bowls of noodles mingled with chunks of meat and the group ate in ragged silence.

Chapter 29

After dinner, the group lingered around the fire, telling stories about the day's events. Nick kept quiet, intently observing each of the group members as he often found himself doing with people. If he studied their typical behavior, he thought he might be able to predict when something was off, or foresee danger.

Beside him, Kate yawned so hard it brought tears to her eyes.

"Why don't you get some sleep?" Nick asked. Kate nodded, her eyelids sagging so that her eyes were hardly open. Nick stood and took her hand in his, then walked beside her as she limped to the tent. He unzipped the flap and braced Kate as she lowered herself to the ground. She wrapped one of Nick's long-sleeved shirts around her arms, closed her eyes, and was asleep at once.

Nick returned to the bonfire and sipped from a bottle of water. Also exhausted, he decided it would be safer if he stayed awake until the group members went to bed.

Jeff and Layla stood up, said goodnight, and retired into the RV. Emily and Phoenix followed suit, leaving Julia, David, and Sam.

David and Sam sat across from Nick on a separate log, passing a bottle of gin back and forth. At the end of the log Nick occupied, Julia sat staring into the fire.

"You were in the military, no?" Sam asked, sparing a moment away from the gin.

"Marine Corps," Nick answered.

"Hell yeah, I knew it! You cut those fuckers up without a second thought," Sam said, throwing a victorious fist in the air. "Have you killed a lot of people?"

Stupid fucking question, Nick groaned internally. *That's okay, take advantage of it.*

"I was a sniper. They called me Fleshkiller," Nick lied, dropping his voice to achieve a sinister tone as he locked eyes with David.

"Damn, man. Remind me not to mess with you." Sam let out a nervous chuckle that Nick hardly heard as he stared David down.

A grisly darkness glowed in David's eyes, and though Nick was uncertain of the reason for this man's grim demeanor, he was confident that his own darkness was more monstrous.

"You got cut up pretty bad." Julia's voice interrupted their stand-off. Nick looked at David a moment longer before turning to Julia. Without a word, David stood and retreated to his tent.

"Fell through some glass. Nothing serious," he said.

"Well, I'm glad you're okay," Julia cooed. Sam capped the bottle of gin and yawned with a dramatic stretch of his arms.

"It was good talking with you, Killer, but I'm tired. And shit-faced. I'm gonna hit the hay. Goodnight." Sam bid the group farewell, and Nick gave a small wave before he went to his tent.

Well, shit, Nick thought. He was sure the men would outlast Julia but here they were, alone together by the bonfire. With reluctance, he noticed she had made her way from the end to the middle of the log they shared.

Inside the tent, Kate stirred from her sleep, an excruciating pain shooting through her ankle. Hoisting herself into a sitting position, she rifled through the pack for the pain pills. The thought of the pill bottle bore an anxious hole in Kate's stomach, but if she could break one in half, maybe even in four pieces, the effects might take the edge off without leaving her in a stupor.

Finding the tablets along with a bottle of water, she twisted the cap on the vial and shook a pill into her hand. With pressure on either side from both her thumbs, the elongated tablet broke in half easily.

As she tried to break it again, voices from outside the tent made her pause. She closed the water, put the tablet pieces back into the orange container, and scooted herself to the front of the tent. Hearing Nick and Julia's voices, Kate listened curiously.

"Marine Corps. That's tough. Did you go overseas?" Julia asked.

Nick all but rolled his eyes. He had learned the hard way to be wary of a woman obsessed with a man in uniform.

"Yeah, three times," he answered, never taking his eyes off the fire. Aware that Julia was inching closer to him, he urged himself to stand up, tell her he was tired, and retreat to his tent.

"Wow, you must've seen some crazy things," she said.

Sitting next to Nick now, her leg touched his. With soft, warm fingers, Julia stroked his shoulder and moved a gentle hand up his neck and through the back of his hair. The physical contact sent chills across his skin, and his eyes started to close without his consent.

"Don't do that," Nick protested. Julia pulled her hand away and turned her body to face his.

"I'm just trying to help you relax a little," her voice dripped with temptation. As she arched toward him so that her breasts were front and center, he trained his gaze on the fire, screaming internally for his feet to pick him up and carry him away from her. Why would the damn things not move?

The heat of Julia's breath on his flesh lit a flame in his lower half as she pressed her lips against his neck. Julia worked a hand up his leg until it reached the place where his thigh and groin met. A fire burned in his loins as he started to stiffen.

"No." Nick stood up. Julia's hand fell away from his body, and he straightened out his pants. Brushing his clothes off, he swiped a hand across his neck as if he could wipe away the interaction.

"You don't have to be so uptight. If you're worried about your girl, I can be quiet." Julia stood up, posing her curvy body as an offering to him. A coy smile formed on her lips—*those* lips—and she raised her eyebrows in seductive questioning.

Nick's body longed for her to touch him, to do all the things to him. He had made no promises to anyone. He was a free man. But the opposition within him reached all the way to his bones. This was one of those traps you learned about as a man. As attractive as Julia was, and the way her touch sent his body into a carnal yearning, she was a distraction. Nick would not risk his and Kate's survival for a night of shallow intimacy.

Nick shook his head, his lips pulled back in disgust, and walked away to his tent, leaving Julia alone and dejected.

Hearing Nick approach, Kate scurried back to her sleeping spot and closed her eyes just as the tent was unzipped.

Nick crawled inside and laid on his back. The pressure woke up every gash obtained by the broken glass. Turning on his side, he faced the backpack barrier that separated him and Kate and rested his hand across one of the packs. The pain from his lacerations relented in his new position.

Though the ground was hard, the aches in his muscles dissipated and Nick relaxed. He closed his eyes, trying to distance himself from the shameful interaction with Julia. Just before the nighttime sounds lulled Nick to sleep, Kate's hand slid on top of his, warm and welcoming. And it felt like home.

As Nick lay there, he realized Julia reminded him of someone, and though he was exhausted, his brain unwillingly revisited a memory

Chapter 30

"Nick, we need to talk," Liv said as she leaned against the wall, arms crossed. Her platinum blond hair hung in perfect ringlets that framed her face, which was set in a tight grimace. A white cotton v-neck hugged her large breasts snuggly, revealing a view of Liv's cleavage that was to die for.

Unable to hear her, he removed one side of his headset and paused the computer game he was playing, though the fingers on his left hand still rested on the keys that moved his character. When he raised his eyebrows and gestured for her to repeat herself, Liv rolled her eyes.

"This is the shit that...ugh," she groaned and pinched the bridge of her nose in frustration. "I'm leaving you, Nick."

"What?" Nick's face soured, and he pulled off his headset, laying it on his desk.

"You've been back for three months. We don't do anything. We don't talk. We've only fucked once since you've been home and it was awkward, like you were doing it because you thought you had to. You just keep to yourself all the time. What are we even doing?"

Nick stood up, his muscles groaning from his morning workout, and took a step toward her. Caressing her forearm, she looked down at his touch, disgusted.

"We can go out. We can talk. Baby, we can do whatever you want." Nick pulled her to him, both hands on the small of her back. Kissing her neck softly, he moved his hands up her waist and toward her breasts. She exhaled with pleasure as he lightly pressed his teeth into her neck. When he cupped her breast and rubbed a thumb across one nipple, she grabbed his hands and pushed them away.

"Stop. I'm seeing someone else. Someone who's actually a functioning human being," she said. Nick assumed she meant a man who took her out and spent time with her, but he noticed she was looking down at his waist. Because after their erotic encounter, though short, he was not even the slightest bit hard. Every bit of masculine dignity left his body with a sigh.

"Someone else? But we live together. I thought we might even get married." Nick sounded desperate, and he hated it

They had been dating for almost three years, and in addition to Liv being gorgeous, she had always been loving and kind toward him. The realization that she had been spending time with other men churned his stomach.

"Married?" Liv laughed. "That would require you to communicate with me." Her nose wrinkled up in disgust as she gazed at him with dead eyes. Nick decided saying anything more would be futile so he would save whatever pride he could maintain.

"Fine. Go." With pursed lips, he shooed her away. Offended by his response, Liv opened her mouth to say more, then closed it and walked away to gather her belongings.

Sitting at his computer, he repositioned the headphones onto his head. Instead of resuming his game, he only stared at the screen, listening to her shuffle around the house, picking up their life together and packing it away in bags.

Liv was right. He had not been much of a companion, but she had been something for him. The sound of her doing routine tasks, watching her curl her hair for a night out, and simply existing in the same house as him gave his loneliness some reprieve. The warmth of her body against his in bed at night was a comfort to him.

Nevertheless, Nick knew he had been selfish, wallowing in his victim mentality, and now she was walking away. Nick's father had been right—he fucked up everything he laid his hands on.

Nick watched Liv pass by the doorway of his office, and then cringed at the sound of the door slamming as she stormed out. The house was exceptionally quiet now. The silence was an ominous war drum in his ears, and tears formed at the corners of his eyes.

Pressing his thumb and forefinger into both eyelids, he wanted to cry but refused to let himself.

What if I just ended the pain? No one would notice if a useless piece of shit like me died. The one person Nick had left in his life just walked out the door.

Nick imagined clutching a switchblade in his hand, digging it into the bulging vein of his wrist, and watching the crimson life trickle out until he was drifting off into eternal sleep in his computer chair.

Envisioning a rope cinched around his neck, Nick saw himself hanging out of the second-story window, gasping for breath until he ran out of air.

He thought about getting his pistol from his nightstand, holding the cold metal barrel to his temple, and painting the wall with blood and brain matter.

The thoughts exhausted him, and he laid his head on his desk.

Nick's inadequacies ran so deep that he could not even do what needed to be done—taking out the trash, doing the world a favor, and ending it all. And so, he carried his weary bones up to his bed and laid down.

Covering himself entirely with blankets, Nick closed his eyes, praying to any god that would listen to let him suffocate on his own carbon dioxide or endure a brain aneurysm and never wake up.

Chapter 31

Nick awoke in the tent, nauseous and covered in sweat. When he rubbed his eyes, his cold fingers chilled his eyelids. Kate's hand must have moved away from his in the night. He sat up and turned his neck from side to side, stretching out the muscles still tight from sleep.

When he twisted his head towards Kate's side, he jumped when he saw her sitting with her arms wrapped around her knees, those hurricane eyes fixated on him.

"Good morning," he greeted, trying to hide his surprise. An eternity passed before she responded, leaving Nick to fidget uncomfortably and attempt to guess her thoughts.

"Why didn't you do it?" Kate finally asked, though her inquiry made no sense to him.

"Do what?" he asked, sounding like an idiot, but he did not have a clue what she was talking about. Had he spoken in his sleep?

"You should've slept with her. Why didn't you? It's not like she wanted to get married."

Nick blinked at Kate several times as he adjusted his train of thought. Julia. She was talking about Julia. Sighing, he ran his fingers through his hair.

"You heard that, last night," Nick stated. Embarrassment and shame washed over him as he thought about the way his body yearned for the strange woman. Kate said nothing, awaiting his answer.

"I didn't want to." Nick shrugged and looked away. He had hoped that would suffice, but Kate replied almost immediately.

"Why not?"

Why was she asking this? What did she *want*? Nick held her gaze this time, trying to pry into her mind, and he was met with desperation, insecurity, and... jealousy?

Careful, Nick. Play this right, he instructed himself.

"People are dangerous these days. No rules. No social norms. No laws. She just throws herself at a guy she doesn't know? Red flag." Nick shook his head. "Besides, she's not my type."

Kate narrowed her eyes at him. Julia was fit, curvy in all the right places, had long flowing hair, and, most importantly, a willingness to be intimate. "I didn't realize the standards for casual sex were so high. Especially given the fact that the world's population is like a tenth of what it was."

Nick laughed. She was not trying to be funny, and laughing was the last thing he should have done at that moment, but he could not help it.

Perhaps it was not jealousy. Maybe she was worried about where her place would be if he became involved with someone else. They had made an unspoken agreement to be traveling companions, to endure the world together. If he developed a relationship with another person, where would that leave Kate?

"We're living in the downfall of society as we know it. Casual sex isn't exactly at the top of my to-do list." Nick offered her a half-smile, impressed with his punny response, but Kate's eyes turned to stone, safeguarding herself against emotions, though he was unclear which ones. She had spent her entire life persisting through betrayal and abandonment, only to be met with Nick's half-hearted responses that only he found humorous.

Nick's smile disintegrated as he relaxed his shoulders and let down his guard. Without hesitation, he faced her cold eyes, inched closer, and thought about taking her hand.

"I know what you're worried about, but I am not easily distracted. I'm not going anywhere. I'm focused on our survival. I'm dedicated to...us." Uncertain if he had said the right words, he watched the icy storm in her eyes melt just a little. The dread that had Kate clenched within its jaws loosened its hold.

Kate's gaze pierced Nick straight to his core. He thought about looking away, considered running and hiding in the familiar comfort of his own misery. It would be easy to fold back into himself and watch Kate leave him, too, as he suffocated.

Instead, Nick took it all in. Every dark affair that unsettled her soul. It was terrifying and beautiful all at once.

Chapter 32

A week passed since Nick and Kate first met the group living in the junkyard. Kate's ankle was nearly healed along with Nick's cuts and gashes. Jeff had been enjoying Nick's leadership and bravery as those qualities benefited their looting missions. Nick was happy to assist the group in gathering supplies while they gave Kate and him a place to stay and kept them well-fed.

Julia had not tried anything further with Nick. Although she hardly looked at him, she often cast reproachful glances at Kate.

Doing chores and braiding each other's hair throughout the day brought Kate and Emily closer. Kate was pleased to help with all the things she was unable to do while injured and eagerly learned new skills. Emily confided in her about life before the group. Kate listened and talked about some of her life, but kept most of her disturbing past quiet.

As the women foraged the woods around them, Emily showed Kate various plants and described their uses. Sassafras roots were used to bring down fevers and relieve stomach issues. Blackberries, other than being delicious, helped alleviate diarrhea.

When they came upon a patch of black-eyed Susans, Emily explained with excitement that a tea made from the roots can help with snake bites and swelling. After Kate arrived, Emily had gone out the next day to look for some, but this was the first of the flowers she had found in months.

Emily showed Kate the ominous white flowers of jimsonweed and explained the severe toxicity of the plant, though her father swore it helped calm the tremors in his hands.

Beaming as she spoke, Emily told Kate that her father used to spend hours with her in the woods imparting his vast knowledge of the flora in the area. They were her happiest memories with him before cancer ate away at his body until there was nothing left.

Emily's mother had already succumbed to the clutches of alcoholism and after her father passed, things got worse. Some nights, she brought home random men at all hours, and others, Emily's mother slept in the bathtub covered in chunks of vomit. Emily pleaded with her to get help on too many occasions to count and after the last intervention resulted in her mother spitting in her face, Emily left home at sixteen. Shortly after, she met the scrapyard group, and they had been a family ever since.

The evening crept over them, and the group settled in around the campfire for dinner, drinks, and stories about the day's adventures. Layla knitted and laughed as Jeff told the group about getting caught up in his own animal trap.

Sam and Phoenix raved about the fish they had caught at the river.

Emily excitedly described the useful vegetation she and Kate had found. David and Julia were the only ones who remained silent.

"What do you make of all this, Nick?" Jeff puffed on a cigar and looked at Nick inquisitively.

"This?" Nick asked.

"The shit that's befallen the world!" Jeff said dramatically, arms in the air like a preacher on doomsday. "We been livin' in these woods quite some time, long before the world went to hell. We ain't keen on news stories or current events. Where did it all go wrong?"

Nick laughed nervously and looked at his hands. "Hell, I don't know. People went fucking crazy. The news, per usual, was just spouting off every ridiculous theory they had. They claimed it was some sort of chemical attack from another country. Then, it was an airborne virus. One story I heard said it was a song. People would hear it and then lose their minds. One of the last reports I heard was something about tainted food. Contaminated brain matter incorporated into a popular food source. I don't know, man. I'm not much of a science person."

Kate thought about the slop she was fed for about a year—a bland mix of beans and rice. She had not been afforded the luxury of dining on the typical foods most people took for granted. Maybe that was how she managed to avoid the disease.

"Damn, spoiled food. I bet it was them fast-food burgers. Always made you wonder what kind of meat was actually in 'em if it was meat at all," Jeff said. "People always thought us livin' out in the woods was strange. May be strange but at least we're still kickin'. You see a lot of 'em out there, these creatures?"

Nick nodded. "Less in the rural areas, of course. Neighborhoods are full of them. They're unpredictable. The ones who haven't lost a lot of function in their legs can move pretty quickly. Others can barely walk. They seem to have lost most cognitive function. They grunt, moan, growl, but they don't speak. Some of them even laugh. It's fucking creepy. And then there's the children..."

Jeff raised an eyebrow. The image of the little girl in the dirty white dress flashed in Kate's mind and she shuddered. Without thinking, she grasped Nick's hand tightly.

"They have the same feral hunger. But not the same weaknesses. Their bodies aren't as deteriorated. They've retained enough mental capacity to perform more actions, such as crying, and sometimes speaking. But the part of their brain that makes them human is gone. They're cunning and, though weaker, considerably more dangerous than the adults."

The group nodded and took in Nick's words, making mental notes for their next trip outside the metal walls.

"I saw something." Phoenix, who couldn't have been older than twenty, shifted in his seat as he recalled a memory. "About a month ago, I traveled to a nearby town for supplies. Infected. Laughers. Whatever you want to call them, they were everywhere. There were other people there, maybe two or three. The Laughers had them cornered in a store."

Phoenix continued, "I wanted to help them, but they were already being eaten. I posted up across the street, hoping I could wait them out. Once they were done feeding, I figured I could loot the store. It was fucked up. I should've just left. But as I sat there, I swear I saw one of the creatures... It was ripping off pieces of its face and, like, forcing it down the person's throat." Phoenix looked to the ground and shrugged. The group stared at him, bewildered.

"That's some wild shit," Sam said, a hint of disbelief coloring his words.

"It was feeding the person? That doesn't even make sense, Phoenix. Why would it do that?" Layla questioned.

"If that's what the boy said he saw, then that's what he saw. I ain't got the foggiest idea what it means, but we all gotta be careful out there," Jeff said. The group relaxed but sat in pensive silence as they ruminated on Phoenix's words.

Noticing the mood had turned ominous, Jeff turned to Nick and changed the subject. "So, now that y'all have healed up nicely, what are your plans? Y'all be staying with us for a while?"

Nick regarded the comforts and safety of the group. They had proved to be trustworthy so far. There were hot meals every night and walls to keep out the Infected, yet he couldn't settle for basic survival. As naive as it probably was, he was hopeful for the regeneration of society, and he wanted to be a part of it.

"I'm sure we'll be moving on after a while but for now, we're comfortable here," Nick answered. Jeff nodded solemnly.

If the group had any hopes for a night of escaping reality and ignoring the decrepit world they lived in, their hopes had been sorely dashed. Each went to bed with heavy thoughts of a crumbled world rife with cackling monsters, sinister children, and people being force-fed bits of rotten flesh.

Chapter 33

A shrill scream ripped through Nick's subconscious, startling him awake. He sat up in the tent and groped for his gun, certain Kate was being attacked. When he readied the pistol in his hand and clicked on the flashlight, Kate was writhing in her sleep, muttering pleas in between agonized shrieks. Nick set aside the gun and gently shook her shoulder. Though she was trembling, her clothes were damp with sweat.

"Kate, you're okay. Wake up," Nick said in a hushed tone. Kate continued to toss and turn.

The flaps of nearby tents unzipped and the door to the RV flung open.

"Kate, you're safe. You're okay," Nick tried again.

Kate took in a sharp breath, her eyes snapping open as she scrambled to sit up.

"What the fuck is going on in there?" Sam shouted.

"Hey, y'all alright?" Jeff's voice boomed across the junkyard.

"Shut her up!" Julia barked.

Nick took Kate's hand, quietly consoling her as the group members closed in on their tent. As Kate steadied her shallow breaths, she laced her fingers with his.

"I'm sorry. I was dreaming. I didn't mean to—"

"Anybody gonna come out here and tell us what the fuck is happening?" Jeff's annoyance had peaked, causing Kate to wince and shrink back.

"Just a minute," Nick replied through clenched teeth and touched a gentle palm to the side of Kate's face. "Hey, everything's okay. You did nothing wrong. I'm going to handle this. I'll be right back."

Nick exited the tent and faced the group members. Looking irritated and expectant, Jeff stood the closest to him. Pinch-faced, with a hand on her hip, Julia stood beside him. David was next to her, arms crossed and anger swimming in his dark eyes. A disinterested glaze covered Sam's eyes, looking as though he wished the ordeal would end so he could return to sleep. Worry covered Emily's face, and Phoenix glanced from person to person, curious.

"Sorry to wake everyone. Kate was having a nightmare."

"We can't have shit like that happen. It'll draw every Laugher for miles," Jeff explained.

"I know, man. It won't happen again."

"How can you promise that? Is she just never going to sleep?" Julia questioned. Nick sighed and ran his fingers through his hair.

"The better question is, who the fuck has nightmares like that? Tell that bitch to get her shit together," David spat. An incendiary anger rose in Nick's chest. He narrowed his eyes at David, and then started laughing.

"God, it's so funny. I must still be half-asleep," Nick said in an amused tone. "Because I swore you just called my girl a bitch." Nick's tone darkened, and he started toward David, the merriment replaced with an ominous glare.

Jeff stepped between the two men. "Okay, we're all tired and freaked out. Let's just take a step back and calm down."

Keeping his icy gaze targeted on David, Nick continued his determined stride until his chest was pressed against Jeff's, serving as a human blockade. When David's lips curled into a smug grin, Nick's fists clenched, and his nails dug into his palms.

"You better watch your disrespectful fucking mouth—"

"Alright, alright," Jeff interjected, pushing back on Nick's chest. Sam moved in to help put distance between the men.

"That girl is going to get us killed," Julia commented as she linked arms with David and pulled him away.

Nick watched until David was out of sight, nostrils flared and panting.

"Don't let him get you worked up like that. He's an asshole but he's all talk. Now, I'm gonna try and get back to sleep." Jeff wrapped an arm around Layla, and they disappeared into the RV. The rest of the group broke apart and retreated into their tents.

Emily approached Nick, nervously clutching the hem of her shirt.

"Is Kate okay?" Emily asked. Releasing the frustration built within him, Nick sighed and met her gaze.

"Yeah, she's okay," he answered.

Emily smiled. "If she needs anything, be sure to let me know. Goodnight."

"Goodnight," Nick replied and held back the tent flap as he crouched inside.

Kate sat against the far wall with her arms wrapped around her knees, casting her eyes toward the ground in a despondent gaze.

"I didn't mean to stir things up. I'm sorry."

Nick knelt beside her, close enough to make out her features in the dark. Tears streamed down her cheeks, igniting Nick's rage further, furious that they had made her feel this way.

"You didn't do anything wrong. You know what? Fuck them," Nick growled, wishing he knew how to unfurl the ball of distress she had become. Although she nodded, shame kept her eyes locked on the ground. Nick placed a hand on her forearm, rubbing his thumb back and forth on her soft skin, and watched some of the tension dissipate.

"What were you dreaming about anyway?" he asked. A shiver passed through Kate as the dream replayed in her mind.

"Bad men doing bad things."

Nick could not fathom what kind of man it took to make a woman feel so small. If it were somehow possible, he would track them all down and punish them—make them suffer. Knowing most of them were likely dead, Nick felt a slight sense of relief. Although he was unable to change the past, he could ensure Kate would be avenged against any bad men going forward.

"You don't have to worry about that anymore."

CHAPTER 34

Something slammed against metal outside, and Nick sat up in the tent. At first, the noises were subtle—gentle thumping against the walls of the junkyard blending with soft puffs of air as Kate breathed in and out, asleep beside him. Then, the sound of something hard raking the rusted metal sent chills up Nick's spine.

Armed with his hunting knife, Nick exited the tent just as Jeff's RV door swung open. Other group members were coming out to investigate the sound, everyone maintaining a mutual silence as they searched.

Then, the laughing began. Eerie chuckles broke through the quiet night air, accompanied by low snarls and labored steps.

"Laughers," Jeff whispered to the group.

Clicking and scraping sounds, followed by heaving grunts caused Nick to pause, perplexed at what the Infected were doing. A tree overhanging the junkyard creaked, then a whoosh of air ended in a heavy thud. Laughter erupted from within the walls, and Nick gasped.

"They're climbing the trees and jumping in!" Nick shouted.

Chaos ensued as the Infected continued to drop into the junkyard, and the group members scrambled in the dark back to their living areas to arm themselves. When Nick rushed back to the tent to wake Kate, she was already sitting up and pulling the machete away from his pack.

Emily screamed as a creature backed her against the tent, and Nick dashed to fight it off. Jeff and Layla were engaged in grappling with a group that had landed behind the RV. Phoenix sped off to help Sam who was pinned to the ground.

Kate clutched the machete, deciding Sam needed her help the most, and started sprinting toward him. Making it only a few feet, a hand wrapped around Kate's mouth and pulled her in the opposite direction. Prying at the hand, Kate thrashed and kicked. The hold on her remained firm as she was towed along the ground to the furthest, darkest corner of the junkyard. Kate was spun around and slammed against a stack of broken cars; glass and metal pierced the skin of her back.

David stood over Kate, his menacing eyes casting dark intentions over her. A helpless panic swam through Kate's veins as he trapped her away from the struggles and screams of the group fighting off the monsters. Another person stood beside David, their identity hidden in the shadows.

"Do you hear it? Listen to them. Hear them die because of you," David whispered harshly into Kate's ear. She screamed behind his hand, which still covered her mouth, and her eyes bulged in fear.

An Infected lumbered toward them and the figure next to David gripped its shoulder and stabbed it in the chest. Brunette hair swung out from the force of the strike, and Kate realized it was Julia. She pulled her knife from the creature and its body fell to the ground.

"Just kidding," David continued. "I don't give a shit about them. I couldn't resist the opportunity to cut up Nick's precious little bitch."

Kate writhed against David's hold on her, pinching and twisting any skin she could grab onto. It did little more than irritate him. His fingers wrapped around strands of Kate's hair and bashed her head against the cars. Stars exploded behind her eyes as pain slithered through her skull. Her vision doubled, and panicked breaths seized her lungs.

Julia leaned into Kate until her face was visible, her lips twisted into a devious sneer. "We're gonna cut you into tiny pieces, and then I'm gonna take your man, stupid cunt."

The thought of Julia's lips pressed to Nick's, her legs straddling his waist made Kate sick to her stomach, and a fiery anger bubbled up in Kate's chest. If she did nothing, these fiends were going to kill her. What she had to do next was going to be loud, and it was going to be fatal but Kate was left without any alternatives.

Kate ripped the revolver from her waistline and squeezed the trigger until the metal cut into her finger. The bullet erupted from the muzzle of the gun into David's gut. The fingers that covered Kate's mouth loosened and trembled around her face until the hand slipped away. Kate pushed David's weak body to the ground and held the revolver at eye level in the direction of Julia's dark form. Kate pulled the trigger again.

The bullet hit Julia's mouth, ripping through her lips and throat. Blood gushed down her chin, sprinkled with pieces of enamel from her shattered teeth. Julia's body stood upright for several seconds, staring blankly into the darkness before falling to the ground without another breath.

The gunshots had rendered the junkyard silent. The clash of blades and fists and laughter had come to a halt. □

"Kate!" Nick screamed, rushing around in the pitch blackness, frantically searching.

Backed against the battered vehicles holding the gun in her shaking hands, Kate was frozen, gazing at the people she had reduced to corpses. A light clicked on and darted around before landing on her.

Nick shone the light from his handgun, casting David and Julia's twisted faces in a spotlight.

"Oh, god," Kate groaned as a strange mixture of anger and horror worked its way up her throat. Rushing up beside her, Nick gently tugged the revolver from her hands and pocketed it. His hand cupped her face, directing her gaze away from the carnage.

A pained moan echoed toward them from the middle of the junkyard, leading Kate to try and look toward the sound.

"Hey, look at me," Nick instructed. "Are you hurt?"

Kate shook her head.

A blade slicing through skin drew their attention away from each other. Nick shined his light toward the sound to see Jeff finishing off an Infected. Jeff's gaze shot toward them and he started to approach.

"Hey, y'all alright?" As Jeff got closer, his eyes fell on David and Julia's bodies. He dropped to his knees beside them, cradling Julia's head in his arms. Her eyes had already glazed over, staring intently at nothing. "No, no, no, no, no." Jeff muttered as he rocked back and forth with her corpse. A piece of skin, likely what remained of her lips, dangled from her face and swayed each time he moved.

Nick tightened his grip on the handgun, his other hand finding Kate's. He slowly started walking them in the direction of the junkyard's gate.

"What the fuck did y'all do?" Jeff shrieked, tears falling down his cheeks. Standing, Jeff held his blade out, shaking and crying. Nick stepped in front of Kate and aimed his pistol at Jeff.

"Don't do this, Jeff. You won't win," Nick warned, backing them farther away from the hysterical man.

"Y'all killed David and Julia. Sam's dead. Phoenix is missin'. Emily's bleedin' out. And the goddamn Laughers found a way into my home! Get the fuck outta here before I lose what little I have left!"

Without hesitation, Nick pulled Kate to their tent. They tossed their belongings into their packs, pulled them around their shoulders, and crept through the metal gates. The pair walked through the night, Nick's flashlight fading as the batteries within began to die. Keeping at a steady pace, they carried on until the junkyard was miles behind them.

Kate halted, bracing herself against a tree to catch her breath. Nick stopped and joined her in taking a break.

"They attacked me. I didn't know what else to do," Kate gasped. "Almost everyone is dead!" Nick reached out a hesitant hand as he considered pulling her in for a hug when Kate wrapped her arms around him.

"It's okay. You did what you had to do. We're okay," he consoled. "Besides, I was ready to leave. This saved us from all the awkward goodbyes." Nick pulled away from her and touched his hand to her cheek, smiling, and though she tried to laugh she could not conjure the sound.

"I'm the sole reason we've been in any danger since we've met." Kate felt like an idiot. *Stupid, careless girl.*

"Keeps things interesting," Nick responded. "Let's keep moving." Kate looked up at him, tears in her eyes, and nodded.

Ignoring aching muscles and parched throats, they pressed on. The pain in Kate's head was hot and throbbing after colliding with the sharp metal of the junked cars. Nick's body was sore from fighting off the Infected.

Dominating both their minds was the junkyard they left in shambles; people who found comfort in an unconventional lifestyle and called themselves a family were left broken apart, most of them dead.

Once again, their world was swimming in chaos.

Keep moving. Don't die.

Chapter 35

After hours of walking, the day shifted into evening. Finding it difficult to stay concealed in the woods, Nick and Kate passed by ghost towns and shopping centers as the trees were replaced by suburbia.

Coming to an intersection, abandoned vehicles sat in the middle of the road. A silver SUV's door handle was painted with blood, and a severed arm peeked out beneath its undercarriage. A small black pick-up truck had crashed into a stop light, a trail of gore leading away from the driver's side door. The wreckage and doors left open along with bodies spilling out of cars resembled a perpetual, nightmarish traffic jam.

Past the cluster of vehicles, a sight caused them to stop dead in their tracks. As many as twenty Infected lumbered about in the street ahead; their pained, maniacal laughter echoed off the asphalt toward the pair.

Nick and Kate slowed from a steady stride to a silent padding across the asphalt. Kate followed carefully in Nick's footfalls as he kept his wary gaze on the group of undead.

For a moment, Nick swore one of the creatures looked directly at them. If one of them saw, all of them would. His forehead flushed with apprehension, and sweat beads formed, trickling down from his hairline.

At the risk of being heard, Nick increased his pace. If the creatures started toward them, he wanted a running start. The monsters remained unaware of their presence as they crept across the intersection. Nick sighed with relief and turned back to see solace on Kate's face.

"Mommy!" A child's voice cried out from the middle of the diseased horde. Kate pivoted and started to follow the plea without thought. Nick grabbed her by the wrist and she shot him an angry look, but he gestured for her to look toward the sound. They watched the group of undead until a break in the crowd revealed the source of the small voice.

"Mommy?" the boy shouted again, walking sluggishly among the dead. Kate was panicked, anxious to help him until she saw his feet. The boy was barefoot, his legs caked in dried blood, and one ankle severed so deeply that the rest of the foot was being dragged behind him.

Kate abandoned her desire to save the child—the boy was already gone. Nick loosened his grasp on her and gently directed her in the opposite direction. The Infected continued to wander aimlessly in the streets, and Nick found a side road for the pair to continue down.

Chapter 36

Walking down a quiet street that ended in a cul-de-sac, Kate excitedly smacked her palm against Nick's shoulder. Turning to her, he raised his eyebrows as she pointed to a house at the end of the street.

The house was nearly the size of a mansion, outlined in gray cobblestones and punctuated with floor-to-ceiling window panes. A surrounding thin layer of trees gave it the illusion of privacy. Embellished with mulch and purple asters, a small koi pond decorated the front lawn.

"Please!" Kate clasped her hands together and clutched them beneath her chin, begging.

Nick looked the house over as if he could see through the walls and deem it safe. Apprehension threatened to tug him to the ground, but when he turned to Kate, she gave him puppy eyes. Her lips turned down in a dramatic frown, and her eyelashes batted in rapid succession. Nick did not stand a chance.

"Fine, one night," Nick said and rolled his eyes, trying not to smile. Kate raced up the brown, stone staircase and stopped short at the ornate, cream-colored, front door.

Glancing around the neighborhood, Nick looked for power lines standing tall in the distance. When there were none, he surmised the electricity must be run underground, protected from the elements, which gave him a glimmer of hope that the power running to these houses was still going strong.

Taking a deep breath, Kate reminded herself that they must be cautious. Nick unsheathed his machete, and Kate produced her revolver. Resting his hand on the doorknob, Nick paused to look at her, awaiting affirmation. She nodded, and he swung the door open.

Clearing this home took much longer than the one they stayed in the first day they met. Almost three times the size and double the number of rooms, it seemed hours before they considered the house safe.

Every room Kate walked into made her love the house more. Each area was well-designed, spacious, and beautifully decorated. She wished they could stay there forever.

In the kitchen, they put together a quick bite to eat. It seemed criminal to prepare plain green beans from a can in such a well-appointed kitchen, but hunger and exhaustion impeded any hopes of a lavish meal.

Nick and Kate retired to the master bedroom which housed a California king-sized bed with a bench at the end, two wardrobes, two armchairs, a bookcase, and a vanity. Two French doors opened up into a master bath with a jacuzzi tub and intricate floor tiles. Kate whirled around and fell into the giant bed, the goose-down duvet swallowing her up.

"This place is amazing," Kate marveled.

Nick sat at the foot of the bed and pulled the first aid supplies from his backpack.

"It'll do. Where are you hurt? There's blood coming through your shirt." Nick had not meant to be short with her. He was tired, but mostly, he worried about how much she loved this place. Afraid to get too comfortable, he knew at any moment they might have to leave, fleeing for their lives.

"You're no fun," Kate pouted, standing up and lifting her shirt. She winced as Nick wiped away the dirt and blood.

Each scrape and gash burned, bringing her back to David hovering over her, holding her mouth shut, the threats they spewed at her, and the revolver screaming at her to be used.

"You okay?" Nick seemed to read her mind. He put away the supplies, closed his pack, and set it on the ground.

"If one more man puts his hands on me..." the words slipped out, and she had to look away though she had meant them. Kate had spent almost an entire year being a slave to a man's every whim and desire and being beaten into submission when she protested.

That had been before the world went to shit. Now, men left their morals in the dust and decided it was survival of the fittest. If they wanted it, they would just take it. Righteousness was no more. Virtues were dead.

As she regarded Nick, Kate admitted, with much guilt, that he seemed to be the only exception, yet she still did not trust him wholly and often wondered about his ulterior motives.

"Hey," he said, examining the look in her eyes. "You know I'd never hurt you, right?" She nodded immediately, but it lacked sincerity. Looking away, she closed her eyes and sighed.

"I... I know," Kate replied, sounding as genuine as possible.

Nick racked his brain for more words but came up short. He wanted Kate to know that she was safe. Surely, he could find some words that would reassure her, and let her know she was in good hands. However, as he gazed at her, Nick could see a deep wounding in Kate's eyes and chose to let it go.

Nick found the linen closet in the hallway and took a thick blanket and a pillow with no case on it. On the floor of the master bedroom, he set up a modest place to sleep.

"What are you doing?" Kate asked.

"I'm pretty tired. I was gonna lay down," Nick explained. "I can sleep in another room if you want. I just figured it was safer to stay in the same one in case something happened."

Kate looked him over, then cast her eyes across the sprawling bed. "This bed is massive. We could fit six of us in here. Plus, we just spent a week sleeping on the ground. Your back's gotta be killing you." Kate scooted away from him in the bed to the farthest side. Uncertain, he gazed at her, then at the five feet of mattress available.

While he could survive sleeping on hard surfaces, his back *was* killing him, and he imagined laying on that bed would feel like a dream. Nick conceded, tossing his blanket on the bed. With Kate beneath the duvet, Nick laid on top, and let out an exaggerated moan of ecstasy.

"See?" Kate laughed. "I'd be an asshole to let you miss out on this."

"God, this is nice." Nick laid his head back and closed his eyes, his tired muscles letting themselves find respite in the comfort of the bed. "Kate, can I ask you something?"

"Sure," Kate hesitated, her voice uneasy.

"How did you avoid the disease?" Nick asked, trying to work it out in his head. If it were an airborne disease, she must not have gone to well-populated places, or anywhere at all. If it were the food, did she grow her own? Did she only eat certain things and happen to miss out on the contaminated culprit?

Kate turned to look at him, her eyes glassed over as tears started to form, and the wounds he had seen there before were wide open.

Nick wanted to take the question back and shield her from the pain of answering except, he needed to know.

To understand her fully, he required the knowledge of her past, and what troubled her so deeply. As much as it pained her heart to dig up the corpses of her past abuse, Nick needed to know what he was up against.

Closing her eyes, Kate took a deep breath and began to explain that day. The day that, for most people, marked the end of their lives but for her, it ushered in a new beginning.

Chapter 37

Kate sat up against the metal cage, the bars leaving deep imprints on her back.

The cage was new. One night, after months of being tied to a queen-size bed, she managed to loosen her restraints, slipping her bruised wrists out of the ropes. What idiot used ropes?

As her legs had lost much of their strength, Kate fell to her knees the moment her feet touched the floor. She straightened up and moved again but slower, teaching herself to walk all over again. Gripping the handrail, she pulled herself up the stairs, but one leg went weak, and her shins hit the splintered wood.

Heavy footsteps lumbered toward the basement door, and it swung open. Connor peered down at her from above, and a sick grin parted his lips.

When Kate attempted to climb a few stairs, she stumbled backward, bouncing down until she hit the unforgiving concrete below. Her head swam as darkness clouded her vision. Connor grabbed her up and slammed her into the bed, launching fists into her head until she lost consciousness.

When Kate woke up, she was locked inside a metal cage Connor had installed in the basement beside the bed.

Kate had been inside the cage for only a few days and Connor had hardly been down to visit since he forced her inside. Hearing his footsteps almost every hour, it seemed he was not leaving the house. Sometimes, she would even hear him laughing though she did not hear the television or evidence that he had company over.

Kate sat in the cage with no activities to bide her time other than thinking, picking at her nails, counting the bruises on her body, or plucking at old scabs. A few times a day she pushed her legs against the metal bars, tightening her leg muscles and then releasing them. If she found another opportunity to escape, she would not let her legs fail her again.

Kate paused when the basement door opened, and low, heavy thuds resounded as Connor descended the stairs. He stumbled through the threshold of the room, holding the door frame for balance.

When Kate looked into Connor's eyes, she always saw evil there. This time was different. The pupils, irises, and even the sclera had been swallowed up by blackness. The grotesque, sexually twisted man was gone and replaced by something even more sinister.

Approaching the cage, he fingered his pocket for the key, crouched on the back of his feet, and put the key into the lock.

Normally, Kate did not bother to fight back. He would only drug her, and she would only earn herself more bruises. Whatever Connor wanted from her this time, it was not going to occur in the bed. It was going to happen right here in the cage.

Positioning herself against the back wall of the cage, she waited until the lock turned and the door swung open with a metallic screech. He reached his hands in, and when his torso blocked most of the doorway, Kate thrust both legs into his chest. Connor lost his balance, shuffled backward and fell flat.

Rushing out of the cage, Kate stepped on Connor's stomach, forcing air from his lungs in a strained heave. Before she could take another stride to meet the concrete past him, Connor grabbed her ankle with an iron grip.

Kate fell to the floor, catching herself on her elbows and forearms. Pain burst from every area of her body; her arms, the ankle where he held her, and even old injuries resurfaced. There would be time for self-pity later.

On her hands and knees, she donkey-kicked him in the head with her free leg, and he released her ankle, groaning in pain.

Kate jumped to her feet, eyes darting over each object in the room in search of a weapon. Connor turned over on his side and pushed himself to a standing position, every action labored and strenuous.

Kate's eyes fell on that damned black chest full of tools made for pleasure but used for torment. Since he caged her, Connor had been leaving it unlocked. In one swift motion, she ran toward it, slid on her knees, and opened the top.

Connor was on his feet now and shuffling toward her. Grabbing the first thing her hands came across, Kate tossed a purple vibrator at him. As it hit him in the chest, he looked down for a moment, then continued his approach.

Taking a leather riding crop, Kate raised it and took a step toward him. She struck his face with the stinging leather until the skin on his cheek burst open. Connor cursed in pain and took a few steps backward, shielding his face with his hands. Kate knew this would not be enough to subdue him, however. As she kept Connor at bay with the crop, she turned her head to search the chest for a more effective weapon.

As Kate rifled through the chest, she knocked over a black, plastic box. She knew this box well. Kate hurled the crop at Connor's head and he batted it away with an annoyed grunt, pressing on toward her.

Grabbing the black box, Kate flung the top off, breaking the cheap hinges. When Connor leaned in to grab her, his legs trembled and he fell to his knees, long enough for Kate to retrieve a needle and syringe from the box and plunge it into a small glass vial.

Flipping the vial upside down, Kate drew the plunger out from the syringe and filled it with liquid. Connor's arms grazed her elbows and just as he grabbed her, she sunk the needle into his neck, shrieking as a ferocious anger exploded from her lungs.

As he pawed at her face, each attempt grew weaker as Connor's body relinquished control to the drug. Kate pushed him away by his shoulders without effort, and he fell to the ground. Connor muttered incoherently before closing his eyes and losing consciousness.

Kate took a pair of metal handcuffs out of the chest, closed one of the bracelets around Connor's wrist, and dragged his body until he was near the head of the bed. She did not have the strength to get him onto it, so she cuffed the other end to the bottom of the bedpost.

As she caught her breath, Kate stood over his body. Connor would never hurt her again. She could just leave him here.

Oh, but he deserves so much more, Kate thought.

Climbing the basement stairs, she entered a kitchen she had not seen in a year. Finding a knife block, she wrapped her fingers around the handle of a butcher's blade and retreated back down the steps.

Standing over his body, she cocked her head to one side, deciding which part of him should bleed first.

Kate thrust the knife into his chest, right where she hoped his heart would be. She would not want him to wake up before the fun was over.

Isn't that right, Connor? It's no fun when your victim is awake and fighting back.

The blade dripped with the satisfying ruby liquid as Kate pulled it from his chest. The smell of dense copper filled her nostrils. She had only ever dreamt of moments like these.

The blade pierced Connor's arms, his legs, his face. Kate dared not view the vile body part that defiled her for so long, yet it deserved the most torment so she stabbed the knife through the crotch of his pants over and over again.

It was not until Kate stopped that she realized she was screaming, her trachea throbbing and sore.

After she cleared her throat and rested her arms, Kate seized the knife in both hands. She held the blade over her head and sliced into Connor's body. Flesh hung loose where the blade separated it from his skin, his nose was gone, and a pool of blood covered most of the basement floor.

Looking over his desecrated figure, the breath from his lungs having left his body long ago, Kate wavered; something was missing. She took a blue dildo from Connor's chest of horrors and shoved it into his mouth.

As Kate looked upon her gruesome masterpiece, a sardonic smile crept across her lips. Her work here was done. She let the knife clatter to the ground and walked up the stairs to greet her newfound freedom.

CHAPTER 38

Nick looked fixedly at Kate, his mouth set in a tight line as he attempted to conceal the unsettling emotions her tale conjured.

"You were imprisoned for a year?" Nick recounted in horrid disbelief.

"Yes."

"Fuck." Nick ran his hands across the top of his head, letting out a lengthy sigh.

The sound of puzzle pieces clicking into place was nearly audible. It was a lot of trauma to take in, and now it all made sense to Nick: the way she cowered and apologized when she felt she did something wrong, her distrust, and yet her willingness to follow him without question. She was an angry, rabid dog backed into a corner, waiting to see if every hand that fed her would offer a meal of poison or nourishment.

"Kate, I'm sorry. I'm so sorry you had to go through all of that."

They sat in delicate, uncomfortable silence for some time. Nick was at a loss for words or actions. Nothing would be acceptable nor was Kate expecting anything. She only waited for time to pass and make her history a memory in his mind, the way it lived in hers.

Closing her eyes, Kate started to drift off to sleep. Nick turned on his side to face her, the woman brave enough to fight with all she had and overcome her captor.

Just before he dozed off, he whispered, "You're a fucking warrior."

Chapter 39

The morning sun broke through the blinds and landed in horizontal stripes on the hardwood. Nick stirred out of his sleep, stretched his sore limbs, and wondered why there was never enough time for sleeping. When he opened his eyes, he assumed to find Kate asleep next to him, but her spot in the bed was empty.

Nick shoved boots on his feet and positioned the handgun in his waistline. After checking the bathroom and finding it vacant, he made his way downstairs thinking she was in the kitchen making food. The kitchen was empty.

Nick's heart sank; Kate was nowhere in the house. Still, he continued searching, calling her name, and moving from room to room.

Nick opened a set of French doors that led from the kitchen to a back patio where the chairs sat empty.

At a loss as to where to search next, Nick stood on the back deck listening to the sounds of the world. Birds chirped and leaves rustled as the wind blew, but there were no signs of human life. The hum of engines or honking horns was non-existent. No one was outside mowing their lawn. No children played basketball in the streets. Life had become a mere blend of nature and silence.

As Nick listened, something disrupted the serenity of the environment—footsteps. Someone was running in his direction from a footpath that led from the backyard and disappeared into the trees.

Nick descended the patio steps, walked across the yard, and drew his pistol. Flanked by trees on either side, the dirt trail had too many twists and turns for him to see to the end. Aiming his gun, he stepped down the path with precision. The footfalls grew closer.

Nick came to a bend in the path, and just as he was about to turn the corner, Kate came from around it. The playful smile on her lips receded when she saw him, and she threw her hands up in the air.

"Don't!" she shouted. "It's me! Don't shoot!"

"Fuck. What the hell are you doing out here?" Nick asked, lowering the gun as he eyed her bitterly. A saturated black t-shirt clung to Kate's small frame, and black yoga pants hugged her thighs. Uncomfortable, Nick averted his eyes back to her face. "What are you—"

"Come with me." Kate grabbed his hand and began pulling him down the dirt path. They ran down the rest of the trail and it ended, opening up into a semi-circle of sand that had been overtaken by grass. Surrounding the beach area were plots of mulch where gardens were choked out by thick weeds.

Beyond the untamed bushes and ragged flower beds was a picturesque harbor. Water rippled in gentle waves and lapped against a sandy bank. The morning sun shone on the water, bathing everything in gold.

Kate shoved both thumbs in her waistband, ready to shed the yoga pants heavy with water to swim comfortably in the shorts underneath. Pausing, she looked down at her body in the clothes she borrowed from the mansion home. Her mind snagged on the scars tarnishing her legs.

Nothing but a disgusting, used-up whore

Insecurities dripped from her brain and into her limbs, weighing her down like the harbor's water anchored the wet clothes to her skin. Allowing her self-doubts to win, she left the pants in place.

Kate ran toward the water and dove in. The clouds reflected in the water broke apart and rippled away from her. Kate emerged from the surface, beads of water rolling off her hair. She gestured for Nick to join her.

Still reeling from panic and frustration, Nick stood there, arms crossed. For a moment, he was captivated by her body moving effortlessly through the water and the way her face gleamed in the sun. The water droplets built up in her eyelashes like diamonds. He forced himself to look away and kicked at a pile of dirt.

"I'm sorry!" she called. "But how beautiful is this?!"

She's being reckless, Nick thought, raising an eyebrow at her. Overcompensating for the revelations she released on him the night before, this was her way of distracting him from her torturous past.

Moving her hands rhythmically with 'come hither' fingers, Kate wore a devilish smile, and Nick could not resist.

"Fuck it." Nick pulled his shirt up over his head, slinging it to the ground, then kicked off his boots and peeled the socks off his feet. Before disrobing any further, he hesitated. Getting into the water with jeans on sounded as pleasant as bathing in honey. This was what she wanted, though. Besides, the water would cover him up once he was in.

Nick unbuttoned his jeans and shook them off one leg at a time, leaving him in nothing but boxer briefs. Carrying his jeans to the water's edge, he folded them and set them in the sand with his pistol on top, leaving it easily accessible. As he approached the shoreline, Nick let the waves wash over his feet, the chill of the water making him shudder.

"It's not *that* cold," Kate laughed, watching him reluctantly come further in.

With most of his skin exposed, Kate looked him over, taking in more of his tattoos. The black ink she had spied on his chest before was a large symbol, some sort of Viking emblem—a circle with eight lines shooting out in every direction, each looking like the fletchings of tribal arrows. Characters from horror movies covered one arm and quotations covered the other. No wonder Nick was so resilient. Anyone who could spend that much time under the tattoo needle had to be.

Nick was in up to his chest now, relaxing as his body adjusted to the temperature. As he floated on his back, soaking up the sun's rays, the water enveloped him.

Kate swam around carelessly, enjoying the serene and quiet atmosphere.

Scanning the shoreline, Nick observed the million-dollar houses sitting empty, rusted boats thumping against docks that would never see their owners again, and sandy beaches eroding from neglect. Once a bustling harbor full of boats, canoes, and swimmers during its peak in the summertime, their bodies were the only ones enjoying the water now.

Water splashed in Nick's face and disrupted his thoughts. Kate grinned at him, getting ready to splash him again.

"Hey!" Nick protested humorously.

"Can't you just get out of your head for a while? Stop thinking and just enjoy this." Kate gestured around the harbor. Not following her gaze, he only offered her a deflated smile. Nick was unsure how to quiet his overworked mind, though he could certainly try.

Kate strode toward him through the water and stopped when their bodies were a foot away. Gazing up at him, she ran her fingers through his hair, water dripping from her fingertips. Focusing on the sensation, he closed his eyes, and let the rest of the world fall away.

When her hands dropped to his chest, he melted beneath her touch. She wrapped her arms around him and laid her head against the place where his heart was thumping steadily. The warmth of her skin, the pressure of her body on his, and the rhythmic crashing of tiny waves soothed his soul.

Nick held her close to him, one hand cupping her head while the other rested on the middle of her back. The caution he took with the placement of his hands was the only tension. After hearing the nightmare of her captivity, touching her was a delicate process, and the last thing Nick wanted was to give the impression of ill intent.

Kate smiled against his bare skin. It was in that moment that she felt at peace. Content. *Safe.*

Chapter 40

After three or four hours of swimming, Nick and Kate retreated to the spacious home. Though they were famished, it had been difficult to pull themselves away from the first bit of fun they had enjoyed in a while.

Nick fixed lunch, his end-of-the-world specialty of canned goods, while Kate dried their clothes.

In the home's basement, Kate discovered a theater equipped with surround sound and an enormous TV that took up the entirety of one wall. Instead of the rigid, plastic seats typically found in public movie theaters, this room had several recliners and a broad, puffy couch that sat central to the widescreen. The walls were lined with display cases that held collectibles from movies and signed memorabilia from music artists.

Along one wall, an impressive CD collection filled an entire bookshelf. There must have been hundreds. Kate read the band names printed on each case, plucked a few from the shelves to turn them over, and scanned the songs listed on the back. She was familiar with most of them.

Thinking back to her childhood, Kate thought about her own music collection. Her mother would offer to reward her for good grades, and she would always request a newly released album from a band she liked. It was almost as good as Christmas morning, coming home from school and finding the new CD on her bed, still wrapped in plastic.

CDs had become the new vinyl record, outdated and almost abolished with the newer generations. Most people used streaming services, paying a monthly fee to listen to an unlimited amount of music from nearly every artist.

Where was all that music now? Lost to the new world, floating around in the airwaves, unreachable. The previous homeowner must have known the value of collecting music you could grasp, music that was almost tangible, music that could outlive even a zombie apocalypse.

The genre present was not what most would expect. In every movie she had seen set in post-apocalyptic times, the survivors only had oldies music. They were stuck with tunes twenty or thirty years older than the present time.

Perhaps it was an artistic gesture at how fast civilization could regress. A world that once relied on technology could very quickly disintegrate into one without cell phones and the internet and annoying talking robots that answered questions and set timers for you. Instead, people were left to collect water from wells, hunt for food, and listen to music made before their time.

Not here, though. What stood before Kate was the largest collection of heavy metal CDs she had ever seen. Without even playing a song, she already felt her anxieties sloughing off of her.

CHAPTER 41

After a pasta dinner, Kate brought Nick down to the basement where she presented the fancy home theater, gesturing around and raising her eyebrows to imply he should be equally impressed. Nervous about indulging in anything that was not pivotal to surviving, he looked around and forced a smile.

Kate picked an album from the collection and opened the top to a CD player on a table beside the shelf. She clicked the disk into place, closed the top, and pressed the "play" button.

A crescendoing guitar riff erupted from the speakers, and the sounds resonated through Nick and Kate—strange yet harmonious. Music had not been a part of their lives in so long.

"All that's missing is a drink in our hands," Nick jested.

"I think I've got that covered," Kate disappeared upstairs for several minutes, returning with the bottle of Casamigos Blanc and two shot glasses. She held up the bottle of tequila to him. "Not just for sterilizing wounds." Kate giggled, and Nick raised his eyebrows, feigning astonishment.

Nick had not truly wanted a drink and cursed himself for making the comment. To maintain a clear state of mind, he intended to decline the liquor. Then, he thought how nice it would be to get out of his mind for a little while. Could it be such a bad thing to spend some time enjoying life instead of merely surviving it?

The plush couch enveloped them as they took several shots each, enjoying the fuzzy feeling that overtook them. All the nightmares of their past were suddenly distant, and the present came into focus, becoming clearer as they drank.

Kate staggered over to the CD player and changed the song. A familiar metal song they recognized from high school blasted from the speakers. The guitar chugged forcefully, and the vocalist's fry screams rang out, causing Nick to nod his head to the rhythm.

"You know this song?" Nick asked, skeptical. Kate returned to her seat and poured two more shots which they gulped down without any forethought. Instead of answering him, she laid her head back against the couch and let the music course through her veins. The heavy guitar and intense vocals always had a way of carrying away her pain and drowning out her anxiety. The song reached the chorus, and she sat up, turning her body towards him.

"It's a love song, you know," Kate commented.

"I know," Nick responded with a coy smile, and she swore her soul evaporated right there, the mist combining with the sound waves coursing through the room.

The vocalist screamed at the top of his lungs about intense, irrational love and growled deeply about fiery commitment.

Kate scooted closer to Nick and picked up the bottle of tequila, taking a swig straight from the bottle. Her closeness and the look in her eyes sent an uncomfortable yearning through Nick's spine.

The breakdown of the song erupted from the speakers. As the vocalist shouted in gritty desperation, Kate slid her hand around the back of Nick's neck.

Kate's lips met his—warmth exploded and rippled through Nick's entire body. Their lips parted and then met again, Kate's hand sliding up his neck and into his hair, ravaging his limbs with an excited heat.

Their tongues intertwined, and Nick could taste the tequila on her breath, reminding him that these were the actions of someone impaired.

Inching closer, Kate draped a leg over his lap, straddling him. The song had ended, and the next was playing but by this time, Kate's body eclipsed everything.

With both hands on the back of his neck, Kate moved her hips into his, softly at first. As the passion of their kiss grew, so did the pressure of her groin on his.

Nick was fully erect now as the crotch of Kate's jeans pressed against his shaft, driving him insane. Though the liquor blurred his movements, the cautious part of his mind remained intact.

In fact, this was all wrong. Putting space between their bodies, he pulled his mouth away from hers. Kate sat back in his lap, puzzled, then the alcohol reclaimed her confidence. Picking up his hands in hers she slid them up her waist, then over her breasts.

Fuuuuck, Nick groaned internally. While his body was completely at her will, his mind was silently pleading for him to stop. This was not how Nick wanted this to happen. Kate had been drinking. If he let this continue, she might hate him in the morning. But, God, she felt so good on top of him.

Stop this now, Nick.

"No, Kate, I can't... we can't..." Nick pulled his hands away from her body, and before she could object, the sound of glass breaking cut through the sound of the music. Straining to hear over the song, their eyes widened as footsteps thunked across the floorboards above them.

CHAPTER 42

Three Infected stumbled down the stairs and into the theater. Kate lifted herself away from Nick, ran to the CD player, and put an abrupt stop to the music.

The music, Nick thought. *The damn music led them straight to us.* He pulled his .45 from the back of his jeans and aimed it at the closest creature staggering toward him.

In his periphery, Kate waved her hands. She shook her head, then pointed to her ear. *Too loud.* He sighed and put the gun away. She was right. There was no telling how many more Infected were in the area. More could be climbing through the window at that very moment and they would surely be drawn to the sound of gunshots.

Nick picked up the tequila bottle by its neck, slammed it on the ground, and expected to be holding a jagged cluster of glass shards to use as a makeshift knife. Instead, the entire bottle disintegrated into tiny fragments and fell on the carpet, leaving him holding a smooth cylinder of glass.

The creatures were only a few feet away from him now, drawn to the sound of the glass shattering, so he tossed it aside and searched for something else.

"Hey, shitheads!" Kate called from across the room, holding a vase in her hands. The Infected stopped their advance toward Nick and paused. All three of their heads turned at the sound of her voice in macabre symmetry, and they started to stagger in her direction.

Hurling the vase at the head of the closest monster, Kate hit her target. The Infected took a step back, stunned and brushing away small pieces of cobalt ceramic from its face.

Another creature approached, swinging its arms wildly at Kate. One of the creature's jagged fingernails connected with her bare arm, slicing her skin. Thrusting her foot into its hips, she sent it tottering backward.

"Over here, douchebags!" Nick shouted. He stood in a combat stance, both clenched fists readied in front of his face as the undead turned on him. Gesturing to Kate, he tipped his chin upward, trying to direct her gaze. Not following, her eyebrows furrowed in confusion.

Throwing powerful punches to the creatures' faces, Nick held them off without doing any fatal damage. The Infected snarled and grabbed at him with desperate swipes, ready to feast.

Kate looked at the wall above her where Nick had been nodding and saw at last what Nick had in mind. A coat of arms was secured to the painted drywall. An elaborately decorated shield featured four sections, adorned with golden lions in various fierce poses and two broadswords welded to the back.

With clumsy motions, she yanked the coat of arms down from the wall. Upon hearing the clanking metal, the Infected lost interest in Nick and pivoted to Kate once again. He continued to engage them with fist and foot, bringing the collective attention back to him.

Kate tugged vigorously at one of the swords attached to the shield, setting one foot on the coat of arms and pulling the blade with all her strength. The metal of the decorative blade bent and cracked with pressure until she separated it from the shield.

Clutching the sword in her hand, Kate realized with dismay that the tip was still attached to the back of the shield. The weapon she held was only jagged teeth of splintered metal; it would have to do.

Kate rushed the figures engaged in fisticuffs and skewered the first Infected between two ribs, surprising the other monsters as it howled in agony.

Stepping over their companion struggling on the ground, they continued in Kate's direction. As she pointed the serrated blade at one of the Infected, Nick kicked it in the back, sending the creature stumbling into the sword and piercing its chest. Nick pulled it off the blade by its shoulders and slung it to the ground.

Kate dodged to her right as the last Infected lunged toward her. She cracked the sword down onto its back, the force sending the monster to its knees.

Nick kicked the back of the Infected's head with tremendous impact, and the bones in its face crunched as it collided with the ground. Kate drove the blade into the soft tissue of its neck, eyeing the figure while it twitched several times, and then sprawled lifeless at her feet.

As Kate turned to check the status of the other Infected, a sturdy hand wrapped around her ankle. Nick drove the heavy sole of his boot into the creature's head repeatedly until it released her. Blood gurgled from its broken jaw as it exerted a final breath.

Though it appeared to be lifeless, they scrutinized the third monster and Kate drove the blade into its skull for good measure.

Nick and Kate rushed upstairs, searching room to room until they discovered broken glass littering the living room floor beneath a shattered window. Frilly curtains billowed about as a nighttime breeze tossed the fabric around; the air outside seemed calm.

Nick handed Kate his pistol, instructing her to shoot anything that tried to enter. He entered the garage and rifled through toolbox drawers, pocketing a box of nails and hanging a hammer from his waistband. Several sheets of plywood lay in one corner, and he carried a few of them back to the living room. Within minutes of boarding up the window, they felt a mild sense of security again.

Maintaining a cautious quietude, they sat at the kitchen table waiting for any more disruptions to their night. The house remained silent.

"I think I actually saved *you* for once," Kate smiled with mock smugness.

"It's about time. Things were starting to seem a little one-sided," Nick teased. Her jaw dropped open as she pretended to be offended, and they laughed. A few moments later he added, "I could've just shot them."

Kate groaned. "Just let me have my moment."

A stinging sensation in Kate's arm put a stop to their laughter. She looked down at her wrist. A small reservoir of partially dried blood had gathered in the crease of her elbow.

"Is that a—"

"Scratch," Kate finished for him. There was no need to play dumb. She gazed at the cut until she went cross-eyed. Everything in sight went out of focus until the gash broke open across her whole arm. Tissue and tendons spewed out and her rich, crimson blood turned black. The viscous fluid poured over her until she was covered in it, head to toe. The liquid cooled down and formed a cast over her body.

Once fully hardened, Kate shook her arms and cracked the mold until it fell away and shattered on the ground. Emerging as mostly herself, her fingernails were ragged, and her mouth tasted of iron. When she spoke, a low growl would escape and Kate would find a hunger within herself that only human flesh could satiate.

A burning liquid splashed across the cut on her arm, rescuing her from the horrific reverie. She blinked away the visual distortion, everything coming back into focus, and saw Nick standing over her, soaking her wound in disinfectant. He nearly poured the whole damn bottle on it as if that made a difference. As if he could simply wash away an infection.

Nick soaked up the excess liquid with paper towels, tingeing them pink. After wrapping the wound in gauze, he placed a large bandage over it and sat back down across from Kate. He had done everything in his power for her. The rest would be a waiting game.

Nick reached his hands across the table, and Kate placed her own within his palms. He clutched them, gazing at her reassuringly.

As many times as music had saved her life, it seemed that it would be the very thing to end it.

Chapter 43

Kate marched upstairs to the master bedroom, flung her pack onto the bed, ripped the zipper open, and rifled through it. Nick eyed her from the doorway.

"What are you doing?" Nick crossed his arms and arched his brows.

"You can stay here. I know you'll eventually move on to search for a refuge, but it's nice here. It'll give you time to regroup and plan."

Picking up the stuffed bat Nick had given her, Kate admired its fluffy black fur and goofy eyes, then shoved it back into the pack, and zipped it up. "I'll head... I don't know, west, I guess. Maybe head towards the mountains."

"What the hell are you talking about?" Nick narrowed his eyes at her. When he tried to place his hand on her forearm, she jerked away, her eyes filling with tears.

"It's only a matter of time before I'm trying to tear open your rib cage and feast on your insides!" She expected to see realization wash over Nick's face along with fear. He would walk her down the stairs and onto the front porch, kiss her goodbye, and say something cliché like, "I'll find you in another life." Instead, he just stared at her and laughed. The bastard laughed at her.

Nick sat on the bed and watched Kate's terror transform into anger. "We don't even know how the infection transmits. You're not going anywhere," he said calmly, like a parent telling a child that they most certainly would not eat dessert *before* dinner. Her anger rose to a boiling degree.

"So, we're just going to wait, huh? Oh, it'll be so much fun. We'll swim and dine and drink and dance around to music until one day, I become sick and rip your fucking face off!"

Laughter bubbled up in Nick's chest, and it took everything in him to stifle it. He thought if he laughed again she would skip the part where she turned into a mindless zombie and rip his face off now. The corners of his lips fighting upward in a smile gave him away.

Letting out a frustrated sigh, Kate threw herself onto the bed, pulling her legs to her chest and resting her chin on one knee. Nick's amusement faded, and remorse took over.

Moving to the spot next to her, Nick rested his back against the headboard and held out his hands. Kate glared at them like he was offering her a snake.

As she looked into his eyes, they took Kate back to the first time she saw Nick, standing over the corpse of her attacker, the bloody hunting knife clutched in one hand. A stark contrast to his shadowed gaze, his blue eyes resonated with kindness.

Kate found solace in their warmth as she fell into Nick's body and wrapped her arms around him. Nick pulled her close and rested his chin on the top of her head.

"Listen, I did several tours overseas. The things I saw, the things I did..." Nick left her to fill in the blanks with scenarios he could not form into words.

"During my last tour, my best friend died in my arms. I almost got myself and two other Marines killed trying to save his life. I returned home empty and distant. I cut off my family and friends. I never left the house. Some days, I wondered why I even bothered using up air that someone else could be breathing. I felt like an incapable waste of space. Had the world not gone to shit, I would've... I'd be gone. When the disease went rampant, I was only surviving out of necessity, driven by some unknown force I wasn't aware of." Nick drew in a deep breath and then exhaled slowly. His next words would be those of a man dropping his defenses for the first time, something Nick believed he would never do. But Kate needed those words.

"Then, I met you. Suddenly, I had a purpose again. I had a reason to wake up every morning, to stay vigilant and protective, to put my all into every single day. You've revived something in me I thought I'd lost. If you want to leave, I can't stop you. But I don't think that's what you want. And that scratch on your arm does not scare me. Come on, it doesn't get more poetic than that. My will to live being the very thing that takes me out?"

Kate was smiling now. Nick gave her body a gentle squeeze and kissed the top of her head.

"Promise me one thing," she said. "At the first sign that I'm afflicted, and not a moment after, you have to kill me."

"I promise, baby. I'll shoot you dead."

Chapter 44

"Nick," his dad's voice came across the phone, gruff and concerned. Sitting at his computer when the phone rang, Nick answered, put his father on speakerphone, and paused the video game he was playing. Just the one syllable from his dad caused his body to tense like drying cement.

"Hey, Dad," Nick said. Though he was unsure why he was calling, he was certain it would not end well, as his father only called to stir up discontent.

The last time they spoke was in regards to his mother. When she had fallen ill, his father urged him to visit her at home, and then at the hospital closer to the end. Another call had informed Nick that his mother had passed.

The last phone call was to give Nick the information for the viewing and funeral. Crushed in a death grip by his depression, Nick did not attend either. He was convinced that any interactions with the people he cared about would cast a shadow around them, and he would somehow make a funeral even more dismal.

There was a long pause as Nick's father considered a way to begin the conversation. Nick was beginning to think that the line disconnected until a heavy sigh resonated from the other side.

"I just spoke with Liv." Another long pause. Nick cradled his forehead in his hands and braced for the lecture. "I called to try and see you both. Even though I wasn't the piece of shit that missed my own mother's funeral, I still tried to reach out. I figured if we could sit down for dinner together, I could figure out what the hell was going through my son's head. But she told me what happened. Told me she left your sorry ass."

Clenching his jaw, tears welled up in Nick's eyes, and he pinched the back of his hand to prevent them from falling. His dad was waiting for a response but what was he supposed to say? What the fuck did he want to hear?

"You're a selfish piece of shit, Nick. You were given so much and you threw it all away, you ungrateful prick." As his father spat out the vitriolic words, Nick nodded, though he could not be seen.

Nick was not gesturing to his father. He was accepting the words into himself, affirming them as part of his character. "You've nothing to say?"

"Dad, I just—I don't know what I'm doing." Nick stuttered, sounding small and pathetic.

"You don't know what you're doing," his father repeated flatly. "Let me tell you what you're doing. Nothing. You're not doing shit. For yourself, for anyone around you, especially not your own goddamn family. In fact, anyone you encounter is left the worst for it, just for having been near you. Everyone thinks you're some hero, but you're nothing but a coward. You won't be hearing from me again."

The call ended, leaving Nick staring at his phone's lock screen. A selfie of him and Liv, standing on a wooden deck overlooking a waterfall, gazed back at him. They smiled wide in one another's embrace as if nothing else existed—just the two of them and the indefinite downpour of water cascading between rocks.

Nick shut off the cell phone and stared blankly at his desk. His dad's words bounced around in his head, chipping away at his sanity with every connection.

Just when he thought maybe he would do the world a favor and leave it, a news notification alerted on his phone.

EMERGENCY ALERT
State of Emergency Declared

Due to widespread reports of violence, the country is now under a state of emergency. Stay inside, keep all windows and doors locked, and avoid contamination with infected individuals. Follow official channels for updates and further instructions.

CHAPTER 45

Kate's head rose and fell, then repeated the motion. The sensation was a rhythmic and comforting transition to wakefulness. Pressed against Nick's chest, the right side of her face was alight with warmth. Though they maintained their habit of sleeping beneath separate blankets, Kate's arm rested across his stomach. The arm.

Kate sat up quickly and inspected the skin around the wound, the portion outside the bandages, though she was not sure what she was looking for. Black veins peering out at her through filmy skin? A purplish dermis throbbing with sickness? There was nothing out of the ordinary, so she sat back against the headboard, taking a deep breath and feeling foolish.

Thinking about the Infected she had encountered so far, Kate wondered how it went for them: the Turning. Did they feel their human selves slipping away? Did they have time to let their loved ones know what was going on and say goodbye? Was it both physically and mentally tormenting? Or was it painless? Did they merely close their eyes as something living and breathing, and open them as a blood-thirsty abomination?

Kate sighed. There were so many questions she would never have answers to, and it was giving her a headache... or perhaps that was a side effect from the heavy drinking the night before.

Nick's eyes were still closed, his body enveloped in a deep sleep and she watched his chest move as his lungs drew in air, then released it in gentle puffs through his nose.

So much had occurred the night before and she hoped some of them would not be discussed. Kate had thrown herself at Nick. The alcohol and the music made her feel... normal. It had temporarily simplified everything; she had felt good, she was attracted to Nick, and she assumed the attraction was mutual.

Then, Nick pushed her away, and Kate thought it was because he had not felt the same until his speech last night.

Kate found that life was starting to look like one big question mark, and the obscurity made her stomach hurt. No, that was also the previous night's alcohol.

Throwing the covers back and launching herself out of bed, Kate raced to the bathroom, lifted the toilet seat, and vomited into the commode. In between violent gagging, she fumbled with the hair hanging in her face. □

A hand grouped her hair into a makeshift ponytail at the base of her neck and she turned to see Nick offering her a sympathetic smile. Before she could return the gesture, she was retching stomach acid into the toilet.

One hand still holding her hair, he sat against the wall next to her. With his other hand, Nick ran his fingers lightly across her back.

After dry-heaving for several minutes more, Kate's stomach released her from its fit of spasms. When she sat back on her feet, Nick let her hair fall from his hand as she took deep, gasping breaths.

Taking a towel that hung next to the double vanity, he dabbed spit from the sides of her mouth. The exertion her body endured left tears clinging to the corners of her eyes. Certain his eyes were on her, she fixed hers to the floor.

"Damn wound cleaner," Nick said. A laugh escaped Kate's lips despite the embarrassment and her face turned red, expecting him to bring up the events she dreaded speaking about. "I don't even remember much of anything before the attack."

The way he cast his gaze away, and the slight pitch in his voice told Kate he was lying. Maybe he was embarrassed for her or maybe, he felt ashamed. Still, he was willing to bury the corpses of the previous night's entanglements, and she was grateful.

In truth, Nick recalled the way his body desperately longed to be one with hers, the way he shivered with desire at the thought of being inside of her, and he hated himself for it. He felt no better than Kate's sadistic captor, letting his hands roam the territory of an incapacitated woman.

Since when was making the right decision so fucking conflicting?

Chapter 46

After washing up and brushing her teeth, Kate joined Nick downstairs in the kitchen. The smells that greeted her were delicious yet nauseating. The grand oak table spread before her was a meaningless slab of wood with only their two souls to fill the chairs.

Nick set a cup of water in front of her and she gulped it down in two swallows. He watched her with an amused grin and brought her a refill. This time, Kate only sipped, returning his smirk with chagrin.

Nick cooked breakfast, pancakes from a box of mix, and canned potatoes. Silence accompanied them as they ate, Kate in famished recovery and Nick in deep thought. He intended to plan out when they would leave this house and begin their next journey. He meant to think about their next steps.

Instead, thoughts of the night before kept creeping in. Images flashed in Nick's mind: Kate's body on his, their lips melting together, the heat between her legs setting his world on fire. It was all he could think about and he wished Kate had never kissed him.

Nick had been doing just fine being around her, staying focused, keeping them safe from the Infected and people alike. He managed to get them safely from one destination to the next.

After she told him about her previous boyfriend and the torture and trauma she endured, it was even easier for him to bury any sexual tension he might have felt. Surely, physical contact was the last thing she wanted. How could she trust anyone with her body?

But the damned alcohol had released inhibitions and opened doorways that could not be shut. If he pretended not to remember, it might be possible to truly forget. He did not want to relive those moments and let the intense, overwhelming emotions consume him again.

Yet here he was, mentally imprisoned on that couch with her legs straddling his. Even now, he could not stop looking at her, the way her black hair fell in subtle ringlets over her shoulders and swayed with every movement. The strength in her small frame defied a lifetime of letdowns and betrayal.

It was the eyes for Nick, though, seeing everything and nothing in them at the same time. They were a prison cell guarding an open book, a wounded deer lying in a field of sunflowers, a child riding their bike through a cemetery.

Nick was in love with the darkness in her eyes because he lived there, too.

Kate looked up from her plate and when she smiled at him, he swore his soul lifted away from his body and materialized on some otherworldly plane where colors were bright, the air was breezy and he was flying.

Chapter 47

Nick and Kate cleaned up the basement theater and moved the bodies of the Infected out to the backyard. Kate was relieved to see that the music collection remained untouched, but mourned the tequila bottle in pieces on the floor.

Nick pretended that he was not worried about Kate turning into one of the monsters, but the way his eyes were constantly on her said otherwise. It made her nervous. She felt like a pariah. They hardly spoke, and once the chores were finished, they went separate ways to find things around the house to keep them busy.

Kate went up to the bedroom and locked the door. If she was going to turn, this would buy Nick some time. Laying on the bed, she stared at the ceiling until the void of the popcorn texture became maddening. Kate sat up and took a visual inventory of the room.

The artifacts of the former residents lay dust-covered around the room like sentimental fossils. Sitting on a nightstand, on what she assumed was the husband's side of the bed, an alarm clock caught her eye. It sat next to a wooden organizer with a place for every man's simple essentials: a watch, a cell phone, and a little dish for change.

On the other side of the clock was a photograph of the man and wife on their wedding day. The wife clung to his arm with both hands, smiling at him with a wide, toothy grin. Golden waves of hair spilled down the front of her lacy, white dress.

The man's smile was darker, less genuine. As he tried to follow a photographer's vague instructions, his eyes strained to look down at her and backward at the same time. Overzealous hair gel kept his combover swept back in a smooth layer on his head. A five-o-clock shadow traveled up into pudgy cheeks and ended at evenly cut sideburns.

Kate wondered why the bride always looked happier than the groom. Why did the man always look as if he were keeping the darkest secret, smiling smugly as if he could not wait to share it with you?

Curious if anything would break through the static, she clicked on the alarm clock's radio and turned the dial though she imagined the radio stations were down with no one to operate them. No one to scream at you about how they play today's hottest hits and then play the same five songs repeatedly.

Static. Static. Nothing came through, and turning the dial became more of something to do rather than a search.

When Kate turned past a set of numbers, she swore there was a break in the static. Grasping for the station once more, she turned the knob backward and forward, the muted sound sucking the static in every time she passed over it.

After turning the dial back and forth several more times, she finally settled on the right numbers. There it was. No crackling. No buzzing static. Just silence. Kate listened intently for a long time until a woman's voice came through.

"Hello! If anyone is out there, we are at the hospital. The building is safe, but we are running out of supplies. A few of us are hurt. We need help," the distressed voice pleaded.

"Nick!" Kate shouted. "Nick, come here!" She rushed to the top of the stairs and called down to Nick again. When he rounded the corner, gun drawn and with so much speed his feet slid on the hardwood, she almost laughed.

When Nick saw her at the top of the stairs, unharmed, he holstered the gun as his alarm dissolved to relief, then molded into curiosity.

Motioning him into the bedroom, they approached the nightstand, and Kate pointed to the alarm clock, afraid to speak and interrupt the transmission. The woman had not spoken in almost a minute, and only dead air emitted from the speakers. Squinting his eyes at her and unsure what he was listening for, Nick kept quiet.

"There was a woman, she was asking for help. She said—"

"Help us!" the voice came across the radio once more. Nick and Kate's heads fixed their eyes to the radio. "We are here, at the hospital. If you can hear us, please come! We are hurt and running out of supplies." The broadcast ended, leaving Nick and Kate listening to empty air once again. Stunned, they looked at each other, processing the woman's words.

"It's west of here, not far," Nick said and clicked off the alarm clock's radio.

"You think we should go?" Kate asked. Deliberating, Nick stared at the ground mapping out every possibility and weighing the risks.

Go. That simple word had been the source of so much grief. And yet it seemed like it was the only option anymore. Go. Keep going. Keep moving.

Would someone suffer because of his decision? Would someone die? Of course, they would. It was just a matter of whom. Who would die next because of the decisions he made?

Running his fingers through his hair, Nick sighed. Self-pity did not become him, and he could spend all day reasoning with himself.

Nick was not sure what the right answer was. Maybe there were no *right* decisions. Maybe opting for one thing or another could not be placed in a box labeled "good" or "bad". "Right" or "wrong". Perhaps there were just decisions.

"I think we should," Nick responded, nodding confidently. As if to punctuate his answer, heavy rain began pelting the roof tiles, and a sharp wind rattled the window panes. "We'll let the storm pass and leave in the morning."

CHAPTER 48

Tucked into a wicker loveseat, Nick and Kate sat on the screened-in back porch, enjoying the storm. Kate was couched between Nick's legs, her head on his chest.

Already three chapters in, Kate had borrowed a novel from a bookcase in the study and was mesmerized by the story of a family staying the winter in a haunted hotel.

Vicious rain thudded heavily on the roof. The sky bathed the world in an ominous golden color that smeared the autumn leaves into an orange and yellow mosaic. Thick, gray clouds passed overhead, slowly releasing themselves onto everything beneath them. A wind chime in the corner of the patio tinkled lazily as a slight wind blew the metal cylinders against each other.

The alarm clock from the bedroom was set up on a small glass table beside the loveseat with its volume turned down low. Periodically, the woman's voice came across, continuing her pleas for help. Nick hoped the people at the hospital could hold out through the stormy night.

The sound of the rain and the warmth of Kate's body caused Nick's eyelids to droop. He felt lazy and listless. Relaxed. It was a feeling he had not enjoyed in some time, and he had to admit, giving this up would be difficult.

Maybe they could stay here a while and play house. Nick could go out a few times a week and loot for supplies, maybe take up hunting.

She could stay back and spend her days reading, maybe even write a book of her own. They would cook delicious meals together in the evening and spend their nights laughing, drinking, and getting lost in old rock tunes.

Nick realized he was smiling, and he swiftly released the happiness from his lips. It was a nice dream, but it was not reality. *Keep moving.*

Another transmission from the woman at the hospital spilled out into the silence of the back porch, waking Nick from his dreamy state. Kate took her eyes away from the pages to listen but returned them once it ended.

"Kate." Nick could not stand it anymore. The things left unspoken were driving him mad. Flagging the page she was on, Kate closed the book and gave him her attention. Inhaling deeply, he took one of her hands in his. "I think we should talk about last night. I know we'd been drinking but there was something there. I care about you. I lo—"

Kate ripped her hand from his before he could utter the words, shaking her head violently. The color drained from her face and her hands trembled. She said nothing but continued her nonverbal rejections. *No, no, no, no, no.* The word filled the room like a thick fog, choking them both and she fled into the house before he understood what was happening.

Nick was left on the back porch by himself, Kate's vehement denials hanging in the air like corpses from a tree. He simply could not leave well enough alone. What did he think was going to happen?

Nick pictured the scene as a black-and-white sitcom from the '50s.

"Well, darlin', I think you're just swell," Nick would say, clad in a gray flannel suit and sporting a trilby hat. Kate would giggle and blush, her white pencil line dress with red polka dots swaying softly from side to side.

"Gee, Nick, I think you're a real dreamboat!" Kate would respond. The pair would share a delightful peck on the lips, then saunter off beneath the enchanting hues of a picturesque sunset.

You're such an asshole, Nick berated himself.

Still, the words had come out, and he could not take them back. In fact, he refused to take them back. The moment Nick had seen her face, everything within him rearranged. His lungs filled with the air of a new life, and he could finally breathe.

Whether he had years or mere days with Kate, he wanted her to spend each moment knowing that although he had rescued her several times, she had pulled him from the brink of certain death.

Chapter 49

"Connor, I'm just not comfortable doing these things. It's not me," Kate plead her case, delicately rejecting Connor's suggestions for new bedroom activities.

When they first became intimate, things were normal. Just the two of them. Missionary, her on top, from behind. Kate assumed Connor was nervous when he had trouble getting into it. She had been, too.

Once, after a dinner party, they had come home heavily intoxicated. Slipping beneath the covers, they began a carnal encounter when his hands slid over her throat and squeezed. Connor's eyes burst alight with pleasure, and he was stiffer than she had ever experienced.

When Kate tried to pry his hand away, he held it there, clenching relentlessly, only releasing his grip the moment he achieved orgasm. Though the act frightened her, Connor held her close for hours afterward, so she chalked up the devious stunt to drunkenness, certain it would never happen again. Instead, it opened a black, oozing door of venereal depravity.

Connor had started to bring home alcohol quicker than she could drink it. One choking hand turned into two. He pulled her hair and scratched deep gouges into her back, her breasts, and her thighs. Each time she tried to stop him, she found herself incapable and clumsy with inebriation.

When his bare hands were no longer able to satisfy him, he bought whips, chains, clamps, restraints, spreaders, the list went on. The engagements had increased to every night, and she was exhausted.

Tonight, Connor had brought up something to do with fire, burning her in some way, and she simply had enough. Kate shut him down before indulging his idea.

Connor stared at her for a long moment, as though she were having a staring contest with a feral dog. She wanted to blink, wanted to look away, but needed to establish her dominance. It was imperceivable that she had to fight for authority over her own body.

"Kate, I love you," Connor said, forcing his voice to sound softer and sweeter than was natural. A dark sickness swirled in his eyes. "Don't you love me?" The inflection of his words was disingenuous and childlike.

"Connor, yes, but I—"

"Then you should want me to be happy. Kate, I do everything I can to make you happy. I buy you anything you want, let you decorate the house any way you want, cook meals when you're tired, and do my best to clean up after myself. I even tolerate those whore friends of yours."

Kate's mouth dropped open, but before a reply could tumble out, she realized what she saw in his eyes—or rather, what she did not see. How could she have missed it? The nothingness.

There were eyeballs in his sockets complete with irises and the whites around them. But if eyes are the windows to the soul, these windows opened up to a disdainful landscape filled with dead trees planted in hard, lifeless soil.

Kate stood up to run, pushing one foot against the ground to propel herself away from Connor. Before she could put distance between them, he grabbed her wrist, spun her around so her back was to him, and caught the other wrist.

Forcing her to the ground with his knee on her back, Connor restrained her arms. With Kate's face squashed against the hardwood floor, he held her wrists in a handcuff grip and leaned down so that his lips were inches from her ear.

"I tried to play nice with you. It's better this way, though. You can make me the happiest man alive." Lifting Kate to her feet, Connor pushed her down the hallway, thrashing in his arms, and kicking her legs behind her. Avoiding each strike, he saw her feet coming every time.

"Let go of me, you piece of shit. Help!" Kate shrieked until his fist connected with the side of her head, and her knees buckled. Cupping his arm around her middle to hold her up, he pushed her to the top of the basement stairs and forced her down each step.

The fight in her rose up again, and Kate attempted to hurl herself down the stairs. She figured his grip was on her so tight that he would certainly fall with her. Instead, he stutter-stepped a few times and regained his balance.

Connor released Kate's wrists and shoved the back of her head until she lost her footing, tumbling down the second half of the stairs. Her face hit the concrete at the bottom, and her vision went dark. The chill of the floor was the only thing that kept her from losing consciousness, and she pushed against it in a feeble attempt to get to her feet.

Connor sent one of his boots into her stomach, and she fell limp again. He pulled her to her feet by her hair and tossed her onto the bed.

Kate willed herself to get up and run from the bed, up the stairs, and out of the house as far as she could go. A whimper escaped her lips, but her muscles would not move. She was going nowhere.

One eye was swollen shut and leaking fiery, anguished tears. Snot ran from Kate's nose, and saliva dripped from the corners of her mouth. Blood streamed down her neck onto her shoulders.

Sweaty and panting, Connor climbed on top of her. When she tried to pull her arms away he used bed sheets to secure her to each bedpost, his strength overpowering her.

The physical abuse, the sexual trauma, and the total disregard for her life were not the most horrifying aspects of this scenario. Kate was certain it was the obscene grin plastered to his face during all of it. Squeezing her eyes shut, she tried to mentally travel far away while he forced himself inside of her.

Chapter 50

A light tapping on the door brought Kate back from the memory. Tears streamed down the sides of her face and onto the comforter below as she lay stiff and motionless on the bed. Concrete depression filled her veins, anchoring her in place.

"Kate," Nick muffled through the thick wooden door, his voice careful and hesitant. She stared at the ceiling, the white popcorn paint swirling into sharp points. A vast hole in her middle opened wide, purging itself of hope and filling up with doubt. Anxiety floated around like butterflies in her stomach, weighty and dripping with disease, fluttering around until suffocating in the noxious fumes of sorrow.

"Kate," Nick tried again, unable to get past saying her name.

Desperation trickled out in his utterance, and Kate's sadness turned to anger. Thrusting herself away from the bed, the lock clicked as it disengaged and she slung open the door, facing him with watery eyes and clenched fists.

"What?" she said, backing away when he half-heartedly reached his hand toward her.

"Can we talk?" Nick asked. Opening the door to him, Kate stepped aside and swung out her arm in a resentful 'come on in' gesture.

Come one. Come all. Step right up and see the freak show. Tonight, we're featuring the tortured woman. Come see her scars. Her fear. You can practically taste it! Don't forget your popcorn!

Nick sat on the edge of the bed as Kate stood in front of him with her arms folded and her eyes to the floor. Unsure how to begin, he fumbled with his hands in his lap.

"Kate, I never meant to upset you. I—"

"We can't do this," Kate nearly shouted. "I... can't do this." Her voice quieted, and she sat defeated on the bed next to him.

Nothing but a whore. A used-up, broken whore. Connor's words played in her head like a bad song on repeat.

"Look, I just can't be what you want me to be, or... do what you expect me to do,"

Nick's eyebrows furrowed in confusion. Turning the words over, he tried to make sense of them. Sex. She was talking about sex.

Since the moment they met, Nick and Kate had formed a connection and started to build a relationship. Nothing had been spoken aloud until he proclaimed his feelings for her, then things became real.

Society's list of rules about relationships clicked into place in her head, and she was stuck on the thing that couples did together, fearful of it. How could he blame her? Had he been through what she had, he was sure he would never want to be touched again.

"Kate, I don't have any expectations." Nick took her hand in his, ignoring the way it trembled at his touch. "What I said, I understand why it took your mind where it did."

Do you, Nick? Do you understand

"But I won't take it back. I meant it. Maybe it could've waited, I don't know. But I'm happy here. Right where we are. I don't want anything else. I don't expect anything else. I'm certainly not going to try and take anything else."

How fucking kind of you, Nick. We've got ourselves a real boy scout here!

Kate gazed at him, the darkness alight in her eyes, the storm in her pupils so powerful, Nick felt the hairs on the back of his neck rise and chills crept down his spine. Kate imagined letting the darkness take over, letting herself respond from the black, putrid corners of her mind.

You understand, huh? You understand where my mind went? YOU UNDERSTAND? She fantasized about screaming as she stood over him. Her voice would be hers but a deep bellow of something inhuman would underline her words. *Did you include the beatings in your comprehension, Nick? How about the burn marks? Me, face planting into concrete right before I was bound to a bed where I would stay for months. HOW ABOUT THE CONSTANT RAPE NICK? DID YOU WRAP YOUR MIND AROUND THAT?*

Kate thought about curling her fingers around his neck and squeezing, watching him struggle, just as he struggled to understand anything that happened to her. If he begged and pleaded for his life, it would mean nothing. Kate had heard it all from her own lips. She had a lot of practice.

Nick might even try and overpower her, but she had played that part, too. Either way, one of them ended up dead in her twisted reverie.

Kate crawled out of the macabre compartment of her brain and stared down at her hands, one empty, one wrapped in Nick's fingers. Those thoughts were entirely unfair to Nick. This man was not her enemy. If he had wanted to hurt Kate, why had he not done so already?

Knowing his words had fallen flat, Nick silently cursed in his desperation to find words that might bring her an ounce of peace. Kate's mind had been somewhere sinister and he had almost expected her to lunge out at him, rip him apart with her fingernails. Had she chosen that route, he would not have intervened.

It had been ignorant of Nick to tell Kate that he understood her trauma when he could not fathom the first thing about it. Atrocious situations were no stranger to him. Being held in captivity, completely powerless with no dominion over his own body, was not one of them.

"Make a deal with me. I'll work out our survival. With your guidance, I'll decide where we go, what we do, and how we stay alive. But when it comes to us, emotionally and physically, you call the shots." Nick leaned in, his lips inches away from her ear, and whispered words she had never been offered before. "You are in control. You have all the power."

Kate's eyes widened at the idea.

I have all the power.

Though usurped by her past and the inadequacy that overshadowed her, it was always there, since they met.

I am in control.

The prospect of this melted away a bit of her uneasiness.

Kate was not daft. The only reason she had power was because he had given it to her. She was weaker, lacked his advanced survival skills, and her proficiency with weapons paled in comparison.

Instead of letting this anger her, Kate embraced it, channeled it. She did not miss the volumes it spoke to Nick's character. A formidable force of strength and cunning, yet he was conceding control of things to *her*. And to think only moments ago, she was daydreaming of killing him. Her lips transformed into an empowered grin.

I have all the power.

Chapter 51

Nick and Kate spent the remainder of their day preparing for their journey. Dipping herself into a hot bath, Kate soaked her body one last time before they found their next place to call home. As she cleaned the wound on her arm, the fear of infection waned.

Gathering supplies, Nick's mind raced like someone packing for vacation, certain he was forgetting something. Questions ravaged his mind. Was he steering them towards a haven, people who could help them? Or would tomorrow be the final page in their story?

Kate finished up with her bath and dressed, glad to cover the scars that decorated her body like pink and flesh-colored confetti. Nick walked in just as she pulled her shirt down and quickly averted his eyes.

"Shit, I'm so sorry. I swore you were reading on the porch," he mumbled and retreated from the bathroom.

"Wait, it's okay. I'm dressed," Kate said, amused at the nervousness she inspired. Then, her eyes fell to the doorknob and the delight faded. Had she forgotten to lock the door? Had she gotten that comfortable?

Nick returned and examined the environment, ensuring he was welcome. Stepping to one of the vanities, he picked up an electric razor and began trimming down his hair.

Kate analyzed the man before her. The man who had saved her life, the man who had killed for her, the man who was *in love* with her. All she had were questions she did not know how to ask.

Lowering the razor, Nick powered it off and turned his head toward her. Kate wanted to look away and pretend her eyes were not absorbing every bit of him. She decided to stand her ground and met his gaze.

Kate sat on the floor between the vanity and the open bathroom door, arms wrapped around her knees as she grasped at thoughtful fragments, trying to string them into sentences that made sense. Instead, she resorted to humor.

"You're not going to embrace the savage, end-of-the-world fashion and let it grow out?" Kate joked.

Nick was silent at first as he assessed her words. He set the razor on the vanity and sat on the floor facing her, legs stretched out, palms resting on the tiles behind him. After lowering himself to the cold, firm floor, his joints cried out in protest but he wanted to give her his full attention. Standing over her was too aggressive a stance.

"Not my style," Nick answered, searching her face. There was more.

"Tell me about your tattoos."

"All of them?" Nick asked, pushing up both shirt sleeves to reveal the black ink that covered most of his arms. He pulled up the legs of his pants as far as they would go, the fabric stopping just below his knees. Tattoos covered his calves and shins, spreading upward beneath his clothes where she could not see.

Adler. The zombie with the swinging dog tags on Nick's back came to mind.

"The one on your chest?" Kate blurted before the thought of Nick, covered in blood and tears, threatened to swallow her whole.

"It's an old Norse symbol. The Helm of Awe. It was used to inspire fear in enemies and summon inner strength. I guess it helped make me feel strong during a time when I felt worthless. Or maybe I thought I deserved the pain that came along with it," Nick expressed, waiting for Kate to laugh at him, mock him.

Instead, Kate gazed at him thoughtfully, even offering a tiny smile as her eyes traveled over the visible ink displayed on Nick's body. She scanned his legs and arms as if trying to read him like a book, but fell short of coming up with new information.

The silence between them pulsed like a heartbeat beneath a rib cage.

Nick scrambled to come up with things to say that would satisfy her questioning mind, grasping for anything that would break the stilted quiet. He could talk more about his time in the military but that would only resurrect things that should remain dead.

Maybe Kate would benefit from knowing more about his relationship with Liv. *Relationship. Sex. Someone else you loved. Someone you had sex with. Great idea, idiot.*

He could talk about Adler. *Depressing.*

Or his strained relationship with his family. *Fucking loser.*

Nick's sense of worthlessness grew so loud that it took up every inch of empty space in the room until he was choking on it.

"Nick, you're a good man," Kate said, punctuating her words with a smile and leaving Nick speechless.

Tears tugged at the corners of his eyes. Before he let his vulnerability fall down his cheeks, Nick jumped to his feet and offered his hand to her, helping Kate up.

Fingers intertwined, Nick could drown in those tumultuous gray eyes and die a happy man.

"You missed a spot," Kate said, stubble prickling the pad of her thumb as she touched a place on his chin. Nick narrowed his eyes at her playfully before returning to the sink to finish his grooming. Kate joined him at the double vanity and brushed through her wet hair.

A good man. Those three syllables echoed in Nick's head. Spending his whole life, pre-apocalypse, trying to be a good man, he painfully strived to make the right decisions and keep everyone around him safe and satisfied.

When Adler died, he blamed himself. He came home from the war and descended into a depression that consumed him completely. Neglecting and failing everyone he loved, Nick had come to believe he was the villain.

Then, the world ended, granting him a second chance to decide what kind of man he would be. At times, he felt as though he still fell short, yet the most beautiful, tormented person he had ever met thought he was a good man.

Desperate to absolve himself from the adversary he had become, Nick anchored Kate's words to his soul.

CHAPTER 52

While trimming the last of the hairs on his chin, Nick listened to the rain outside pounding against the window panes, wondering when it would stop and how it would impact their travels. After shaking the hair from the razor into the sink, Nick secured it in his pocket and walked downstairs.

Entering the three-car garage, Nick looked over a black Chevy facing the garage doors. The pristine paint job, rugged tires, and sleek design called to him. What if they could put the vehicle to use? The rain smacked against the roof louder as if to cheer on Nick's idea.

Nick peered into the windows of the SUV, finding it absurdly clean. When he tried the driver's side door handle, it was locked. Searching through the house, Nick surveyed the counters in the kitchen, finding only expensive kitchen appliances, junk mail, and the dishes they had dirtied during their stay.

Toward the front door, Nick eyed a wooden shelf—a key ring with multiple house keys and one black key fob adorned with a bow tie hung from its tiny hooks. He swiped the keys and headed back to the garage.

Nick clicked the unlock button, opened the driver's side door of the vehicle, and sat inside. Though it had been months since he had been behind the wheel, every action came naturally. Pressing his foot on the brake, he pushed the button that ignited the engine. The SUV came roaring to life, the sounds of the motor echoing throughout the garage. The gas gauge started at empty, climbed to full, then settled on half of a tank. That would be plenty to get them where they needed to go.

Nick shut off the vehicle, hoping the sound had not attracted unwanted attention. As he pocketed the key, Nick concluded that driving would be their means of escape if the rain persisted.

CHAPTER 53

"This is NBC news anchor Helen Whitlock reporting from Raleigh, North Carolina. I'm here in front of Duke Regional Hospital where the number of intakes has exceeded twice the hospital's limit. People are out here lying on the grass, on benches, and even in the street as they await medical attention. As patients grow increasingly violent, the National Guard has been called in to provide order. The president has deployed FEMA to most major cities."

After hanging up the phone with his father, Nick sat at his computer investigating the emergency situation around the country. The news clip in front of the hospital displayed a professionally dressed woman standing on a sidewalk littered with people. Some held their heads in pain. Others jerked around involuntarily like puppets controlled by invisible strings. A few of them erupted with frenzied laughter.

When Nick checked the date of the video, he found it was from a week prior. In search of something more recent, only videos taken from people's phones emerged.

Nick selected a video with over 2 million views and watched in horror as people ran down the streets of Baltimore. Cars sped through the streets without regard for pedestrians. People chased others down, biting and clawing through them until the asphalt was slick with blood. Windows of businesses were smashed open, and people jumped through, taking all they could get their hands on. Sirens blared from all around as officers stormed the streets.

The person recording was hit with force letting out an audible "oomph". The phone fell to the ground and recorded nothing but a smoky sky, the corners of skyscrapers, and what appeared to be a person's shoulder in the corner of the frame. The shoulder moved back and forth without pattern.

Nick leaned closer to the computer screen. His headphones emitted the sickening sound of skin tearing away from the bone. Revulsed, he realized the shoulder bobbing up and down belonged to some feral human, ripping apart the person who the phone belonged to.

Nick paused the video and looked for the date it was uploaded. It was posted two days ago, and Baltimore was only a couple of hours away.

The area Nick lived in was rural and secluded, his closest neighbor being five miles away. He stepped out onto his front porch and saw smoke clouds billowing up from the direction of the nearest city. The madness would extend to his area before long.

Nick had the means to stay at home for a month, maybe two, but winter was coming. The days of electricity were numbered, and he had enough gas to run the generator for a week, at most.

Grabbing a hiking backpack from the upstairs bedroom, Nick packed everything he thought would be essential to someone about to leave their home, never to return. Sitting around and waiting for something to happen was not how he operated.

Nick thought of calling his dad or Liv but his father would ignore the call, and Liv had already found someone else to take care of her.

It was a strange feeling, witnessing the world descend into turmoil without a single soul to call on. Everyone he ever cared about had gone from his life one way or the other.

So, Nick set off into the wilderness with minimal supplies and no idea where he was going.

Keep moving.

Chapter 54

Early morning passed by as Nick and Kate slept on. The sky barely lightened as the sun rose, hidden behind thick clouds. The rain persisted and the dark bedroom remained still and lifeless until a clap of thunder stirred Nick from his sleep. He awoke and examined the room through sluggish, hazy eyes. Kate slept on her side facing away from him, breathing a slow, delicate melody he could get lost in.

As Nick suspected, the rain had not let up. He sat up in bed, taking in the lazy silence of the house, absorbing the opportunity to enjoy the nothingness of the morning. There were no dangers and no problems, only rainfall.

Nick ran a hand gently across Kate's back. His touch startled her, but as wakefulness brought her back to the present, she settled. Clumsily stretching her arms, she turned toward him and yawned. She wrapped her arms around a pillow and snuggled into it, pretending to go back to sleep.

"Hey," Nick admonished. Eyes still closed, Kate smiled and pulled the comforter over her head.

"Go away," Kate groaned. Nick laughed and pulled the blanket away from her face. Her lips were tugged down at the corners, pouting. Curling an arm around his waist, she laid her head on his chest, forcing him back into a lying position. "Can't we just lay here for a while?"

Nick closed his eyes, Kate's body spreading warm comfort across his skin like standing in front of a fireplace in the dead of winter. The bed covers lulled him with the tune of never leaving this home, resounding in his ears like sweet background music. Until the transmissions from the hospital played their siren song, luring him away.

"We have to go." Nick kissed the top of her head and pulled away.

"It's still raining."

"I've got it covered," Nick grinned. "Get your stuff together."

Nick and Kate made their way around the house, collecting their belongings and anything else they might need. Kate snuck down to the theater in the basement and stuffed her backpack with CDs. She even considered taking the CD player, but it would not fit. As she passed the couch in the theater, memories tugged at her—the taste of the liquor, his lips pressed to hers. Resentment mixed with a sickening desire poured into her, so she put the thoughts away for later.

Their packs were bursting when they felt comfortable enough to leave. The day landed somewhere around noon, though time mattered little now that they would be driving. Nick grabbed the keys from his pocket and led Kate to the garage. She stood on the stairs that led down to the concrete floor and stared at the vehicle.

"We're driving?" she asked after a hesitant pause.

"I imagine my license is expired. I'll keep to the speed limit, so we don't get pulled over." Nick cut her a playful smile that did not affect her serious mood.

Remembering their agreement, Kate would trust him with their survival, so she threw her backpack into the SUV and took her place in the passenger seat.

Nick entered the driver's side and started the vehicle. The engine was quieter than Kate imagined it would be, even in the cavernous garage.

When Nick clicked a button on a remote hanging from the sun visor, the garage door moved upward, revealing the gray, wet world outside. The door groaned as the chains pulled it up along the tracks. Nick inched the SUV forward until it cleared the door and pulled out onto the driveway.

Once the garage door was open to its full extent, Nick pressed the remote again. Chains and metal complained as they shifted direction, and the door made its descent toward the ground.

Just as the large home was almost out of sight, Kate spotted two Infected lumbering toward the garage from her side-view mirror. Sighing, she shifted in her seat, looking forward and leaving the danger behind.

They must have passed twenty or thirty homes like the one they had been staying in, million-dollar structures with large brick columns and picturesque windows facing the harbor. Embellished dwellings with three or four-car garages, in-ground swimming pools, and fountains amid paved circle driveways.

Kate thought about the kind of money it took to afford homes like these—for all the good it did now. Wealthy families had been reduced to mindless, cackling cannibals. Fancy cars collected dust. Dark green algae floated in swimming pools. Thousand-dollar suits hung in closets without having touched skin in months. All those numbers in bank accounts while the account holders roamed about, moaning and hunting their prey.

The rain picked up as Nick drove, and he was right. The rainfall was so heavy that the vehicle was but a whisper on the road. They turned out of the neighborhood onto a main road, the stop lights blinking like forlorn party lights.

Kate stared fixedly out of the passenger side window, taking in what she could see through the pane spattered with droplets of rain.

Though it was midday, the clouds cast a shadow over the city. Everything was soaked, concrete buildings and brick sidewalks all a shade darker. Some buildings simply looked empty, as if closed for the day with doors shut tight and parking lots deserted. Other buildings were left in ruined, looted states.

Half of the lights on a gas station's sky-high sign blinked dutifully while the others were broken and dark. The lot was littered with vehicles—Kate was sure bodies were in them, people so afraid to leave their cars in fear of the Infected that they chose the fate of starving in metal coffins with wheels.

Laying on the ground in front of the gas station's wide-open doors was a body—age, and gender far from being identifiable. Its flesh was torn away at the bone, strips of clothing trailed off in every direction, and a pile of entrails led away from it.

Next, they passed a hotel, and Kate shuddered at the thought of what horrors lay inside. Hundreds of people trapped in one living space, each one passing the disease to the next until only a few were left uncontaminated. Those few fighting for their lives until the hotel's renovations of skin and blood and intestines were complete.

Kate gasped as she noticed one of the cars in the hotel's lot. The back window was rolled down a few inches, and a tiny hand hung through the opening, a small wrist resting on the glass as if reaching for help. Watching until the hand was out of sight, part of her expected it to move, flinch, curl its fingers. It remained still.

Even when Kate closed her eyes, she was haunted by images of a small child sitting in the back of that car, screaming and pleading for someone to help them only for their cries to attract the horrors and end up a decaying statue in the back of a run-down sedan.

Kate turned her focus to the inside of the car, watching Nick as he drove, his eyes focused on the road.

"You okay?" Nick asked, keeping both hands on the wheel. He cast his eyes in her direction while keeping his focus on the road. Though most perils of driving were no more, Nick feared running into a stopped vehicle or a horde of Infected. The dangers of the post-apocalyptic roadways were new—less common but more hazardous.

"I'm okay," Kate said. And for the most part, she meant it. The macabre sights of the road were fading away, and the gentle hum of the SUV inspired a sense of normalcy; just two people on a road trip.

Of course, Nick's presence brought about a feeling of security on its own. The only shadow in her mind was the looming destination, the hospital, and whatever atrocities awaited there.

Chapter 55

The massive brick hospital emerged into view, twisting Kate's stomach into fearful knots. Though the world was dimmed by rain, the hospital stood tall—a modern, and bright monolith. Enormous blue panes of glass fronted the building, only broken up by the white emblem. Kate assumed it was supposed to look like an anatomically correct heart bordered by olive branches. An eagle stood proud over top of the heart, its wings spread wide. Solar panels topped the hospital's roof, raindrops pelting the black rectangles and sliding off in steady streams.

The parking lot was a carbon copy of others they had passed since beginning their journey. Cars crashed or abandoned, doors left open, and blood spattered on the upholstery. Kate willed herself not to think too much about the scenarios that preceded what she saw now, including the black coupe with a string of intestines wrapped around one of the headrests inside. Perhaps her own desensitization was not so far off.

Nick slid the SUV into a parking spot and shut the vehicle off, leaving the rain a deafening drumbeat on the windshield.

The hospital was shuttered and lifeless. The windows, appearing larger now, loomed over them like cautious eyes. Kate took a deep breath, readying herself for whatever they would find inside.

"You ready?" Nick asked. Kate wondered how, even at this moment, he exuded nothing but confidence.

"Yeah," Kate said, her voice quivering. "Let's do this."

Nick kissed the back of her hand, let it go, and exited the vehicle. Kate followed suit, making sure to close the car door without making a sound.

The sidewalk leading to the front entrance was smothered with overgrown juniper bushes. The automatic sliding doors did not sense their presence and remained closed. Peering through the glass panes, the long, dim hallway was never-ending, the doors at the end barely visible. Emergency lights bathed the interior in an eerie glow.

Nick pried at the doors, pulling them away from each other until they gave way and allowed them in. The two stepped inside, and Nick closed the doors quietly.

The front desk appeared as if the admissions clerk had only stepped away for a break. An old, stained coffee cup sat among a pile of papers.

The door to the nurses' lounge was partly open. Cardigans spilled out of lockers, and take-out boxes decorated the faux oak table. A half-eaten sandwich sat on top of plastic wrap, the bread moldy and wilting.

At the end of the main hall, the building split into two corridors. Nick surveyed both thoughtfully, considering where this group in need of help might be, and chose the right wing without reason.

Moving down the hall, they found only more patient rooms, another nurses' lounge, and a pair of restrooms. At the end of this passage was an elevator.

Next to the elevator was a stairwell. Nick and Kate took the steps up to the second floor which must have been used for surgeries. Sizeable, open rooms with glass walls stood one after another. Each room contained an operating table, metal machinery, computers, and tools used for opening up the body and repairing it. Nick continued his steady, tactical stride down the hallway.

Kate paused as she peered into one of the operating rooms. Except for the dead bodies, this room was set up like the others. A thin brunette woman wearing a hospital gown lay on the floor next to the bed, leg splayed out, crooked and broken. Her decaying skin was gray and mottled with bruising and coagulation. A long, precise incision was still visible in the awkward leg.

A surgeon's body clad in the notable, white lab coat was sprawled out beside her, except the top half of the coat was maroon with blood. The doctor's jaw was separated and hanging by a thin tendon. His eyes bulged in frozen terror. A wide, bloody cavity replaced his midsection where an Infected had feasted.

Kate's eyes fixated on the woman, conjuring up her backstory. Given the purposeful gash opening up to her shin, Kate surmised she was having surgery on her leg until it was interrupted by an onslaught of the plagued monsters.

Though foggy at first, the sounds of the hospital sprang to life, emerging from Kate's memory.

CHAPTER 56

"Good evening, miss. How are you feeling?" the doctor asked as he entered her modest triage room.

Beneath his lab coat, he wore a white cotton shirt and a bright blue tie that swung out between the lapels as he walked. His trousers were black and neatly pressed, hugging his lower half in all the right places.

The doctor's dark hair was plastered against his scalp except for a single lock that hung over his forehead. Though Kate found it charming, he probably pressed it back every time he caught a glimpse of his reflection, frustrated with how unkempt it made him look.

Kate imagined the doctor asking for her number, calling and inviting her out on a date. She lost herself in a daydream where her dating life was normal and her evenings were spent with a dignified, respectful man, laughing over wine and awful movies.

"Miss?" the doctor repeated. Kate shut her eyes and scoffed internally. *Respectful man? What a joke.*

"Sorry, I'm in pain. But I'm okay," Kate answered. The doctor nodded and glanced down at his clipboard.

"I'll have the nurse bring you something for the pain shortly, and then we'll take some X-rays. Can you tell me what happened?" The doctor looked at her awaiting some scenario where she fell out of a tree or had a car accident. Kate tensed up and looked at her hands.

"I... fell down the stairs," Kate said with as much conviction as she could muster.

The doctor eyed her for a moment that turned over in the room until a lifetime passed. Then, he nodded and jotted down some notes on his clipboard. He put a hand on her unbroken leg and mentioned something about pain meds again, but Kate had stopped listening.

The doctor left the room, and Kate laid back on the bed she had raised into a sitting position. Her leg throbbed with pain, and she tried to keep it as still as she could. Every time it moved, a grinding sensation that hurt like hell sent chills through her body.

A nurse entered the room with a small paper cup and held it out to Kate.

"This will help with the pain, honey," the nurse said.

Kate downed the two, white tablets while the nurse scribbled on the whiteboard next to the door. When she stepped away, Kate read the scrawling words: *Hydro-APAP 5-325mg 2 tabs 4:45 pm.* She could not make sense of them.

Kate set the empty paper cup on the small table, and the nurse promptly discarded it into a nearby trashcan. She sat on the edge of Kate's bed and looked at her solemnly.

"The doctor says you fell down the stairs." The sentence came out in the form of a statement, yet doubt dripped from every word.

"That's right," Kate said. Tension climbed the walls of her throat and took hold. The nurse carried a gaze that aimed to chisel away at Kate until only the truth remained.

"Listen, honey. I see lots of women come in here that have... fallen down the stairs. And I'm not going to preach to you. But I just want you to know, those... stairs, they don't have to hurt you anymore. There's help out there, you know."

While Kate could not remember what had started the argument in the first place, she would always remember the ending. Connor accused her of fucking someone, which Kate denied with tireless vehemence. Refusing to believe her, Connor asked her to let him know how difficult it was to fuck with a broken leg.

And that was when he crushed her calf under his boot, pulling up on her ankle until the bone splintered in half. It had taken her almost forty minutes to lift herself to her feet and limp to the car.

Though it was bereft of joy, Kate smiled at the nurse. Cocking her head, the nurse looked Kate over with such a pitying look it disgusted her.

Kate thought of saying something, asking for help, crying out to be rid of this man and this situation, but if Connor was willing to break her leg over nothing, he would certainly kill her for ratting him out.

Slumping back in the hospital bed, Kate lowered her head in defeat. The nurse came to terms with the fact that Kate was another battered woman who refused to blow the whistle on her partner, and left the room, taking every ounce of warmth and hope with her.

Kate stared at the white walls, hopelessness bubbling up into her throat until she choked on tears. She was alone. And once she left here, she would be worse off than alone. She would be with him.

Chapter 57

The recollection slipped away along with the sights and sounds until Kate was staring into the gruesome operating room once again. As tears streamed down her cheeks, Kate realized she had been sobbing.

As Kate looked around for Nick, a hand covered her mouth from behind and pulled her into a janitor's closet. One hand remained on her mouth while the other shut the closet door without a sound, diminishing any bit of light in the small area.

Wide-eyed and consumed in blackness, she was pressed into a warm body she assumed to be Nick's. Despite the brevity of their companionship, she knew him—his scent, his movements, his inhales and exhales.

With one hand firmly wrapped across her lips to keep her quiet, his other hand wrapped around her waist, pulling her close to him so they both fit inside the small room. Nick leaned his head against the side of Kate's, his breath drawing on her neck and ear.

Kate fixed her eyes on the small rectangular window set in the middle of the closet door. Several minutes passed until she heard a faint shuffling sound.

The shuffling grew louder until a heavily decayed Infected passed, a distorted gait causing its body to heave in exaggerated back-and-forth motions.

The two remained stationary in the closet for several minutes after the walking corpse had gone out of sight, awaiting the possibility of more Infected. None came.

Removing his hand from Kate's mouth, Nick leaned over her, turned the doorknob, and pushed it open. They emerged, glancing around with apprehension. The hallway was clear in both directions.

Nick paused, deciding which way to go, toward the direction the Infected went or back the way it came, where more might be staggering around. Not wanting to backtrack, they pushed on in the afflicted creature's path.

Turning to Kate, Nick stopped and surveyed her face where he could still see the tracks her tears made.

"You were crying." Nick reached out to her, then thought better of it and let his hand fall. Kate caught it halfway and touched it to her cheek, nestling her face into it.

"Dead things reminding me of other dead things. Doesn't matter now," Kate said. After studying her a moment longer, Nick nodded, and they carried on.

They arrived at a place where the hallway split off towards the middle of the hospital and saw an Infected dragging its feet down the corridor. Keeping quiet, they continued their search for the survivors.

Ascending another staircase, they arrived at the third floor. The walls were decorated with colorful decals of cartoon characters and superheroes; they were in the children's ward.

The layout remained the same. The middle of the level housed the nurses' stations, break lounges, and restrooms. The outer rooms, intended to host tiny patients, stood with closed doors decorated in fairy tale scenery.

One room was different from the others. Past the first nurses' desk was a massive room with glass walls, filled with toys and puzzles. Kate jumped back and grabbed hold of Nick's forearm when she spotted a figure kneeling in the corner of the room. Pausing, they observed the tiny form playing with a superhero action figure.

Both recalled the diseased little girl they came across when they first met and shuddered at a reenactment of the morbid event. Gripping the handle of his machete, Nick pulled the blade from its sheath with prudence.

The soft hissing of metal sliding against leather caused the little boy before them to stiffen. All movement in the room ceased as Nick and Kate watched the boy, and the boy listened for them. He set down the toy and turned around to them hesitantly.

"Are you here to see my dad?" the boy asked. Nick and Kate sighed and their fright dissipated. Nick entered the room toward the boy, noting that he did not appear afflicted. His skin was intact, and his eyes housed irises of a brilliant blue rather than the soulless black of the dead.

"I think so," Nick answered. "What are you doing down here by yourself? It's not safe." The boy only smiled a knowing grin.

"Can you take us to your dad?" Kate asked. The boy shrugged and walked past them out of the door. Nick and Kate followed him down the hall, cautious of any Infected roaming around, though the boy seemed untroubled by the possibility of their presence.

The trio strolled down the hallway under the fluorescent lights, passing by what seemed the same room over and over until they reached the end of the hall. Piling into an elevator, the boy pressed the button to the basement floor. The elevator trembled, groaned, and then began its descent. The light over top of the buttons read "2" and then "1" until finally, it halted on "B".

The doors creaked open to hallways that looked vastly different from the rest of the building. Instead of the expected parking garage or maintenance rooms, a long hall stretched out before them. Shiny metal walls reflected the halogen lights giving the area a bright and futuristic appearance. After stepping out, the elevator door closed, sitting idle until called for by more passengers.

Footsteps rounded the corner and three figures appeared holding automatic rifles and pointing them in Nick and Kate's direction.

"Woah, hey, we heard your message across the radio, and we came to see how we could help," Nick explained, hands raised in surrender. By instinct, Kate stepped in toward Nick who kept one hand in the air and used the other to push Kate behind him.

The figures, dressed in tactical gear, moved in toward them as one unit.

"Up against the wall," the one in front ordered.

Nick and Kate complied, turning to the wall and pressing their bodies against the cold metal. The guards searched them, taking their weapons and backpacks. Despite the tools and food they had acquired, Kate's first thought was the stuffed bat Nick had given her.

Kate pulled away from the guard holding her. "Wait, can I just have my—"

The man knocked her back against the wall, her cheek hitting the metal with force. Nick ripped his arms away from the guard holding him.

"Keep your fucking hands off her!" Nick shouted and was met with the butt of a rifle to his eye. Dazed, he was overtaken and secured against the wall again until they were ready to proceed.

The armed men marched them down the hallway until they reached a room with a metal door and a small window. They directed them into it and shut the door. The lock turned, and they were trapped within. The room was empty. No bed, no toilet, not even a bucket.

Nick and Kate stared at each other in shock. What started as a trip in search of refuge and possibly aiding other humans, led them to imprisonment. Locked inside an impenetrable chamber without their weapons, they were now at the will of strangers.

A conquered feeling settled over Nick like dirt being poured into a grave. It was clear to him now that there *were* wrong decisions, and he had made the worst one of all. He had failed them both.

Chapter 58

"Bro, thank God you don't shoot like this in real life. You'd get us killed," Adler laughed, taking a quick sip of soda before returning his hand to the game controller.

After returning home from their last deployment, Adler and Nick moved into a house on base. Moving out of the cramped, overly regulated barracks had been a relief. The tensions with other Marines after their capture of the Afghani woman became a distant memory, and they were able to enjoy greater privacy and find more ways to keep themselves occupied.

The two sat on a black leather couch playing a split-screen, first-person shooting game on the television. After working all week, their bodies and minds were grateful for a period of mindless fun.

"What are you talking about? I have more kills than you!" Nick lashed back, getting irritated.

"Yeah, and twice as many deaths," Adler said, laughing harder now. Nick rolled his eyes and continued playing.

The match ended, and Adler whooped loudly as the screen presented their scores. "Five more kills than you, bitch!"

"Whatever, that map sucks," Nick said. He set down his controller and went to the kitchen in search of something to snack on when the unmistakable sound of a gunshot rang out. Just one. The men looked at each other solemnly, then started for the front door, only stopping to pull on their boots.

Stepping out onto the street, Nick and Adler tried to discern where the sound had come from. Other Marines were doing the same, looking wildly from face to face hoping someone had an answer.

Nick's first thought, and probably everyone else's, was an active shooter in the community, but when no other shots rang out, his theory dissipated.

"Here! It was here!" a man called from several houses down. It was Zachary Dawson, a man serving in his and Adler's unit and Morris's roommate.

An echo of Nick holding his pistol to Morris's head while the Afghani woman pleaded for her life resonated through his mind.

Nick and Adler ran to Dawson who frantically explained that Morris had come home the evening before with a six-pack of beer, went up to his room, and had not been out since. When he knocked on the door and asked if everything was okay, there was no response. Then, a few moments ago, he heard the gunshot ring out from Morris's room.

Dawson explained which room belonged to Morris, and the pair entered the home, cautious and fearful of what they would find.

Nick and Adler ascended the stairs and paused just outside Morris's door. Adler knocked. Nothing, not even a stir of movement in response.

"Morris, it's Nick." No answer.

Nick and Adler's eyes met, building each other up with silent fortitude as they prepared to enter. Nick tried the knob though he knew it would be locked.

Taking turns, they kicked the door until the wood gave way. Splinters of white and brown shrapnel flew into the room, commingling with the disorder within.

"Shit," Adler said, his voice small and tinged with despair.

Resisting their limbs, which implored them to flee from the room, they stepped in and relied on every bit of strength they had not to fall to their knees.

Morris's body sat upright in a desk chair. His head hung inert, mouth agape, and his chin slumped against his chest. Enlarged pupils stared at the floor through a white film.

Between his feet, a black handgun pointed innocently at one of the chair's legs, just a piece of decor or clutter that needed cleaning.

Morris had shot himself through the roof of his mouth, and the bullet exploded through the back of his head, ripping apart every bit of flesh and bone in its path.

The wall behind him was painted in brain matter and blood. The dripping sound was sickening, as pieces of his cerebellum slid off the wall and onto the floor. A small trickle of blood from his mouth pooled on the collar of his otherwise pristine uniform—as if the grim reaper was going to perform an inspection.

The six-pack of beer sat beside the chair, six empty slots in a cardboard carrier. Nick regarded the frame of mind and planning required to carry this out. How long had Morris known that one day he would buy six beers, and ride the inebriation until he was confident enough to pull the trigger?

What if Nick *was* to blame? Their confrontation overseas—had it sent Morris over the edge? Had Nick been too harsh on him? He thought he had done the right thing, protecting the foreign woman, but maybe it had been another nail in Morris's coffin.

"This is my fault," Nick said aloud, though he did not mean to.

"Woah! No, it's not! Look at me, bro!" Adler turned Nick's body away from the gruesome scene and put his hands on both shoulders. Nick looked through him, ensnared by guilty thoughts. "Dude had a lot of issues. We saw that overseas. You did the right thing. You can't control the decisions other people make."

Nick tried to focus on Adler's words, but his heart was wrenched with remorse.

"I should've talked to him. I should've been there."

Chapter 59

Kate awoke in a confused stupor, her back leaning against the cold metal wall with her head resting on Nick's shoulder. Blinking until her vision was clear, the steel walls came into view, reminding her of their imprisonment.

Kate stood, careful not to wake Nick, and approached the locked metal door. Peering through the small window, she was not sure what she expected to see on the other side. Some sort of explanation as to why they were there? Instead, she saw only a long hallway, coated in metal from floor to ceiling, and sighed.

Nick's body shot up, gasping as he awakened from a terrible dream. Kate sat beside him, and he collapsed into her lap, resting his head on her thighs while she moved her fingers up and down his back.

After a while, he sat up looking renewed. The nightmare faded away and paled in comparison to the horrific reality of their situation.

The pair sat in silence for hours. There were no signs of life outside the room. They listened for footsteps, voices, maybe even a cough or the clearing of a throat but came up short.

Kate wished they would hear something, and for the sake of her sanity, she longed for the sound of crickets chirping or elevator music. Even a clock ticking would help set her mind at ease; it would be proof that she was still alive and not captured in some sort of purgatory. Yet, maybe that was the point. Perhaps these people had imprisoned them here intending to drive them insane.

The room appeared to close in on her, and she swore every time she looked around, the walls were a few inches nearer. As if she were back in the cage, Kate stared at the wall, counting the seconds that ticked by, awaiting her next round of torment. She half-expected to see Connor's face appear in the small window on the door.

Kate jumped when she looked up and saw, not Connor's face, but an unfamiliar man looking in at them. Nick got to his feet and stood tall, clenching his fists. One of the guards in tactical gear opened the door and stepped inside, followed by a man wearing a lab coat, along with three additional guards. Kate positioned herself behind Nick, though she knew he could not shield her from whatever would come next.

"Good evening, I'm Dr. Chamberlain. Please excuse the harsh treatment but you can't trust anyone these days. Am I right?" the man in the lab coat said, gazing at Nick and Kate for a moment, perhaps expecting an answer to his question. They responded with a bitter silence. "Anyway, I'm afraid the treatment will have to remain harsh. We aren't going to harm you, but we do need you to be part of some vital research. You're going to play an integral role at the forefront of science."

The guards advanced toward Nick and Kate, securing their arms behind their backs and leading them down the hallway. Nick toyed with the idea of fighting them off, however, the automatic weapons in their hands were a convincing deterrent.

The journey down the hallway was dreadful as their anxious minds played out scenarios of their looming fate. When they reached their destination, the guards ushered them into another empty, metal room, positioning Nick and Kate standing in the middle across from each other.

Though Nick could not bear to meet Kate's eyes, he forced himself to drink her in. If these were their final moments, regardless of the failure he turned out to be, Nick wanted every detail of Kate tattooed on his soul.

Dr. Chamberlain greeted two other doctors as they entered the room. One of them held a syringe, and Kate's body caved in on itself with terror. The guards released her and surrounded Nick while the doctor with the syringe approached him.

"What the fuck is that?" Nick asked. The guards took hold of him while the doctor held the syringe up in the air and depressed the plunger so that a few droplets trickled from the needle.

"Injecting the contaminated prion protein," the doctor stated in a monotone voice. Dr. Chamberlain nodded, his eyes wide and focused on Nick.

"No!" Kate screamed and started toward Nick but one of the guards held her in place. As she tried to pry his hands away, his strength overpowered her. The doctor injected the needle into the crease of Nick's elbow and slowly pushed the clear liquid into his veins until the syringe was empty. Nick stared down at it in horror, panting as fear swept through his body. The needle was removed, and both doctors left the room.

"Was that—am I infected?" Nick asked, gasping breaths interjecting each phrase. No one answered.

"Let him go," Dr. Chamberlain ordered, studying Nick closely. The guards released Nick's arms and took a few steps back, placing their hands on their weapons, and never taking their eyes off him.

The door to the room opened, turning everyone's attention toward it, and the doctors reentered. As the door swung closed, Kate noticed several more armed guards standing outside. The doctors had notepads in their hands, and they stood beside Dr. Chamberlain, jotting down their observations.

Nick grunted as the liquid worked its way through his body. Unable to slow his breathing, his throat felt coarse. Every vein bulged from his skin, and his face grew hot.

"No, no, no, no, no," Nick muttered. "It can't end like this. It can't fucking end like this."

While the doctors scribbled notes on their pads, Dr. Chamberlain fixated on Nick further, fascinated by what was unfolding before him.

A gnawing pain rushed through Nick's body, and he wanted to punch something, everything. As anger washed over him like a torrential downpour, his fists tightened into balls until the knuckles turned white.

Tears welled up in Kate's eyes as she looked on in helpless dread. Nick was turning, and she could only watch.

"Nick," Kate rasped. The doctors and guards turned their attention toward her, though she remained invisible to Dr. Chamberlain.

Kate cleared her throat and tried again. "Nick, I thought escaping that cage was the best thing to happen to me. Even though the world was a complete shitshow, I was free. I thought life couldn't get any better. Then, I met you. You didn't know me. You could've done anything without consequence. But you rescued me and made me feel as if I were worth saving."

Nick trained his eyes on her as his breathing grew ragged. The fight against the fury building inside was taking everything out of him. Still, he concentrated on her beautiful face, her mesmerizing words.

"All I did was put up walls, compare you to every man I've ever known, and push you away. I shouldn't have taken it for granted. I'm so sorry. I'd go back to that cage for another year if I could trade it for five more minutes with you. Nick... I love you."

When Nick tried to say it back, tried to force the words out, only a hostile bellow emerged. Sweat trickled down his temples, and though he was unable to say it, he tried to center his mind on the fact that he loved her, too.

As his mind slipped away, Nick could feel everything that made him human disintegrate into rage and hunger. Pale and crooked fingers jutted out in front of him as if grabbing at something.

It was as if he were trapped inside a body controlled by someone else.

I'm still here. I'm still me.

Nick's bloodthirsty limbs devoured the screaming in his head piece by piece as he understood that these doctors wanted him to hurt Kate; they wanted him to tear her apart while they watched. Uncertain if he could stop himself, he could make it a hell of a lot harder.

With a quick jerk, Nick pulled at the guard's hold on his arm. When the guard's grip tightened, Nick twisted around until the bone in his upper arm snapped, dislocating the shoulder. Pain radiated through his body, causing the anger within him to surge again. It was not enough. He needed to damage himself more.

"He's trying to break his arm! Grab him! Get her out of here," Dr. Chamberlain barked. Three guards grabbed Nick under the arms and pushed him against the wall.

One guard subdued Kate's arms behind her back and led her out of the room. She craned her neck, trying to get a glimpse of what they were doing to Nick, but the guards blocked her line of vision.

Kate was led a few doors down into a hospital room complete with a modest bed, a television hanging on the wall, a side table with wheels, and an attached bathroom. The only difference was the bed contained restraints which the guard promptly secured her in.

Kate struggled against the straps, violently jerking and pulling to no avail. She fell back into the bed, sobbing, her throat sore from shrieking.

Kate steadied her breathing and stared up at the white-speckled ceiling tiles, a piece of hair matted to her face from tears and sweat. Thinking she knew hopelessness before, nothing compared to the sensation paralyzing her now.

When Kate was held captive, imprisoned by cold metal and sexual depravity, she had never known intimacy, never felt the heartwarming tenderness of a man. All she had known was sorrow and torment, degradation and agony. Kate had never hoped for a better situation simply because she knew not what to hope for. There were no Prince Charmings. No happily ever afters. Those were just things made up in fairytales and romantic comedies.

When Kate met Nick, she was convinced he had an ulterior motive and assumed there was something he aimed to gain from their time together. Yet, over and over he proved to be selfless and loving.

Kate's cold heart was melting. She was coming down from the mountain, and it scared the hell out of her. So, she bottled up her feelings, and stuffed them way down inside, supposing there would be time to get used to her new emotions. There would be time to warm up and admit how she truly felt.

Regret and despair ripped open a vast hole in her stomach as she wept. Kate never imagined it would be too late. She thought there would be more time, yet there she lay, tied to a hospital bed, left to suffer her uncertain fate.

Nick.

If they had not killed his body yet,

his mind,

his heart,

everything that made him the most beautiful person she had ever known,

was dead.

Chapter 60

Kate awoke, sweating and uneasy from a nightmare where she dreamt of being chased by a faceless pursuer, the trees went on forever as though running through a time loop, repeating the same section of dark, foggy trees.

Hands broke through the dirt, trying to catch her ankles. The dream figure held out a knife, slashing through the air as they hunted her. She sensed them closing in and woke up just as the heat of their breath connected with the back of her neck.

As she re-oriented herself with the basement's dingy walls and the ties around her wrists, Kate longed to be back in her dream. At least there she still had a chance. And if not, being sliced to pieces was still the preferable circumstance.

The front door upstairs creaked open, and more than one set of footsteps shuffled inside. Kate listened, praying that whoever Connor had over as company would stay far away from the basement. As usual, her prayers evaporated into the horrid atmosphere she shared a space with. Connor, along with a man she had never seen, descended the stairs.

"Where are we going?" the stranger asked. Connor reached the bottom of the stairs and let the view do the talking. The stranger stepped off the last step, head swiveling around the room as he took everything in.

Kate only lay there, staring at the ceiling. She used to cry whenever Connor brought others into their vile scenarios. That part of her soul had dried up.

"What the fuck is this?" the stranger asked. Connor's smug smile faded away, replaced with irritation.

"Come on, Aaron. I thought you'd be down for a good time." Connor crossed his arms and eyed the man with disapproval.

"Connor, you have a fucking girl tied to a bed. Miss, can you hear me?" Aaron walked toward the bed, but Connor stepped in his path. Assuming an alpha male posture, Aaron lifted his head and broadened his shoulders, though he stood several inches shorter. "What's going on here? Look, if this is some kind of kink you guys are into, I'll just walk away. No judgment. But... she does not look okay. She's covered in cuts and bruises, looks way too thin. She looks completely traumatized, dude."

"This is what they're into now, man. Women like her, they just can't help themselves. This one, always throwing herself at everyone. She's hungry for it. I'm giving her exactly what she wants, just in a more controlled environment," Connor explained, looking certain that Aaron would understand.

Instead, Aaron scrunched up his nose, bewildered and horrified. His nervous gaze landed on Kate who was fixated on them now, interested in their interaction. When she made no attempts to ask for help, not even subtly, this seemed to frighten Aaron even more.

"I can't let this continue. Miss, I'm gonna get you out of here," Aaron said and pulled out his cell phone as he started for the door, his fingers moving about the screen as he pressed buttons.

Kate could not believe it. The weight of all those torturous months lessened, and a pang of hope ignited in her heart.

Kate could see it already. Aaron would call the police. The officers would storm the house and take her away to safety. Connor would resist them, and they would beat him until he complied. They would take him away to prison where he would live a pathetic, sexless life. He would die alone there, a disgusting, old man. This was it. It was finally over.

"Put the phone down, Aaron," Connor demanded. Aaron turned around, phone in hand, and scoffed. Before he could turn and start up the stairs, Connor grabbed him by the shirt and shoved him against the wall, knocking the phone out of Aaron's hands. As it hit the concrete, fragments from the shattered screen flew in every direction.

"You're not going to get away with this," Aaron said, fear and doubt layered beneath his intimidating tone.

"I will but you won't be around to see it." Connor pulled a switch-blade knife out of his pocket, clicked the blade open, and thrust it deep into Aaron's chest. Aaron's eyes widened, and he raised his arms to defend himself. Before he could make any moves, the knife cut through him again.

Aaron groped at his chest, gasping for air like a fish out of water as blood spilled out between his fingers.

Though Aaron no longer posed a threat, Connor stabbed him again and again until he crumpled to the ground.

Connor stood looking down at Aaron taking his last laborious breaths until a final gust of air exited his mouth. His clenched fingers went limp; his body lay unmoving. Kate's mouth twisted in a horrified grimace as she stared at her only hope, dead on the floor.

Against every instinct, Kate's eyes landed on Connor, still staring at the body. He was grinning, one hand massaging the crotch of his jeans. Kate realized she was caught in the clutches of a true psychopath.

Kate's story would end, and before long, she would also be nothing more than a crumpled pile of blood, tattered limbs, and violated body parts. Leaving nothing of importance behind, her life would be gone.

Kate would never wake up next to a man she loved. She would never hear the patter of tiny feet as her children ran across the floor. She would never create or accomplish anything. And no one could save her.

Chapter 61

The door to the hospital room opened, a pleasant interruption to another of Kate's dark memories. A female doctor, one that had been in the room when Nick received the injection, crept in and quietly shut the door behind her.

Greasy brown hair framed the face of a plain-looking woman in her upper thirties. Her lab coat diminished her womanly figure and gave her an air of authority. She set down a small tray with bland mashed potatoes and some square of meat on the table next to Kate's bed.

"You must be famished," the doctor said.

Kate said nothing and stared at the ceiling. The doctor pulled up a chair next to Kate's bed and sat, crossing a denim leg over the other.

The leather weighed on Kate's wrists—a constant reminder of her confinement. The paper-thin hospital blanket bristled against her chilled skin. A sharp ache spread its icy tendrils throughout her lower body as laying in the same position took its toll.

"Listen, I know you must feel—"

Kate tuned her out. Feeling. What was she feeling? Kate lay there searching for an emotion. She tried to feel something, anything—anger, hurt, sorrow. Yet, her mind failed to land on a single thing. She was a crumpled piece of paper, a heaping waste of space.

"Kate?" The doctor tried to get her attention. For a moment, Kate wondered how she knew her name, then decided it did not matter.

The doctor droned on about grief and how Nick's death was not in vain, and a ton of other stupid shit Kate did not want to hear. Then, she stayed silent for a long while.

"My name's Charlotte, by the way."

Kate turned her head slowly towards the doctor, her eyes empty and overcast.

"Stupid name," Kate said, her words dripping with venom. The doctor retracted from her a bit, then tried to hide that she was taken aback.

"Listen, Charlotte. I'd like to tell you that what I've experienced has formed me into a stronger being. I'd like to say that it's fueled a fire in me. One that's forged a more prominent and independent human. I'd like to tell you that I've learned how to survive. That I will overcome all of these difficulties and traumas I've faced and will push through and fight until my final day. I wish I could say that. Truth is, I simply don't give a shit. I'd be more than happy just to lie here until my body gives up, as my mind already has. I'm not angry about what you all have done to Nick. I'm not frightened by the restraints keeping me here in this bed. In fact, I feel nothing and I'm... tired."

Chapter 62

Murmuring amongst themselves, doctors filed into a room and took their seats behind a two-way mirror. When Dr. Chamberlain entered the room on the other side, their voices quieted, and they turned their attention to him. Two armed guards escorted the infected Nick into the room, followed by two more doctors.

Positioning Nick in the center, hands and ankles bound by heavy chains, his head bobbed unsteadily as a sedative put his feral brain in slow motion. Black, lifeless eyes struggled to focus on any one thing.

Nick stood looking about from one subject to another, the veins in his temples sticking out like tiny roadways. Cracked lips curled into a hungry sneer, and his nostrils flared with each breath. A navy henley clung to his heaving chest, speckled in dirt, sweat, and blood. His hunched shoulders swayed his body from side to side. Clenched fists hung idly at his waist, fingers bruised and caked with dirt.

"Good afternoon, ladies and gentlemen," Dr. Chamberlain spoke to the mirror in the room, addressing the doctors on the other side. "Today's presentation will be short, but I wanted to give everyone an update on our progress. Some of you who aren't working directly with the infected subject may feel far away from this project, so I wanted to bring you a little closer. Meet Nick. A Caucasian male around 30 years old, he appears to be prior military with no visible health issues. We are currently awaiting results on labs, bloodwork, and a whole exome

DNA test to get an idea of his medical and ancestral past. He arrived with a female companion. Though we had no intention of setting him upon her, it seems he thought that was the plan, and he tried to break his arms. We have the female resting in her own room until the experiments are complete."

The doctor continued. "For this presentation, we have our subject on a high dose of benzodiazepines for sedation. However, in order to obtain pure results, he will be unmedicated for our experiments which will include observations of his physical and mental states during different scenarios. Other than some stress, he will be unharmed unless necessary to ensure the safety of our staff. Once the experiments are complete, he will be given the final protein inoculation. Based on those results, we will determine the likelihood of our ability to proceed to phase three. If there are any questions, you may direct them to Charlotte or myself. Thanks, everyone, for being here."

Dr. Chamberlain concluded his speech with a firm nod toward the mirror and turned his attention toward Nick. Subtle grunts escaped Nick's lips in breathy intervals as his eyes washed over the doctor.

Lips that once spoke intelligent sentences and expressed emotions had become mute vessels for infectious transmission.

Eyes that once conveyed love and sorrow, pain and triumph, now only held a ravenous glow, a starving desperation.

Arms that once protected, now only searched for flesh.

And legs that once carried the man into battle now struggled to hold steady an undead, empty casing of a former human.

Dr. Chamberlain gestured toward the door. The guards led Nick out into the hallway and back to his holding cell. After securing him to the hospital bed, they replaced IVs, wrapped a blood pressure cuff around his bicep, and pasted electrodes on his forehead and chest.

After triple-checking Nick's restraints, the doctors exited the room, leaving him alone.

Nick stared at the ceiling feeling the sedatives lift a veil away from his body and mind. Instead of being replaced with complex emotions and thoughts, only a longing for violence filled the void. His breathing intensified as his eyes bulged out ahead of him.

Nick pulled at the straps around his wrists, straining against the resistance. Trying to lift himself into a sitting position, a leather band across his forehead held him in place, just above the electrodes measuring his brain waves.

Nick's efforts were futile, and he would remain there, hungry and yearning until the doctors decided to begin their tests on him. Relaxing his muscles, Nick gave in to his captivity, and a single tear streamed down his cheek.

Chapter 63

Charlotte entered Kate's room wearing the same white lab coat and holding another tray of food. Day after day was the same, empty and monotonous.

The bags under Charlotte's eyes were thick purple pillows, and pieces of her hair had escaped her messy bun. Kate wondered if her disordered appearance was due to a tussle with the newly infected Nick.

Were they baiting him, antagonizing him to attack, observing his actions, then beating him until he retreated? Or was he already dead? Had he gotten out of their control, assaulted one of the doctors, and earned a bullet to the temple?

Anger rose in the pit of her stomach from the ashes of hopelessness. Kate felt something. She grasped the feeling and held onto it, drinking in every ounce of it. If she did not use this emotion, act upon it, Kate would wither away into nothing. Nick's death would be in vain.

"Charlotte?" Kate forced her voice to sound small and innocent. Charlotte looked up at her, surprised and awaiting her next words. "I hate just lying here. My body hurts. I can't just give up like this. Could I maybe go for a walk?"

Charlotte considered her request, examining her appearance and noting the numbers that her vitals displayed. Nodding, she rolled the bedside table away and unclasped the leather straps that held Kate to the bed.

Rubbing her wrists marked by purple rings where the restraints dug in, Kate sat up slowly, weak and unsure of her movements.

Making a show of imbalance, she got to her feet. Even after all the time spent strapped to the bed, longing for death, she felt unshakeable.

You're a fucking warrior

Nick's words, the sound of his voice, swam through her veins, eviscerating every ounce of weakness it passed through. Doubt and fear disintegrated into mangled afterthoughts.

Kate straightened up and faced Charlotte, setting the woman on fire with the intensity in her eyes. Before the doctor could second-guess her decision, Kate gripped the woman's head with both hands and pulled down on it with force until it connected with her kneecap. Staggering backward, Charlotte held her face and moaned in pain and confusion. Kate pushed her to the ground and burst through the door.

Jerking her head left, then right, Kate broke into a sprint once she was sure the hallway was clear.

Door after door passed by as she ran. She turned left down a hallway. Then, right. Left again. Her lungs seized inside her for air, and just when she started to think she was going in the wrong direction, Kate turned a corner and saw an elevator at the end. The sight renewed her, and she ran toward it until it was only feet away. To the right of the elevator, Kate saw what she was looking for—a stairwell.

Kate dashed up the stairs, taking two or three of them at a time. As she rounded a landing, she gripped the handrail, swinging around to the next set of steps. The sight at the top of the stairs was unexpected.

Instead of opening up to the first level of the hospital, there was only a metal panel in the ceiling studded with thick bolts framing a door.

Expecting to hear footsteps chasing after her, voices encouraging each other to capture the escapee, Kate stopped to listen. When she heard nothing, she examined the sliding bolt that secured the door. The latch squealed as she depressed the sturdy metal and slid it away from the hole. The door popped with ease as the bolt released the pressure of its firm grip.

Kate pushed upward on the slat of metal, testing its weight. Dull aches sprouted from her shoulders, her back, and the top of her head as she hoisted the bulky door open. With a final heave, the door creaked until it rested open on its hinges.

Kate climbed through the opening and found herself in a tiny, dark closet somewhere on the hospital's first floor. Looking thoughtfully at the trap door, she almost reached out to lower the door back in place. It was instinct. When you open something, you make sure to close it. Except... *fuck those doctors and their sick experiments.*

Kate left the trap door and the closet which housed it wide open.

Kate's fists tightened and relaxed as anxiety ripped through her body. Exhausted, her muscles throbbed like a weary heartbeat. Still, she pushed through the vacant hospital, across the parking lot, down the street, and into a gas station.

With only a few fluorescent bulbs protruding from the ceiling, the station was dim. Listening to the sounds within the walls, she waited for grunts or moans or decrepit feet dragging along the floor. She was met with a welcome silence.

Pressing her back against the wall, Kate sighed deeply and ran her fingers across her face to see if she was real. Had she actually escaped? Was this all a dream?

This time yesterday, she was inclined to let her body and mind decompose in that hospital bed until she was no more. Kate's trauma, her dreams, her insecurities, her passions; she had let them go until they were maggots feasting on her worthless corpse.

Today a fire burned inside of her, and she felt driven to carry on. Dying tied up to a bed would be Connor's ultimate success, though a posthumous one. And Connor's win would be the undoing of everything Nick worked so hard for. No, Kate would persist.

Whether today, tomorrow, next month, or years from now, when it was her time to pass from this life to the next, Kate would do what she had spent all her life doing—fighting like hell.

Chapter 64

Scanning the gas station, reality hit Kate like a ton of bricks, and she stood there terrified, wondering what the hell she was doing there.

What was the big plan? Where would she go? What would she eat? How would she defend herself? Where would she sleep at night?

The thoughts circled her, closing in until they were suffocating. Panic rose inside her chest, and her throat tightened. These were the decisions Nick made effortlessly.

An indifferent wanderer, she was right back where she had begun after escaping Connor. Merely surviving. *Don't die.*

Deep and slow, Kate inhaled and exhaled. She repeated this until the trepidation lessened. Trying to push away the fear of things she could not control, she resolved to take it one moment at a time. She could do this.

Kate picked up a cloth tote from behind the checkout counter. Smaller and less durable than a backpack, it would have to do. She slung it over one shoulder and filled it with food items still fit for consumption.

Kate tossed in other items she thought might be needed: a lighter, a pocket knife, and Tylenol. Sifting through the toiletry section, she grabbed a pack of baby wipes and a travel-sized bottle of soap.

An electric razor sat between shaving cream and toothpaste, and she gazed at it longingly. A soft chuckle escaped her lips as she pictured Nick keeping his hair so well-groomed even after an apocalypse depleted the world as they knew it. Tears streaked her cheeks, and she wiped them away. If she allowed herself to sink into that dark place, she may never come out.

A scraping sound drew her attention toward the large glass windows facing the street. At first, she saw nothing until the sound grew louder in intervals. Her heartbeat picked up speed as she awaited a terrible fate. Expecting something pale and hungry to come crashing through the doors, she stood unmoving, hardly breathing.

An Infected pulled itself into her view, using its hands to drag itself along. Tattered fingernails scratched the concrete with every movement. Chills danced up Kate's spine with every advance.

The lower half of the creature came into sight, and Kate gasped. It had no lower half. Entrails spilled out from where a torso and legs had once been attached. Intestines trailed it like a macabre wedding dress train. The Infected's insides left a wet stream that stained the sidewalk, like the path of an overgrown slug.

Kate watched, paralyzed until the morbid thing was out of sight. Clutching the tote bag tightly, she tiptoed toward the back of the convenience store and escaped out of a door labeled 'emergency exit'.

Kate stood behind the store, scanning the alley. Black trash bags drooped from green garbage bins, wilting in the autumn warmth. She imagined setting the dumpster on fire to perfectly represent her pathetic existence, then chided herself for wallowing in self-pity.

One block over, a five-story apartment building loomed overhead. Kate considered the number of people that may have died within it and the amount of undead that could be roaming its halls. Nevertheless, she set off in that direction. Perhaps, she had a death wish.

Keep moving. Don't die.

Chapter 65

Entering the apartment building through its yellow double doors, Kate was careful to avoid the broken glass splintering out from the window frames. The doors creaked and the sound, though barely a whisper, exploded in the quiet atmosphere.

Standing in the lobby, Kate peered down the dark corridor and glanced toward the flight of stairs leading to other hallways that mimicked this one. Couches, tables, and bookshelves blocked off the stairs like an oversized Tetris game.

Kate climbed on top of an end table and pulled herself through a small gap between the furniture blockade. With no destination in mind, she tiptoed up the stairs and walked down the second floor across the dingy yellow-brown floral carpet. The place looked as though it had not been updated since the late '70s which was evident in its earthy tones and wood paneling.

The stillness of the building should have been reassuring, yet it only set flame to Kate's uneasiness. Every apartment door was closed tight. There were no sounds. The usual smell of rotting flesh was absent. She stopped her advancement down the hallway, ready to turn and leave when an apartment door behind her swung open—unit 213.

As Kate turned around with caution, the barrel of a pistol emerged from the gap in the door, followed by a man holding it. He trained the gun on her, eyeing her, waiting to see what she would do. Kate only stood there like a deer caught in a hunter's crosshairs.

After a lifetime of seconds passed, he lowered the weapon, let out a deep breath, and started laughing.

"Oh, shit. Sorry about that. Thought one of those things wandered in here. Grace, it's okay. It's just a girl," the man called to someone in the apartment. Bewildered by his calm demeanor, Kate relaxed, grateful to have the gun barrel pointed elsewhere.

A small, thin woman peered around the doorframe at Kate. Her blonde hair was pinned up into two pigtails, giving her an even younger appearance, though Kate imagined she must have been around her age. Relaxing as Kate stood there, unthreatening and unarmed, the woman offered a nervous smile.

"Name's Ryan. This is Grace. You hungry?" The man holstered his pistol and gestured into the apartment. Though Kate aimed to be wary, the rumbling in her stomach clouded her senses, and she started toward the couple.

"I'm Kate," she offered a shy smile that she hoped appeared pleasant.

The apartment was furnished with aged decor. Torn fabric pulled away from the arms of a shabby yellow couch. Faded paintings of various farm scenes hung on the walls, some of them askew. Chipped laminate peeled away from the top of a particleboard dining room table.

Grace showed Kate to an empty chair at the table and divvied up food onto plates, setting one at each of their spots. Kate could feel their stares as she devoured the hamburger meat and green beans, but the hollow hunger overtook any insecurities.

Their clinking forks and muffled chewing were the only sounds as they ate. Ryan took his final bite and rested the fork on his plate, sitting back in his chair and sighing with satisfaction.

"So, what brings you to this shithole town?" Ryan asked.

"Just passing through."

Ryan nodded slowly, processing her answer that was not really an answer. The disappointment in his eyes spurred guilt within Kate. They brought her into their home and fed her a warm meal, only to be met with her vague, guarded answers. "I was traveling with... a loved one, looking for a refuge. But... he's gone. So now I'm just a tumbleweed, drifting from place to place. I don't really have a plan."

Though Kate skirted close to the truth, she dared not think of Nick. She gave little thought to the meaning of her words: *loved one*. Instead, she pictured a sibling, a cousin, an uncle—anyone other than him. The mention of Kate losing someone provoked Grace's hand to find Ryan's and squeeze it.

"Sorry for your loss, Tumbleweed," Ryan said, his features grim and sincere. Kate nodded, accepting his condolences, and amused with her newly given nickname.

"You can stay here." Grace's eyes were soft and filled with concern. "There are a few others here in this building. We cleared it out and keep it that way. We all mostly keep to ourselves. Some folks have real trust issues. But we're always around if anyone needs anything."

Kate smiled at her. Aside from Nick, this was the only kindness she had been shown since she had escaped from Connor. Warm gestures were few and far between.

"I just might take you up on that," Kate said.

Chapter 66

"How long do you think you'll stay?" Grace asked as she pushed open the door to the unit adjacent to hers, and the pair entered. Kate was not sure how to answer. This apartment building seemed like a great setup. Others were there to assist her if necessary. The building was secure. It was centered in the middle of the city which meant supplies should be easy enough to acquire. □

Yet, there it was. Kate could see it from the place she would call home for now, the apartment window. The hospital stood in the distance, dark and looming. To most, it was made of brick and concrete. To her, it was made of despair, and she hated having to breathe and sleep under its shadow.

"I don't know yet," Kate said.

"Well, if you decide to stay awhile, there are plenty of other apartments. You don't have to stay right next door to us. I just figured this would be best for now. In case you need anything." Grace mindlessly dusted off one of the kitchen counters with her hands.

Kate nodded, taking in the modest apartment. Although everything was covered in dust, it contained the necessities. The kitchen, dining room, and living room were combined into one large area. There was a table she could eat at and a worn, olive-green couch to sit on. A black, particleboard bookshelf overflowing with novels sat beside a TV with a busted screen.

"You and Ryan seem pretty comfortable taking in a stranger," Kate commented.

Grace shot her a knowing smile. "It's Ryan. He has this way about him. He just reads people so easily. It's been a useful skill these days. The moment someone passes his vibe check, I know they're okay. He's never wrong."

The door leading into the bedroom stood ajar, and Kate glanced in. A plush mattress lay on a pine bed frame covered in a navy blue comforter that appeared lighter in color due to the layer of dust.

Images of her and Nick cuddled together in the bed at the mansion home invaded her thoughts, making this worn, full-sized bed seem desolate. She closed the door to the bedroom and decided she would sleep on the couch.

"Is it bad out there?" Grace asked, sitting down on the couch and gazing out the window. Kate joined her, peering through the dirty pane of glass that looked out toward the gas station, the main road, and the hospital behind it all.

Flashbacks of every terrible thing flooded Kate's mind: the blood, the murder, the rape, the Infected relentlessly hungry for carnage. What few people remained taking what they wanted without consequence. Death was around every corner, and death was not even the worst thing that could happen to a person.

Kate closed her eyes, pressed her fingers against her eyelids, and wished it all away, then nodded. Grace turned to her with somber, apologetic eyes. □

"We've lived in that apartment for years, Ryan and me. We haven't been far. When everyone started to turn, we teamed up with a few other residents of the building and cleared it out. That was tough. You know, in the movies, it's always big, scary zombie men. But here, it was families. It was women, children, babies, the elderly. It didn't matter.

They were all on the same mission. They all wanted us dead. I know you've probably seen so much worse but... it still haunts me."

"Tragedy is tragedy, no matter how much or how little. They say what's important is how you deal with it, what you learn from it, and what you do to come back from it. But I don't think those people could've fathomed a world like this one," Kate said.

Tears formed in Grace's eyes, and Kate felt as if that was her cue to offer consolation, a comforting hand on the shoulder, but it would do her no good, so she spared Grace the wasted sentiments.

Grace wiped her cheeks with the back of her hand and stood up. "Sorry to dampen the mood. I'll leave you to get settled in and get some sleep. Is it okay to knock in the morning when breakfast is ready?"

"Of course. Thank you, Grace." Kate closed the door behind Grace as she left. She clicked the lock on the doorknob, turned the deadbolt, and slid the door chain into place.

Kate turned around and faced the empty apartment. Though hardly big enough to comfortably house a couple, the place was far too large for Kate alone. She felt small and bereft.

Kate opened the bedroom door long enough to retrieve the blue comforter and shake away most of the dust. She closed the door again, comforter in hand, and settled down onto the couch. □

The blanket was the color of one of Nick's long-sleeve shirts. She stared at it, became lost in it, then wrapped it around her shoulders, imagining it was Nick's sturdy embrace. Her heart ached and a deep sorrow welled up in her throat until she was choked with sobs.

Kate's eyelids drooped now, and a weariness clouded her mind. She welcomed it, fearing she might otherwise lie awake for hours. Yet, in a matter of minutes, she succumbed to a night of deep sleep.

Chapter 67

A gentle tapping at the door stirred Kate from her sleep. Was it morning already? Opening her eyes, she lay there in silence, waiting for the sound to recur. She surveyed the pitch-black sky through the window and the few stars that dotted the night. The tapping sounded again. Kate pulled the covers away from her body and sat up.

Kate conjured up every scenario as to why she would hear knocking in an apartment building in the middle of the night. A pipe? A neighboring resident repairing something?

Knock. Knock. Knock. Fear tingled through Kate's veins, leaving her weak and ice cold. The sound had not come from the front door. It was coming from the bedroom. She stood up slowly on shaky legs. Each step she took was like walking through sand.

After several painstaking steps, her hand was on the bedroom doorknob. Opening the door, Kate expected to see something terrible standing behind it. Instead, there were no changes since the last time she had been in the room.

Releasing a breath she had been holding for too long, Kate almost laughed at herself until her eyes adjusted to the darkness in the bedroom. There was a lump in the bed. Something lying under the sheets. Something shaped like a body.

"Come here, baby, lay down with me." Nick's voice cut through the darkness like a machete. *It couldn't be him.* Kate's internal voice screamed danger while her feet carried her toward the bed.

As Kate came closer, she was able to make out his features. His brown hair created a dark contrast against the white pillowcase. The sheet conformed to his abs and thick leg muscles. Some of the darker lines of his tattoos peeked through the fabric. Nick was smiling at her, and she thought she would melt.

"What are you doing here?" Kate asked. Though it was the strangest question, she was unable come up with anything else. Nick laughed and pulled her into the bed next to him. Propping himself up on his elbow, he traced a gentle finger down her face. Kate cupped his cheek with her hand and Nick leaned down, pressing his lips to hers.

The warmth of their mouths joined together sent shivers across her skin. Her heart fluttered with elation inside her chest. To hear him again, to feel him again—she felt all the fissures in her soul mend.

When they parted, Kate let the taste of him settle on her lips before she opened her eyes. Her lids fluttered open. Panic struck her in the chest, and she jumped back because Nick was gone. A face Kate never expected to see again, outside of her memories, replaced him.

"You ready to have some fun, baby?" Connor grinned at her wickedly. Kate screamed and turned to her side, desperate to propel herself from the bed, but Connor grabbed her by the wrist. Twisting and jerking, she used all her strength trying to free herself from his fingers clamped around her arm.

Connor managed to pull her back to him, and when he spun her around, he had disappeared.

Kate was face to face with an Infected, rotting flesh dangling loosely from its cheeks. Watery, dark eyes stared lifelessly at her.

With surprising speed, the creature seized her throat and squeezed, cutting off her cries for help. Kate's windpipe began to fold, crushed within its tightened grip. Her eyes rolled to the back of her head as her vision faded to black.

Kate hit the floor next to the couch with a heavy thud. Entangled in the comforter, she kicked her feet frantically until they were free. Sweat dampened her skin, and her hands trembled with anxiety.

Just a dream, she told herself. *Just a horrible fucking dream.* Sitting against the couch, Kate played the dream over and over in her head. She recalled Nick's voice, and how his kiss sent her reeling into euphoria.

Although Kate tried to allow only the good part to thrive in her mind, Connor's face and her certain death barged in. Instead of shivering in ecstasy, she found herself quaking with sobs.

Pulling herself back onto the couch, Kate sunk deep into the cushions and lay there staring at the floor until the sun began to peek over the horizon.

Chapter 68

Kate joined Ryan and Grace for breakfast, a modest bowl of beans. Kate's eyes were heavy from a lack of sleep and an abundance of crying. As the couple carried on a conversation, Kate tuned them out.

The morning sun was blinding and invasive as it cast its auspicious rays everywhere, exhausting any chance of rest or relaxation. What was the sun so damn cheerful about so early anyway?

The three finished their meals, and Grace collected plates and silverware. Ryan may have asked Kate something, but she was lost in thought, staring at the golden beams of sun spilling out onto the floor.

Wood splintered, and a tumultuous crash caused their heads to swivel toward the front door. Grace grabbed the shotgun lying on the kitchen counter.

"No, you'll risk crossfire. Grab a melee weapon. Nothing projectile," Ryan instructed.

Apartment doors swung open as other neighbors came out to investigate the commotion. Ryan handed Grace a crowbar and Kate a metal baseball bat.

Ryan faced the door, holding a katana ready, and Grace swung it open. Ryan walked a few paces out into the hall where the barrage of footsteps grew louder, ascending the stairs. He ushered the women out of the apartment, and they ran for the stairs leading up to the third floor.

At the top of the stairs, several people stood armed with non-projectile weapons. Forming a semi-circle, they awaited the creatures' arrival.

As many as fifteen Infected stampeded up the stairs and straight for the group. Ryan and another man, large and burly with a long, thick beard, were the first to battle the monsters.

Little by little, the group was broken up and separated into smaller skirmishes throughout the hallway.

Kate found herself backed against the wall by three Infected, closing in too close for her to swing the bat effectively. She pushed past them and sprinted down the hallway until she reached the end. The creatures' diseased legs carried them toward Kate, faster than should be possible. Glancing around with panic, her only surroundings were closed apartment doors and a window leading out to a fire escape.

Kate pushed the window up, the glass and wood groaning with the motion that had not been performed in years. She stepped through the opening and stood back against the black metal railing with the bat ready. The Infected followed in her wake.

Kate drew back as the first creature outstretched its arms to grab at her. Before she could swing, the monster's palm shoved her shoulder hard, and her waist tilted over the metal railing. She tried to lean forward, but her feet had lifted off the ground and she slid over the barrier of the fire escape.

Kate was upside down now, the Infected's grungy fingers grasping at her feet until they were out of its reach, and she plummeted toward the ground.

As Kate fell, she strained to right her body, to become perpendicular to the ground. Just before she connected with the pavement, her body tilted, and she landed hard on her left arm. Her head bounced off the concrete, leaving Kate dazed. Pain shot through her arm from the elbow in both directions. The bones in her arm made a sickening crunch, like a boot stepping on fresh snow.

Once the impact had reached its climax, Kate's body fell backward. The chill of the concrete seeped through her shirt as she lay on her back, helpless. The Infected looked down over the railing at her, snarling and gnashing its teeth. Tears streamed down her cheeks as the pain burned unbearably through her.

A spurt of blood erupted from the Infected's mouth as a blade seared through its chest from behind. The creature's body toppled over the railing and crashed to the ground nearby. Ryan looked down at her from the fire escape above, yelled something inaudible, and then disappeared.

Moments later, Ryan, Grace, and several others were leaning over Kate speaking in hurried, frantic voices and Kate tried to decipher what they were saying.

"Shit."

"Her arm sure as hell ain't supposed to bend that way."

"Can you hear me, Tumbleweed?"

"What do we do?"

"She hit her head. It could be serious."

"What about the hospital?"

"It's worth a try. Pull the truck around. We can lay her in the back and take her there."

Kate opened her mouth to protest. She could not go back there. She did not get this far just to end up back in that place. As their frenzied chatter continued, her voice was lost beneath the chaos.

The sounds of the approaching motor revved her heart into a panic. Kate was afraid to move, and her objections were assumed to be reactions to the physical pain, not the unease of returning to the hospital.

"Here." Someone slipped a tablet into Kate's mouth and held a bottle of water to her lips to wash it down. She presumed, hoped to God, it was something to help with the anguish spreading over her like wildfire.

Then, several sets of hands lifted her carefully off the ground and into the truck bed. Kate meant to refuse the transport, telling them what had happened there. However, she considered the state of her arm, the head injury sustained, and the quality of life she would have if left untreated. □

Maybe the doctors would infect her, too. Or maybe they would help her.

Kate lay against the cold metal truck bed and surrendered to her fate. The tires began to move and despite all that Kate had been through—the pain, the degradation, the torture, the atrocities—she considered the hospital to be the venue of her greatest loss.

Chapter 69

As Kate opened her eyes, a grogginess set in that was followed by blinding pain. She winced, squeezing her eyes shut, willing the agony to subside. Exhaling deeply, Kate tried to stabilize the throbbing in her arm. After several minutes, either the discomfort slackened, or she grew accustomed to it.

Kate gazed around. She was back in a hospital room though it was hard to determine if it was the same one as before since they all looked identical.

Kate's eyes followed the clear tubing protruding from the top of her right hand until it ended at several computers monitoring her vitals. The machines beeped and whirred in a soothing, repetitious manner. A thick, plaster cast concealed her arm, and her head was wrapped with bandages. Several cuts and bruises had been treated, sterilized, and covered.

Kate sighed. She was behind the safety of the hospital walls, and her injuries had been tended to. However, her recovery would likely be a long one. The thought of spending the next several weeks or even months prisoner to this bed with nothing to do filled her with dread. She could do nothing else but lie there with no purpose other than to stay alive. *Don't die.*

The door burst open, and Charlotte entered with a tray containing liquid nourishment and syringes filled with medicine. Kate prayed it was for pain.

"Oh, good. You're awake!" Charlotte chimed cheerfully. A tender splotch of purple was painted across her forehead where Kate had attacked her just a few days previous. She sat the tray down and observed Kate's vitals. □

"You took quite a fall, but everything looks good." Charlotte picked up the syringe and injected it into Kate's IV. "This is morphine, for pain. I'm sure you're feeling a lot of it. We wanted you to wake up fully from the anesthesia before giving you any pain medications."

Kate nodded and managed a tiny "thank you." While she was thankful for the care they had provided, what they had done to Nick lived beneath her skin like an infectious disease, setting her flesh on fire with untamed scorn.

Kate was not restrained to the bed this time, not physically. Now, she was restrained by pain, drugs, and her inability to survive on her own with only one good arm.

"You're welcome, Kate. Our best surgeon spent several hours on you in the OR. You suffered several types of fractures in your left arm. He put screws in to hold the bone together.

"We performed some brain imaging. No swelling or bleeding, but your recovery will require time and rest in order to heal correctly. I know you don't want to be here but please, take advantage of our resources and expertise. Let us help you get back on your feet."

Kate nodded, unable to call forth a response, her mind already clouding over from the morphine. The pain ebbed leaving her body heavy and tired.

"How long have I been here?" Kate asked.

"You arrived yesterday. Late morning. The surgery went on until six or seven in the evening. You've been asleep since. It's almost 4 p.m., now," Charlotte answered, opening a cup of something gelatinous and inserting a spoon into it.

As Kate's eyelids drooped, she wondered what else Charlotte had introduced into her bloodstream. The room was spinning, and she could hardly keep her eyes open. The thoughts in her head were swimming around, a strange mosaic of reality and fiction, past and present.

"When will I see him?" Kate asked. Her voice sounded distant as if it had come from someone else's lips. She scrunched up her nose in confusion. Who was she even talking about? Nick was dead, right? He had fallen... No, that was her. Had she killed him? Every event blurred together.

Kate's head fell against the hospital bed, rolling from side to side until the medication had taken over completely. Charlotte stepped away toward the door and started to pull it shut. Before closing it completely, the nurse uttered something Kate could not make sense of in her stupor.

"You'll see him soon enough."

Chapter 70

The next several hours were spent in a deep, psychedelic sleep full of faces and colors and remnants of memories. It was not until she felt hands on her arm and pain surge through one side of her body that Kate was able to grasp hold of consciousness.

Panic swept through her, and her body jerked from left to right. Her efforts to break free were futile.

When Kate finally pried open her eyes, her breathing calmed. Doctors stood over her, examining her injuries, replacing bandages, and jotting down notes about her recovery.

Charlotte was among those present. Despite their history, her presence gave Kate a small shred of comfort. She was a kindly, familiar face, even with the bruises.

Perhaps Charlotte's persona was always under oath, staying neutral even in the toughest situations—anything for the Hippocratic promise she had made when she became a medical professional. Whatever her reasons, Kate was glad to have her in the room.

"Everything is looking good, Kate," Charlotte said. A syringe emerged from somewhere in her lab coat. She held up the needle inches away from her face and tapped a pen against it several times, freeing the liquid of bubbles.

"Please, don't put me to sleep again," Kate pleaded. Charlotte looked at her sympathetically, just for a moment. Then, she pulled the cap off the syringe, inserted the needle into Kate's IV, and plunged the liquid sleep through the tube.

Tears formed at the corner of Kate's eyes as she watched the world become hazy once more. She longed for a moment to catch up, to assess what was happening to her, but her conscious moments kept getting stolen.

Drowsiness took hold. Her mind and body shut down, giving into the narcosis. Once her world had gone black, everything lit up again, like the opening of a play. The stage was her subconscious, and everything was mixed up. Characters blended together, and the plot was nonsense. Still, Kate would watch like a dutiful audience member until the morphine released her.

Chapter 71

The sound of gunfire roused Kate from her sleep. Her eyes fluttered open and shut until she realized what she heard was not coming from the peculiar reveries of her drugged mind. The gunshots were real, and they were nearby.

Kate's body jolted upright, and her broken arm ached from the sudden movement. Her eyes performed a wild dance around the room, assessing what to do amid the impending chaos. Panicked voices and shuffling bodies sounded off at the end of the hall toward the elevator and stairs.

Ignoring her body's painful cries, Kate rose into a sitting position and swung her legs off the side of the bed. Breathing in and out several times, she inhaled the confidence to act, rather than lay motionless in white sheets until the danger passed.

Screams exploded down the corridor, echoing, bouncing off the walls, and gaining momentum until they stopped at her door like bad omens.

Kate got to her weak, unsteady feet and held the side of the bed until blood rushed into her legs, giving them the strength to move. Taking several labored steps toward the door, she gripped the handle and tugged it open.

Opening the door just enough for one eye to peer through, she looked up and down the hall. Blood smeared the walls and trailed along the floor tiles. Bodies wearing lab coats lay mangled on the ground. The corpses of a few Infected lay not far from them.

The trap door. She had left that damn door open, and now she was center stage for the oncoming disaster.

For a moment, Kate thought maybe the invading creatures were all dead. Then again, she knew the risks of hoping for the best.

Pulling the door open a few inches more, Kate slipped through the narrow opening. The hallway was empty for the moment. She turned opposite the carnage and walked toward the observation and testing rooms: the last place she had seen Nick.

Shuffling, uncoordinated footsteps descending the stairs sent her into a panic. A dense thud made her turn, and a pile of Infected lay at the foot of the stairs. They had tripped and fallen over each other, stumbling about trying to get to their feet.

Kate's pace intensified, willing her feet to carry her faster down the hall and cursing them when they did not move quickly enough.

Turning the corner, armed guards ushered Charlotte and a few male doctors, including Dr. Chamberlain, into a room. Kate paused when she saw them, unsure of how they would react to her presence. Would they consider her an enemy, too?

The guards stared at her as vital seconds passed. The Infected, whose group was growing, rounded the corner just behind Kate. One of the guards gestured for her to come to them, and she broke out into a sprint.

Once Kate passed the guards, they began shooting into the crowd of Infected. The number of creatures rounding the corner was never-ending, and their bullets were not enough to stop the tide of undead.

The Infected took out the guards, one by one. Once their situation was deemed dire, Dr. Chamberlain pulled the door closed, separating their group from the horde of Infected and leaving the remaining guards to their fate. They blockaded the door with furniture and heavy equipment.

Kate leaned against the cold metal wall, catching her breath. The room appeared to be some sort of headquarters for the doctors. Computer terminals and medical machinery lined the walls. Notepads and files were scattered across desks. A television hung from one wall though Kate figured it was not for watching sitcoms.

Kate's eyes fell upon a window at the back of the room. The large pane opened up to a view of a hospital room, one that looked much like hers. A man lay in the bed, restrained by his arms and legs. A gray hue colored his body, stretching over engorged muscles. Deep purple veins snaked across his damp skin. A whiteboard hanging next to the door read "Patient 67". How many people's lives had they destroyed?

As Kate looked closer at the man, she gasped aloud, and her lips trembled in realization. It was Nick.

Attracted to the commotion, he had begun thrashing wildly in an attempt to free himself. Vigorous grunts bellowed from his chest.

Kate's heart shattered to pieces as she stared at him—the man who once cared for her reduced to a barbaric state. She pressed her palm and forehead to the glass, unable to take her eyes away.

Dr. Chamberlain caught Kate's gaze and watched tears cascade down her cheeks as she observed Nick in his undead state. The doctor scanned the room for what survivors were left: Charlotte, a few male doctors, and Kate. Hardly an army. He knew what needed to be done.

Chapter 72

Dr. Chamberlain left Kate to gaze fixedly at Nick and approached a door off one side of the room. Swiping a keycard, the door swung open, revealing a spacious, illuminated room. Looming metal shelves containing hundreds, maybe thousands, of vials stood reflecting the fluorescent lights.

Dr. Chamberlain retrieved a syringe from a desk covered in medical supplies. Taking a vial from a shelf labeled "PrPc", he shoved the needle into the top and drew the liquid into the syringe. He capped the needle and approached Nick's door.

"Doctors, I'm going to need some help," Chamberlain said, holding up the syringe. He entered Nick's room, and the doctors filed in. Kate drifted in behind them, horrified and uncertain about what was happening.

Dr. Chamberlain held out the syringe and prepped it for injection. Though Nick was strapped down, the doctors held his arms tightly. Chamberlain plunged the needle deep into Nick's vein and depressed the plunger until all of the liquid was coursing through him.

Every eye in the room fixated on Nick. The doctors hardly breathed as they stood in fascinated observation.

At first, Nick's movements appeared more aggressive. His body writhed on the bed, and his arms tugged against the restraints so hard

Kate was sure the leather would snap at any moment. Little by little, however, his resistance decreased.

Nick could almost feel the molecules in his body realigning, the proteins in his brain folding and unfolding. The anger, the hunger, the bloodlust, all of it dissipated as quickly as it had come on.

As Nick looked around the room at the doctors, the desire to tear them apart faded, replaced with fear and confusion.

With great epiphany, he realized he was having rational thoughts. Something was wrong. They had not wanted to bring him back. At least, not this soon. The doctors were engrossed in his transformation while a subtle wariness glimmered in their eyes.

Resting his head back against the hospital bed, Nick let the rest of his metamorphosis take place. His body felt electric as life came back to it. Like puzzle pieces being set into place, his humanity rejoined with his body, making him whole again.

Kate shrunk further into the safe nook of the room. Her heart dared, just for a moment, to hope. Nick appeared to be changing, to be coming back to her, but how could that be possible? She stomped out the optimism like the remaining ashes of a bonfire, ready to kill or die at the hands of the monster she once loved.

As Nick's body normalized, his breathing steadied, and an emptiness filled him. He was human once again. Now what was his purpose?

Once able to handle his surroundings, he turned his head into the room. The doctors were agape as they stared at a man who had come back to life; a man who had been to the other side and returned to tell the tale.

Nick caught sight of something in the corner. Looking past the lab coats that surrounded him, his heart almost stopped. It was the final piece he needed to seal his revival. Nick's eyes found Kate.

Chapter 73

Kate cowered at the edge of the room, hands pressed against the wall to hold herself up. She watched in disbelief as the doctors untethered Nick's restraints, his eyes never leaving hers. So captivated by his recovery, no one heard the Infected throwing themselves at the door, desperate to break in.

"Nick, welcome back to us," Dr. Chamberlain greeted. Nick looked up at him warily. Pain covered his body like a thin veil. Though rife with sore muscles and bruised tendons, something kept most of the unpleasant sensation at bay.

Standing, Nick anticipated his limbs to falter, yet his muscles lifted him without effort. He felt stronger than ever. When his eyes met Kate's in an intense gaze, she was frozen against the wall, holding her arm in pain.

Kate let out a whimper as he walked to her with purpose. Squeezing her eyes shut and turning her face away, she waited for teeth to tear through her flesh.

Instead, he ran his fingers across her cast, then pressed his palm to her face, stroking her cheek with his thumb. Kate leaned into his touch, closed her eyes, and wept.

Careful not to squeeze her arm too tight, Nick pulled Kate into his chest, wrapped his arms around her, and kissed the top of her head.

Tears drenched his sternum as she cried into his shirt. He pressed his lips to her forehead for a long moment charged with raw elation.

A million thoughts fought their way to words, but Nick had not quite found his voice. His throat burned, and he was unsure what odd noises might come out if he tried to talk. Besides, when he spoke to her for the first time, after she thought he was dead, he wanted it to be perfect.

The Infected grew more determined in their attempts to break down the door, and finally, everyone in the room was stirred from their compulsive observation.

Dr. Chamberlain swiped the keycard again and entered the room with all the vials, walking past them to another room that required special access. This room was smaller and contained gear for the armed guards that had not survived the onslaught.

Dr. Chamberlain passed out rifles with loaded magazines, armor, and helmets. The doctors held the weapons in their hands as if holding newborn babies, understanding their delicacy but not how to properly handle them. □

Suiting up in a ballistics vest, Nick almost laughed out loud as he pictured the Infected running around carrying M-16s, then wondered if any sound would come out if he did laugh.

Nick strapped a tactical helmet on, picked up an automatic rifle, jammed a fully loaded magazine into it, and holstered several others into the nylon webbing across his chest.

"We weren't planning on bringing you back yet but... look at us. As a team, we spent months doing studies, running tests, and inspecting and dissecting the brain until we found a cure for this disease. And we succeeded. We're more apt at saving lives, not taking them. We need your help." Dr. Chamberlain fiddled with his rifle, clumsily loading it.

Anger tried to force itself to the forefront of his brain. These people had captured him and Kate and turned him into one of the monsters he had worked to keep her safe from. However, that had to be a secondary emotion. Pushing that feeling down somewhere undiscovered, he focused on the situation at hand. If he let his rage get the better of him, more people would die.

Nick equipped Kate with a pistol, something she could fire with one hand. Kate regarded the heavy piece of deadly metal in her palm, thinking how few times she had fired a gun in her past, yet now it had become second nature. A handgun was now an essential extension of oneself.

Chapter 74

The blockades were moved away from the door, and Nick positioned himself behind it. Kate stood behind him to one side, pistol ready. Situated diagonally from the door to avoid crossfire, the doctors rallied in a corner.

The Infected were feral and thrashing wildly against the door. Like moths to flames, they were drawn to the hot blood coursing through the veins of the living and were ready for a feast.

Nick unlocked the door and swung it wide open. The creatures that were pressed against the door fell across the threshold at his feet. The remainder of the horde wasted no time, stepping on the bodies of their fellow undead to swarm the group of survivors.

Nick unloaded a full magazine into the oncoming creatures within seconds. Riddled with bullets, they fell to the floor, but for every Infected that hit the ground, one more was behind it. Nick ejected the magazine and slammed another into the bottom of his rifle.

The doctors were taking shots at what they could, but their aim was clumsy, and their rounds missed more than they hit, even at such close range.

The multitude of creatures only grew along with a cacophony of disturbed laughter. Nick backed up to avoid their outstretched arms, though they seemed to be groping for Kate and ignoring him. He brushed off the notion and continued holding them off.

A group of Infected ran past Nick, directly toward the doctors. Kate turned her pistol towards them and killed what she could, but she feared shooting through or past the creatures and into the doctors themselves.

The first to meet their end was Charlotte. An Infected clamped down on her throat, its fingers digging in until its nails pierced the skin. Blood shot from her neck, showering the Infected and one of the doctors close by. Her hands weakly groped at the Infected's grasp, her eyes wide with terror until her throat was butchered. The creature released its grip, and Charlotte crumpled to the ground.

One of the male doctors fired rounds furiously into the onslaught until two ragged arms broke through the wall of bodies and slammed into him. The Infected wrenched the rifle from his hands and slung it to the ground. The doctor's arms flailed in desperation as the monster gripped his shirt and sunk its teeth into his neck, ripping away veins and tendons until the life drained out of him.

Nick reloaded his rifle again, finally seeing an end to the surge of the Infected. After finishing them off, he turned to see Kate striking one of the creatures with the butt of her handgun. It had moved in too close for her to shoot.

Slinging the rifle around to his back, Nick picked up a scalpel from a nearby desk and pulled the creature away by its shoulder. As it stumbled backward, he swiped the blade across its throat, severing everything vital. He pushed its body to the ground, confirmed Kate's safety, and turned his attention to the doctors.

It was too late. The Infected had already minimized them to a massacred pile of red pulp.

The last of the creatures stumbled toward Kate, blood dripping from their teeth and hands. The pair fired their weapons into the crowd of undead until their backs were against the door to the room full of vials. Kate fired a final shot, and at last, all of the creatures were sprawled out on the floor, lifeless.

Nick and Kate fell to the ground, their strength and endurance giving way now that it was no longer needed. Surveying the carnage, blood painted the entire room, a scene only imagined in horror movies.

"Hey," Nick tested his voice, worried he might not produce a sound. Instead, his voice came out husky and strong. Kate turned her head toward him, hungry for every word. "I'm sorry. I'm so sorry I left you."

Kate smiled at him, though tears stung her eyes. All the most cliché things to say came to mind. She thought she had lost him. She thought he was gone for good. She loved him. She hated him for going away. She was in disbelief that he was truly human again. However, the idea of beginning any one of those sentences was exhausting. Nothing she could say in that moment would cover the multitude of emotions she felt.

Besides, her eyes said it all. Instead, she leaned over and pressed her lips to his. Closing their eyes, they savored the kiss, the warmth, and the life that detonated between them.

After pulling away, they sat in victorious silence for several moments. Inhale. Exhale. Inhale. Exhale. Though the sound of their breathing was unremarkable, it was a glorious symphony of survival to Nick and Kate.

Nick thought he should feel guilty. He was unable to protect the doctors. His unit was torn apart. The majority of his soldiers lay dead in the other room. He failed them.

Maybe his transformation had deadened the part of him that felt sympathy. Or maybe it was the end of the world that had desensitized him. □

Nevertheless, Nick was content. He had been turned into the thing he had spent so much time escaping—the grotesque creature he had killed so many of. Though he felt he had not come back the same, he had still come back.

As they regained their motivation, Nick and Kate scanned the room. Their eyes seemed to move across it at the same time. The tall metal shelves with thousands of vials. Thousands of cures. Thousands of opportunities.

Chapter 75

A muffled groan traveled from the room full of bodies into an atmosphere that had become too quiet. Nick and Kate paused and turned to each other with wide eyes and tense bodies. Nick grabbed his rifle, though he was sure he was almost out of rounds.

Another sound broke the stillness, this time a small whimper, and the pair jumped to their feet. Nick readied his weapon, and Kate followed close behind as they reentered the room of carnage. Taking slow paces, they inspected each body, watching for chests rising and falling, any sign of movement.

"Help," a quiet, strained voice whispered from the corner, under a pile of corpses. Nick approached, sights trained on the gory mass of limbs.

With one arm, he pulled bodies from the accumulation and tossed them aside. Kate marveled at his strength, wondering how he could maneuver the bodies without effort.

Finally, Nick uncovered the source of the sounds as Dr. Chamberlain lay gasping for breath underneath the bodies of the slain Infected. Other than a gunshot wound to the arm, likely the result of crossfire, he appeared unharmed.

"Take me in there." Dr. Chamberlain pointed to the hospital room where Nick had been held. Nick helped the doctor to his feet, supported him as they shuffled to the destination, and sat him down on the bed.

"Doc, we should take care of that bullet wound," Nick said.

"That can wait. If I've been contaminated, there's not much time," Dr. Chamberlain replied and walked Nick through the process of preparing the inoculation he received only hours before. Nick injected the liquid into the doctor's veins and discarded the needle. The doctor nodded in satisfaction.

Dr. Chamberlain laid back on the bed with his palm facing upward, giving Nick access to the bullet wound in his forearm. As Nick cut away the fabric around the injury, Kate grabbed a rag from a table nearby and placed it between the doctor's teeth. The doctor bit down, preparing for the pain he was about to endure.

Nick poured isopropyl alcohol on the doctor's forearm. The liquid mixed with the viscous blood and dripped on the ground. Dr. Chamberlain squeezed his eyes shut, wincing as the alcohol bubbled on the wound and obliterated any impurities. Kate handed Nick a pair of small, metal tweezers which were also doused in the disinfectant.

Uncertain of what he was about to do, Nick looked up at Dr. Chamberlain with a troubled gaze. The doctor nodded and continued giving directives. Nick pushed the forceps into the open wound, moving them around until they found something hard. He maneuvered the tool until both sides were gripping the bullet. The doctor writhed in pain, forcing his eyes to stay open to offer instructions.

Kate rested a hand on Dr. Chamberlain's shoulder, offering what little consolation she could. With a swift, steady tug, Nick withdrew the metal projectile. Kate passed Nick a pile of gauze as blood spewed from the bullet hole. After covering the wound and applying pressure until the bleeding slowed to a trickle, Nick bandaged the injury and let out an immense sigh of relief.

"Not bad, doc." Dr. Chamberlain's humor prevailed through the pain. Nick laughed nervously, thankful the procedure was over with.

Dr. Chamberlain's smile faded, his eyes serious and features sharp. "Thank you. Given our... strained relationship, I would've understood if you had left me to die or waited until I became infected and then shot me. I appreciate that more than you know."

"It was the right thing to do," Nick said, putting his arm around Kate and pulling her body into his. "Besides, having a doctor around seems to be pretty useful." Nick kissed Kate's temple, and she smiled.

Chapter 76

Dr. Chamberlain shuffled into the room populated with the mysterious vials with Nick and Kate following curiously.

"While we're on the topic of being useful, I was hoping you all could help me." The doctor's gaze scanned the shelves, eyes full of hope and wonder. "Call it a mission of... restoration."

Nick and Kate looked over the clear ampules and then back to the doctor.

"What exactly are you suggesting?" Nick asked.

"It is here. We have the cure. And it works." The doctor turned to them, a furious ambition burning in his eyes. "We'll repair and safeguard our headquarters. I'll work at making more of the prion protein: the cure. After Kate has taken some time to heal, the two of you can take it out into the world. You'll be the harbinger of this world's rehabilitation. It'll be our own Reconstruction Era."

Kate was a whirlwind of emotions. A surge of fears broke down the doors of her mind. They could bring people back from the purgatory of their undead state, but what would they do once they regained their life? They would have nothing, no one. No goals, no homes, no purpose. Then again, she had been in the same predicament after escaping from Connor, and Kate had triumphed thus far.

Furthermore, would they be breathing life back into the Connors of the world? They might revive people with honor, people willing to fight alongside them, people inclined to help others with their newfound rebirth. But that meant resurrecting the thieves and liars and murderers.

Kate thought of the little girl she and Nick had come across just after meeting: the sweet, small child she saw so much of herself in. With this cure, with this power, they could bring back so many of them—every innocent being. They had to take this chance, no matter the repercussions. They had to risk it to resuscitate those worth saving.

Nick was aware of the dangers. Though not every soul would be worth reclaiming, he was mission-driven. Rather than hideous monsters, he now saw every Infected as a civilian, a person with a soul. And civilians were meant to be kept safe. Protected.

Nick would execute the mission and deal accordingly with the world created as a result of his actions. He saw this as an opportunity for his own redemption. Every Infected he cleansed would somehow represent someone he had failed in his life: Adler, Morris, his ex-girlfriend, his mother and father, all of those doctors that had been reduced to carcasses in the other room. He could atone tenfold for every person he had let down.

Dr. Chamberlain observed the pair, watching every emotion play out on their faces. Fear morphed into anticipation. Then, worry faded into acceptance, even eagerness.

After a while, Nick and Kate looked to each other, nodding. Nick took her in his arms and held her, certain he would never let go.

Kate succumbed to his touch as all mistrust dissolved, and she clung to the only person who had ever protected her, the man willing to burn down the whole world for her.

They were uncertain of this feat. The challenges would be great. The odds of success were undetermined. While they might not make it out alive, they knew one thing for sure. Together, Nick and Kate were ready to take on the world.

Note From the Author

Thank you for going on this adventure with me. We laughed, we cried, we sat on the edge of our seats. Most importantly, we fell in love with Nick and Kate. While I didn't live the lives of either character, pieces of myself were sprinkled into their creation. Depression and anxiety have been a companion of mine since I was young. We delved into a lot of tough topics in this book, many dark themes that you, or someone you know, may struggle with. I want to let you know that you are seen, you are known, and you are loved. There is help out there in many forms, and I encourage anyone struggling to reach out and ask for support. Lean on music, wrap yourself up in a great book (insert cheeky wink here), talk it out with friends and family, and speak with a professional if your time and funds allow it. For those times that are especially difficult, I've included some resources below.

Suicide and Crisis Lifeline

988

This phone number will also direct those with a military background to more specific mental health care. (They even offer texting services for those of us who cringe at the thought of making a phone call.)

National Sexual Assault Hotline

1-800-656-4673

You are incredible; the world needs you in it.

Dark Bloom Soundtrack

Music is incredibly important to me and was integral in the writing of this book—either to inspire a certain mood, help keep me focused, or drown out the noises of my household. I have included songs that either fit perfectly with the themes of this book or helped spark a certain emotion that aided in the writing process. I hope you enjoy them as much as I do.

O.G. Loko- **Of Mice & Men**

Face Me- **the Plot in You**

Control- **Halsey**

Chokehold- **Sleep Token**

Baba Yaga- **Slaughter To Prevail**

The Reaper- **Dark Divine**

If Tomorrow Never Comes- **Wage War**

How To Be Me- **Ren, CHINCHILLA**

Polarize- **Twentyonepilots**

Parasite Eve- **Bring Me the Horizon**

Never There-**Currents**

Akudama- **Alpha Wolf**

Doomswitch- **Make Them Suffer**

Darkbloom- **We Came As Romans, Brand of Sacrifice**

Pride- **Soil**

Easy- **Camila Cabello**

The Price of Grace- **Convictions**

Try Hard- **Patient Sixty-Seven**

My Father's Son- **the Amity Affliction**

Acknowledgements

This book was the definition of a labor of love. Though I've been writing since elementary school, I randomly decided at the age of 30 to start this novel.

The story has lived in my head for a long time, and perhaps putting it to paper was a bit of catharsis for me. It took me about 2 years to write—picking it up, putting it away, and finding time in between all that life throws at a full-time wife, mom, and employee. Of course, I had much help and inspiration throughout the process, thus the purpose of this page.

To my mom, thank you for reading this book over and over, editing thoroughly for grammar and situational inconsistencies, and ceaselessly offering your unconditional support.

To my husband, a Marine Corps veteran and my hero, thank you for believing in me and always answering my random questions regarding military normalities and war instances.

To my sister, thank you for your neverending love and support, for reading my book as a beta reader, and for showering me with suggestions and praise.

To my children, for always reminding me how beautiful and colorful a make-believe world can be, even if you decide to pepper it with zombies and emotional traumas.

Thanks to my editor, Bill, for giving Dark Bloom a lot of loving attention, and for helping me make this book as beautiful as possible.

To my electricity expert, Stormy, thank you for providing me with valuable information about the likelihood of electricity during an apocalypse.

I thank my beta readers, especially Sobo, Sharon, Vickie, Ashleigh, Alyssa, and Tonya. You all spent many years on a wild journey with me. You hung in there through my writing ups and downs and made me feel like I had a book worth sharing. Thank you for being there!

To my coworkers who stayed excited about this project with me for two years. You all never stopped believing in me, gave me advice when I needed it, and endured the insufferable horrors of the workplace with me. Special thanks to my shift bestie, Gary. You listened to me drone on about this book almost every day, offered me insight into the medical aspects of this book, and remain the only person I can carry a conversation with about prion diseases.

Thanks to Bob for spending time with Dark Bloom and giving me a lot of insightful writing advice.

Printed in Great Britain
by Amazon

59380470R00169